playing
for pi

John Grisham is the author
one work of non-fiction, a collection of stories,
and a novel for young readers. He is on the Board
of Directors of the Innocence Project in New
York and is the Chairman of the Board of Directors
of the Mississippi Innocence Project at the
University of Mississippi School of Law. He lives
in Virginia and Mississippi.

Also available by John Grisham

Fiction
A Time to Kill
The Firm
The Pelican Brief
The Client
The Chamber
The Rainmaker
The Runaway Jury
The Partner
The Street Lawyer
The Testament
The Brethren
A Painted House
Skipping Christmas
The Summons
The King of Torts
Bleachers
The Last Juror
The Broker
The Appeal
The Associate
Ford County
Theodore Boone: Young Lawyer
The Confession

Non-fiction
The Innocent Man

john grisham

playing for pizza

arrow books

Reissued in the United Kingdom by Arrow Books in 2011

8 10 9 7

First published in the United Kingdom in 2007 by Century
First published in paperback in 2008 by Arrow books

Arrow Books
The Random House Group Limited
20 Vauxhall Bridge Road, London, SW1V 2SA

www.randomhouse.co.uk

Addresses for companies within The Random House Group Limited can
be found at: www.randomhouse.co.uk/offices.htm

The Random House Group Limited Reg. No. 954009

A CIP catalogue record for this book
is available from the British Library

ISBN 9780099557265

Penguin Random House is committed to a sustainable future for
our business, our readers and our planet. This book is made from
Forest Stewardship Council® certified paper.

Printed and bound in Great Britain by Clays Ltd, St Ives plc

Typeset by SX Composing DTP, Rayleigh, Essex

This book is dedicated to my longtime publisher, Stephen Rubin, a great lover of all things Italian – opera, food, wine, fashion, language, and culture. Perhaps not football.

Playing for Pizza

Chapter 1

It was a hospital bed, that much appeared certain, though certainty was coming and going. It was narrow and hard and there were shiny metal railings standing sentrylike along the sides, preventing escape. The sheets were plain and very white. Sanitary. The room was dark, but sunlight was trying to creep around the blinds covering the window.

He closed his eyes again; even that was painful. Then he opened them, and for a long silent minute or so he managed to keep the lids apart and focus on his cloudy little world. He was lying on his back and pinned down by firmly tucked sheets. He noticed a tube dangling to his left, running down to his hand, then disappearing up somewhere behind him. There was a voice in the distance, out in the hallway. Then he made the mistake of trying to move, just a slight adjustment of the head, and it didn't work. Hot bolts of pain hit his skull and neck and he groaned loudly.

'Rick. Are you awake?'

The voice was familiar, and quickly a face followed it. Arnie was breathing on him.

'Arnie?' he said with a weak, scratchy voice, then he swallowed.

'It's me, Rick, thank God you're awake.'

Arnie the agent, always there at the important moments.

'Where am I, Arnie?'

'You're in the hospital, Rick.'

'Got that. But why?'

'When did you wake up?' Arnie found a switch, and a light came on beside the bed.

'I don't know. A few minutes ago.'

'How do you feel?'

'Like someone crushed my skull.'

'Close. You're gonna be fine, trust me.'

Trust me, trust me. How many times had he heard Arnie ask for trust? Truth was, he'd never completely trusted Arnie and there was no plausible reason to start now. What did Arnie know about traumatic head injuries or whatever mortal wound someone had inflicted?

Rick closed his eyes again and breathed deeply. 'What happened?' he asked softly.

Arnie hesitated and ran a hand over his hairless head. He glanced at his watch, 4:00 p.m., so his client had been knocked out for almost twenty-four hours. Not long enough, he thought, sadly.

'What's the last thing you remember?' Arnie asked as he carefully put both elbows on the bed's railing and leaned forward.

After a pause, Rick managed to say, 'I remember Bannister coming at me.'

Arnie smacked his lips and said, 'No, Rick. That was the second concussion, two years ago in Dallas, when you were with the Cowboys.' Rick groaned at the memory, and it wasn't pleasant for Arnie either, because his client had been squatting on the sideline looking at a certain cheerleader when the play came his way and he was squashed, helmetless, by a ton of flying bodies. Dallas cut him two weeks later and found another third-string quarterback.

'Last year you were in Seattle, Rick, and now you're in Cleveland, the Browns, remember?'

Rick remembered and groaned a bit louder. 'What day is it?' he asked, eyes open now.

'Monday. The game was yesterday. Do you recall any of it?' Not if you're lucky, Arnie wanted to say. 'I'll get a nurse. They've been waiting.'

'Not yet, Arnie. Talk to me. What happened?'

'You threw a pass, then you got sandwiched. Purcell came on a weak-side blitz and took your head off. You never saw him.'

'Why was I in the game?'

Now, that was an excellent question, one that was raging on every sports radio show in Cleveland and the upper Midwest. Why was HE in the game? Why was HE on the team? Where in the hell did HE come from?

'Let's talk about it later,' Arnie said, and Rick was too weak to argue. With great reluctance, his wounded brain was stirring slightly, shaking itself from its coma and trying to awaken. The Browns. Browns Stadium, on a very cold Sunday afternoon before a record crowd. The play-offs, no, more than that – the AFC title game.

The ground was frozen, hard as concrete and just as cold.

A nurse was in the room, and Arnie was announcing, 'I think he's snapped out of it.'

'That's great,' she said, without much enthusiasm. 'I'll go find a doctor.' With even less enthusiasm.

Rick watched her leave without moving his head. Arnie was cracking his knuckles and ready to bolt. 'Look, Rick, I need to get going.'

'Sure, Arnie. Thanks.'

'No problem. Look, there's no easy way to say this, so I'll just be blunt. The Browns called this morning – Wacker – and, well, they've released you.' It was almost an annual ritual now, this postseason cutting.

'I'm sorry,' Arnie said, but only because he had to say it.

'Call the other teams,' Rick said, and certainly not for the first time.

'Evidently I won't have to. They're already calling me.'

'That's great.'

'Not really. They're calling to warn me not to call them. I'm afraid this might be the end of the line, kid.'

There was no doubt it was the end of the line,

but Arnie just couldn't find the candor. Maybe tomorrow. Eight teams in six years. Only the Toronto Argonauts dared to sign him for a second season. Every team needed a backup to their backup quarterback, and Rick was perfect for the role. Problems started, though, when he ventured onto the field.

'Gotta run,' Arnie said, glancing at his watch again. 'And listen, do yourself a favor and keep the television turned off. It's brutal, especially ESPN.' He patted his knee and darted from the room. Outside the door there were two thick security guards sitting in folding chairs, trying to stay awake.

Arnie stopped at the nurses' station and spoke to the doctor, who eventually made his way down the hall, past the security guards, and into Rick's room. His bedside manner lacked warmth – a quick check of the basics without much conversation. Neurological work to follow. Just another garden-variety brain concussion, isn't this the third one?

'I think so,' Rick said.

'Thought about finding another job?' the doctor asked.

'No.'

Perhaps you should, the doctor thought, and not just because of your bruised brain. Three interceptions in eleven minutes should be a clear sign that football is not your calling. Two nurses appeared quietly and helped with the tests and paperwork. Neither said a word to the patient, though he was an unmarried professional athlete with notable good looks and a hard body. And at that moment, when he needed them, they could not have cared less.

As soon as he was alone again, Rick very carefully began looking for the remote. A large television hung from the wall in the corner. He planned to go straight to ESPN and get it over with. Every movement hurt, and not just his head and neck. Something close to a fresh knife wound ached in his lower back. His left elbow, the non-throwing one, throbbed with pain.

Sandwiched? He felt like he'd been flattened by a cement truck.

The nurse was back, holding a tray with some pills. 'Where's the remote?' Rick asked.

'Uh, the television's broke.'

'Arnie pulled the plug, didn't he?'

'Which plug?'

'The television.'

'Who's Arnie?' she asked as she tinkered with a rather large needle.

'What's that?' Rick asked, forgetting Arnie for a second.

'Vicodin. It'll help you sleep.'

'I'm tired of sleeping.'

'Doctor's orders, okay. You need rest, and lots of it.' She drained the Vicodin into his IV bag and watched the clear liquids for a moment.

'Are you a Browns fan?' Rick asked.

'My husband is.'

'Was he at the game yesterday?'

'Yes.'

'How bad was it?'

'You don't want to know.'

★ ★ ★

When he awoke, Arnie was there again, sitting in a chair beside the bed and reading the *Cleveland Post*. At the bottom of the front page, Rick could barely make out the headline 'Fans Storm Hospital.'

'What!' Rick said as forcefully as possible.

Arnie snatched the paper down and bolted to his feet. 'Are you okay, kid?'

'Wonderful, Arnie. What day is it?'

'Tuesday, early Tuesday morning. How do you feel, kid?'

'Give me that newspaper.'

'What do you want to know?'

'What's going on, Arnie?'

'What do you want to know?'

'Everything.'

'Have you watched television?'

'No. You pulled the plug. Talk to me, Arnie.'

Arnie cracked his knuckles, then walked slowly to the window, where he barely opened the blinds. He peered through them, as if trouble were out there. 'Yesterday some hooligans came here and made a scene. Cops handled it well, arrested a dozen or so. Just a bunch of thugs. Browns fans.'

'How many?'

'Paper said about twenty. Just drunks.'

'And why did they come here, Arnie? It's just you and me – agent and player. The door's closed. Please fill in the blanks.'

'They found out you were here. A lot of folks would like to take a shot at you these days. You've had a hundred death threats. Folks are upset. They're even threatening me.' Arnie leaned against the wall, a flash of smugness because his life was now worth being threatened. 'You still don't remember?' he asked.

'No.'

'Browns are up seventeen to zip over the Broncos with eleven minutes to go. Zip doesn't come close to describing the ass-kicking. After three quarters, the Broncos have eighty-one yards in total offense, and three, count 'em, three first downs. Anything?'

'No.'

'Ben Marroon is at quarterback because Nagle pulled a hamstring in the first quarter.'

'I remember that now.'

'With eleven minutes to go, Marroon gets drilled on a late hit. They carry him off. No one's worried because the Browns' defense could stop General Patton and his tanks. You take the field, third and twelve, you throw a beautiful pass in the flat to Sweeney, who, of course, plays for the Broncos, and forty yards later he's in the end zone. Remember any of this?'

Rick slowly closed his eyes and said, 'No.'

'Don't try too hard.

'Both teams punt, then the Broncos fumble. With six minutes to go, on a third and eight, you check off at the line and throw to Bryce on a hook, but the ball is high and is picked off by somebody in a white jersey, can't recall his name but he sure can run, all the way. Seventeen to fourteen. The place is getting tense, eighty thousand plus. A few minutes earlier they were celebrating. First Super Bowl ever, all that jazz. Broncos kick off, Browns run the ball three times because Cooley ain't about to send in a pass play, and so the Browns punt. Or try to. Snap gets fumbled, Broncos get the ball on the Browns' thirty-four-yard line, which is no problem whatsoever because in three plays the Browns' defense, which is really, really pissed at this point, stuffs them for fifteen yards, out of field goal range. Broncos punt, you take over at your own 6, and for the next four minutes manage to cram the ball into the middle of the defensive line. The drive stalls at midfield, third and ten, forty seconds to go. Browns are afraid to pass and even more afraid to punt. I don't know what Cooley sends in, but you check off again, fire a missile to the right sideline for Bryce, who's wide open. Right on target.'

Rick tried to sit up, and for a moment forgot about his injuries. 'I still don't remember.'

'Right on target, but much too hard. It hits Bryce in the chest, bounces up, and Goodson grabs it, gallops to the promised land. Browns lose twenty-one to seventeen. You're on the

9

ground, almost sawed in half. They put you on a stretcher, and as they roll you off the field, half the crowd is booing and the other half is cheering wildly. Quite a noise, never heard anything like it. A couple of drunks jump from the stands and rush the stretcher – they would've killed you – but security steps in. A nice brawl ensues, and it, too, is all over the talk shows.'

Rick was slumped over, low in the bed, lower than ever, with his eyes closed and his breathing quite labored. The headaches were back, along with the sharp pains in the neck and along the spine. Where were the drugs?

'Sorry, kid,' Arnie said. The room was nicer in the darkness, so Arnie closed the blinds and reassumed his position in the chair, with his newspaper. His client appeared to be dead.

The doctors were ready to release him, but Arnie had argued strongly that he needed a few more days of rest and protection. The Browns were paying for the security guards, and they were not happy about it. The team was also covering the medicals, and it wouldn't be long before they complained.

And Arnie was fed up, too. Rick's career, if you could call it that, was over. Arnie got 5 percent, and 5 percent of Rick's salary wasn't enough to cover expenses. 'Are you awake, Rick?'

'Yes,' he said, with his eyes still closed.

'Listen to me, okay.'

'I'm listening.'

'The hardest part of my job is telling a player

that it's time to quit. You've played all your life, it's all you know, all you dream about. No one is ever ready to quit. But, Rick, ole buddy, it's time to call it quits. There are no options.'

'I'm twenty-eight years old, Arnie,' Rick said, with his eyes open. Very sad eyes. 'What do you suggest I do?'

'A lot of guys go into coaching. And real estate. You were smart – you got your degree.'

'My degree is in phys ed, Arnie. That means I can get a job teaching volleyball to sixth graders for forty thousand a year. I'm not ready for that.'

Arnie stood and walked around the end of the bed, as if deep in thought. 'Why don't you go home, get some rest, and think about it?'

'Home? Where is home? I've lived in so many different places.'

'Home is Iowa, Rick. They still love you there.' And they really love you in Denver, Arnie thought, but wisely kept it to himself.

The idea of being seen on the streets of Davenport, Iowa, terrified Rick, and he let out a soft groan. The town was probably humiliated by the play of its native son. Ouch. He thought of his poor parents, and closed his eyes.

Arnie glanced at his watch, then for some reason finally noticed that there were no get-well cards or flowers in the room. The nurses told him that no friends had stopped by, no family, no teammates, no one even remotely connected to the Cleveland Browns. 'I gotta run, kid. I'll drop by tomorrow.'

Walking out, he nonchalantly tossed the newspaper on Rick's bed. As soon as the door closed behind him, Rick grabbed it, and soon wished he had not. The police estimated a crowd of fifty had staged a rowdy demonstration outside the hospital. Things got ugly when a TV news crew showed up and began filming. A window was smashed, and a few of the drunker fans stormed the ER check-in, supposedly looking for Rick Dockery. Eight were arrested. A large photo – front page beneath the fold – captured the crowd before the arrests. Two crude signs could be read clearly: 'Pull the Plug Now!' and 'Legalize Euthanasia.'

It got worse. The *Post* had a notorious sports-writer named Charley Cray, a nasty hack whose specialty was attack journalism. Just clever enough to be credible, Cray was widely read because he delighted in the missteps and foibles of professional athletes who earned millions yet were not perfect. He was an expert on everything and never missed a chance for a cheap shot. His Tuesday column – front-page sports – began with the headline: 'Could Dockery Top All-Time Goat List?'

Knowing Cray, there was no doubt Rick Dockery would top the list.

The column, well researched and savagely written, was structured around Cray's opinions about the greatest individual chokes, screwups, and collapses in the history of sports. There was Bill Buckner's booted ground ball in the '86

World Series. Jackie Smith's dropped TD pass in Super Bowl XIII, and so on.

But, as Cray screamed at his readers, those were only single plays.

Mr. Dockery, on the other hand, managed three – Count Them! – three horrible passes in only eleven minutes.

Clearly, therefore, Rick Dockery is the unquestioned Greatest Goat in the history of professional sports. The verdict was undisputed, and Cray challenged anyone to argue with him.

Rick flung the newspaper against the wall and called for another pill. In the darkness, alone with the door closed, he waited for the drug to work its magic, to knock him out clean, then, hopefully, to take him away forever.

He slipped lower in the bed, pulled the sheet over his head, and began crying.

Chapter 2

It was snowing and Arnie was tired of Cleveland. He was at the airport, waiting for a flight to Las Vegas, his home, and against his better judgment he made a call to a lesser vice president of the Arizona Cardinals.

At the moment, and not including Rick Dockery, Arnie had seven players in the NFL and four in Canada. He was, if he could be forced to admit it, a mid-list agent who, of course, had bigger ambitions. Making phone calls for Rick Dockery was not going to help his credibility. Rick was arguably the most-talked-about player in the country at that dismal moment, but it wasn't the kind of buzz that Arnie needed. The vice president was polite but brief and couldn't wait to get off the phone.

Arnie went to a bar, got a drink, and managed to find a seat far away from any television, since the only story still raging in Cleveland was the three interceptions by a quarterback no one even knew was on the team. The Browns had rolled through the season with a sputtering offense but a bruising defense, one that shattered records for yielding so few yards and points. They lost only once, and with each win a city starved for a Super Bowl became more and more enthralled with their old lovable losers. Suddenly, in one quick season, the Browns were the slayers.

Had they won the previous Sunday, their Super Bowl opponent would be the Minnesota Vikings, a team they shut out and routed back in November.

The entire city could taste the sweetness of a championship.

It all vanished in eleven horrifying minutes.

Arnie ordered a second drink. Two salesmen at the next table were getting drunk and relishing the Browns' collapse. They were from Detroit.

The hottest story of the day had been the firing of the Browns' general manager, Clyde Wacker, a man who had been hailed as a genius as recently as the preceding Saturday but was now the perfect scapegoat. Someone had to be fired, and not just Rick Dockery. When it was finally determined that Wacker had signed Dockery off waivers, back in October, the owner fired him. The execution was public – big press conference, lots of frowns and promises to run a tighter ship, et cetera. The Browns would be back!

Arnie met Rick during his senior year at Iowa, at the end of a season that had begun with much promise but was fading into a third-tier bowl game. Rick started at quarterback his last two seasons, and he seemed well suited for a drop-back, open-style offense so rare in the Big Ten. At times he was brilliant – reading defenses, coolly checking off at the line, firing the ball with incredible velocity. His arm was amazing, undoubtedly the best in the upcoming draft. He could throw long and hard with a lightning-quick release. But he was too erratic to be trusted, and when Buffalo picked him in the last round, it should have been a clear sign that he needed to pursue a master's degree or a stockbroker's license.

Instead, he went to Toronto for two miserable seasons, then began bouncing around the NFL. With a great arm, Rick was just barely good enough to make a roster. Every team needs a third-string quarterback. In tryouts, and there had been many, he'd often dazzled coaches with his arm. Arnie watched one day in Kansas City when Rick threw a football eighty yards, then a few minutes later clocked a bullet at ninety miles an hour.

But Arnie knew what most coaches now strongly suspected. Rick, for a football player, was afraid of contact. Not the incidental contact, not the quick and harmless tackle of a scrambling quarterback. Rick, with good reason, feared the rushing tackles and the blitzing linebackers.

There is a moment or two in every game when

a quarterback has a receiver open, a split second to throw the ball, and a massive, roaring lineman charging the pocket unblocked. The quarterback has a choice. He can grit his teeth, sacrifice his body, put his team first, throw the damned ball, make the play, and get crushed, or he can tuck it and run and pray he lives for another play. Rick, as long as Arnie had watched him play, had never, not once, put the team first. At the first hint of a sack, Rick flinched and ran frantically for the sideline.

And with a propensity for concussions, Arnie really couldn't blame him.

He called a nephew of the owner of the Rams, who answered the phone with an icy 'I hope this is not about Dockery.'

'Well, yes, it is,' Arnie managed to say.

'The answer is hell no.'

Since Sunday, Arnie had spoken with about half of the NFL teams. The response from the Rams was pretty typical. Rick had no idea how completely his sad little career had been terminated.

Watching a monitor on the wall, Arnie saw his flight get delayed. One more call, he vowed. One more effort to find Rick a job, and then he would move on to his other players.

* * *

The clients were from Portland, and though his last name was Webb and she was as pale as a

17

Swede, they both claimed Italian blood and were keen to see the old country where it all began. Each spoke about six words of the language, and spoke them badly. Sam suspected they had picked up a travel book at the airport and memorized a few of the basics over the Atlantic. On their previous trip to Italy their driver/guide had been a native with 'dreadful' English, and so they had insisted on an American this time around, a good Yank who could arrange meals and find tickets. After two days together, Sam was ready to ship them back to Portland.

Sam was neither a driver nor a guide. He was, however, very much an American, and since his primary job paid little, he moonlighted occasionally when his countrymen passed through and needed someone to hold their hands.

He waited outside in the car while they had a very long dinner at Lazzaro's, an old trattoria in the center of the city. It was cold and snowing lightly, and as he sipped strong coffee, his thoughts returned to his roster, as they always did. His cell phone startled him. The call was from the United States. He said hello.

'Sam Russo please,' came a crisp greeting.

'This is Sam.'

'Coach Russo?'

'Yes, that's me.'

The caller identified himself as Arnie something or other, said he was an agent of some sort, and claimed to have been a manager on the 1988 Bucknell football team, a few years after Sam played there. Since they both went to Bucknell, they quickly found common ground, and after a few minutes of Do-You-Know-So-and-So they were friendly. For Sam, it was nice to chat with someone from his old school, albeit a total stranger.

And it was rare that he got calls from agents.

Arnie finally got to the point.

'Sure I watched the play-offs,' Sam said.

'Well, I represent Rick Dockery, and, well, the Browns let him go,' Arnie said.

No surprise there, Sam thought, but kept listening. 'And he's looking around, considering his options. I heard the rumor that you need a quarterback.'

Sam almost dropped the phone. A real NFL quarterback playing in Parma? 'It's not a rumor,' he said. 'My quarterback quit last week and took a coaching job somewhere in upstate New York. We'd love to have Dockery. Is he okay? Physically I mean?'

'Sure, just bruised a little, but he's ready to go.'

'And he wants to play in Italy?'

'Maybe. We haven't discussed it yet, you know, he's still in the hospital, but we're looking at all the possibilities. Frankly, he needs a change of scenery.'

'Do you know the game over here?' Sam asked nervously. 'It's good football, but it's a far cry from the NFL and the Big Ten. I mean, these guys are not professionals in the true sense of the word.'

19

'What level?'

'I don't know. Tough to say. Ever hear of a school called Washington and Lee, down in Virginia? A nice school, good football, Division III?'

'Sure.'

'They came over last year during spring break and we scrimmaged them a couple of times. Pretty even matchup.'

'Division III, huh?' Arnie said, his voice losing some steam.

But then, Rick needed a softer game. Another concussion and he might indeed suffer the brain damage so often joked about. Truthfully, Arnie didn't care. Just another phone call or two and Rick Dockery was history.

'Look, Arnie,' Sam began earnestly. Time for the truth. 'It's a club sport over here, or maybe a notch above that. Each team in the Series A gets three American players, and they usually get meal money, maybe some rent. The quarterbacks are typically American and they get a small salary. The rest of the roster is a bunch of tough Italians who play because they love football. If they're lucky and the owner is in a good mood, they might get pizza and beer after the game. We play an eight-game schedule, with play-offs, then a chance for the Italian Super Bowl. Our field is old but nice, well maintained, seats about three thousand, and for a big game we might fill it. We have corporate sponsors, cool uniforms, but no TV contract and no real money to speak of.

soccer, so our football has more of a cult following.'

'How did you get there?'

'I love Italy. My grandparents emigrated from this region, settled in Baltimore, where I grew up. But I have lots of cousins around here. My wife is Italian and so on. It's a delightful place to live. Can't make any money coaching American football, but we're having fun.'

'So the coaches get paid?'

'Yes, you could say that.'

'Any other NFL rejects?'

'Occasionally one passes through, some lost soul still dreaming of a Super Bowl ring. But the Americans are usually small college players who love the game and have a sense of adventure.'

'How much can you pay my man?'

'Let me check with the owner.'

'Do that, and I'll check with my client.'

They signed off after another Bucknell story, and Sam returned to his coffee. An NFL quarterback playing football in Italy? It was hard to imagine, though not without precedent. The Bologna Warriors were in the Italian Super Bowl two years earlier with a forty-year-old quarterback who'd once played briefly for Oakland. He quit after two seasons and went to Canada.

Sam turned the car heater down a notch and replayed the final minutes of the Browns-Broncos game. Never in his memory had he watched one player so completely engineer a

21

defeat and lose a game that was so clearly won. He himself had almost cheered when Dockery was carried off the field.

Nevertheless, the idea of coaching him in Parma was intriguing.

Chapter 3

Though the packing and leaving was somewhat of a ritual, the departure from Cleveland was a bit more stressful than usual. Someone found out that he had leased a condo on the seventh floor of a glass building near the lake, and there were two shaggy reporter types with cameras loitering near the guardhouse when Rick wheeled through in his black Tahoe. He parked underground and hurried up the elevator. The phone in the kitchen was ringing when he unlocked the door. A pleasant voice mail was left behind by none other than Charley Cray.

Three hours later the SUV was packed with clothes and golf clubs and a stereo. Thirteen trips – he counted them – up and down the elevator, and his neck and shoulders were killing him. His head ached and throbbed and the painkillers did little to help. He wasn't supposed to drive while drugged, but Rick was driving.

Rick was leaving, running away from the lease

on the condo and the rented furniture therein, fleeing Cleveland and the Browns and their awful fans, scampering away to somewhere. He wasn't quite sure where.

Wisely, he had signed only a six-month lease on the condo. Since college he'd lived a life of short leases and rented furniture and learned not to accumulate too many things.

He fought the downtown traffic and managed to glance in the mirror for one last look at the Cleveland skyline. Good riddance. He was thrilled to be leaving. He vowed to never return, unless, of course, he was playing against the Browns, but then he'd promised himself that he would not think about the future. Not for another week anyway.

As he raced through the suburbs, he admitted to himself that Cleveland was undoubtedly happier with his departure than he was.

He was drifting west, in the general direction of Iowa, not with any enthusiasm, because he was not excited about going home. He'd called his parents once from the hospital. His mother asked about his head and begged him to stop playing. His father asked him what the hell he was thinking when he threw that last pass.

'How are things in Davenport?' Rick had finally asked his father. Both knew what he was after. He wasn't curious about the local economy.

'Not too good,' his father said.

A weather bulletin caught his attention. Heavy

snow to the west, a blizzard in Iowa, and Rick happily turned left and headed south.

An hour later his cell phone buzzed. It was Arnie, in Vegas, sounding much happier.

'Where are you, kid?' he asked.

'I'm out of Cleveland.'

'Thank God. Going home?'

'No, I'm just driving, going south. Maybe I'll go to Florida and play some golf.'

'Great idea. How's your head?'

'Fine.'

'Any additional brain damage?' Arnie asked with a fake laugh. It was a punch line Rick had heard at least a hundred times.

'Severe damage,' he said.

'Look, kid, I'm onto something here, a spot on a roster, guaranteed starting position. Gorgeous cheerleaders. Wanna hear it?'

Rick repeated it slowly, certain that he had misunderstood the details. The Vicodin was soaking a few areas of his tender brain. 'Okay,' he finally said.

'I just talked to the head coach of the Panthers, and they will offer a contract right now, on the spot, no questions asked. It's not a lot of money, but it's a job. You'll still be the quarterback, the starting quarterback! A done deal. It's all you, baby.'

'The Panthers?'

'You got it. The Parma Panthers.'

There was a long pause as Rick struggled with geography. Obviously it was some minor-league outfit, some independent bush league so far from the NFL that it was a joke. Surely it wasn't arena football. Arnie knew better than to think about that.

But he couldn't place Parma. 'Did you say Carolina Panthers, Arnie?'

'Listen to me, Rick. Parma Panthers.'

There was a Parma in the Cleveland suburbs. It was all very confusing.

'Okay, Arnie, pardon the brain damage, but why don't you tell me exactly where Parma is.'

'It's in northern Italy, about an hour from Milan.'

'Where's Milan?'

'It's in northern Italy, too. I'll buy you an atlas. Anyway—'

'Football is soccer over there, Arnie. Wrong sport.'

'Listen to me. They have some well-established leagues in Europe. It's big in Germany, Austria, Italy. It could be fun. Where's your sense of adventure?'

Rick's head began throbbing and he needed another pill. But he was practically stoned anyway and a DUI was the last thing he needed. The cop would probably look at his license and go for the handcuffs or maybe even his nightstick. 'I don't think so,' he said.

'You should do it, Rick, take a year off, go play in Europe, let the dust settle over here. I gotta tell you, kid, I don't mind making phone calls but the timing is lousy, really lousy.'

'I don't want to hear it, Arnie. Look, let's talk later. My head is killing me.'

'Sure, kid. Sleep on it, but we need to move fast. The team in Parma is looking for a quarter-back. Their season starts soon and they're desperate. I mean, not desperate to sign just anybody, but—'

'Got it, Arnie. Later.'

'You've heard of Parmesan cheese?'

'Sure.'

'That's where they make it. In Parma. Get it?'

'If I wanted cheese, I'd go to Green Bay,' Rick said, and thought himself clever in spite of the drugs.

'I called the Packers, but they haven't called back.'

'I don't want to hear it.'

* * *

Near Mansfield he settled into a booth in the restaurant of a crowded truck stop and ordered french fries and a Coke. The words on the menu were slightly blurred, but he took another pill anyway because of the pain at the top of his spine. In the hospital, once the television was working, he'd made the mistake of finally watching the highlights on ESPN. He cringed and even flinched at the sight of his own body getting hit so hard and crumbling to the ground in a heap.

Two truckers at a nearby table began glancing

at him. Oh, great. Why didn't I wear a cap and some sunglasses?

They whispered and pointed, and before long others were looking, even glaring at him. Rick wanted to leave, but the Vicodin said no, take it easy for a while. He ordered another plate of french fries and tried to call his parents. They were either out or ignoring him. He called a college friend in Boca to make sure he had a place to stay for a few days.

The truckers were laughing about something. He tried to ignore them.

On a white paper napkin, he began scribbling numbers. The Browns owed him $50,000 for the play-offs. (Surely the team would pay him.) He had about $40,000 in the bank in Davenport. Due to his nomadic career, he had not purchased any real estate. The SUV was being leased – $700 a month. There were no other assets. He studied the numbers, and his best guess was that he could escape with about $80,000.

To leave the game with three concussions and $80,000 was not as bad as it seemed. The average NFL running back lasted three years, retired with all manner of leg injuries, and owed about $500,000.

Rick's financial problems came from disastrous investments. He and a teammate from Iowa had tried to corner the car-wash market in Des Moines. Lawsuits had followed and his name was still on bank loans. He owned one-third of a Mexican restaurant in Fort Worth, and the other two owners, former friends, were screaming for more capital. The last time he ate there the burritos made him sick.

With Arnie's help he had managed to avoid bankruptcy – the headlines would've been brutal – but the debts had piled up.

A rather large trucker with an amazing beer belly drew near, stopped, and sneered at Rick. He was the whole package – thick sideburns, trucker cap, toothpick dangling from his lips. 'You're Dockery, aren't you?'

For a split second Rick thought of denying it, then he decided to simply ignore him.

'You suck, you know that,' the trucker said loudly and for the benefit of his audience. 'You sucked at Iowa and you still suck.' There was heavy laughter in the background as the others joined in.

One shot to the beer belly and the dude would be on the floor, squealing, and the fact that Rick even thought about it made him sad. The headlines – why was he so concerned with the headlines? – would be great. 'Dockery Brawls with Truckers.' And, of course, everyone who read the story would be pulling for the truckers. Charley Cray would have a field day.

Rick smiled at his napkin and bit his tongue.

'Why don't you move to Denver? Bet they love you there.' Even more laughter.

Rick added some meaningless numbers to his tally and pretended as if he heard nothing. Finally, the trucker moved on, with quite a swagger now. It's not every day that you get the chance to berate an NFL quarterback.

★ ★ ★

He took I-71 south to Columbus, home of the Buckeyes. There, not too many years ago, in front of 100,000 fans, on a gorgeous autumn afternoon, he'd thrown four touchdown passes and picked the defense apart like a surgeon. Big Ten Player of the Week. More honors would certainly follow. The future was so bright it blinded him.

Three hours later he stopped for gas and saw a new motel next door. He'd driven enough. He fell on the bed and planned to sleep for days when his cell phone rang.

Arnie said, 'Where are you now?'

'I don't know. London.'

'What? Where?'

'London, Kentucky, Arnie.'

'Let's talk about Parma,' Arnie said, crisp and businesslike. Something was up.

'I thought we agreed to do that later.' Rick pinched his nose and slowly stretched his legs.

'This is later. They need a decision.'

'Okay. Give me the details.'

'They'll pay three thousand euros a month for five months, plus an apartment and a car.'

'What's a euro?'

'That's the currency in Europe. Hello? It's

30

worth about a third more than the dollar these days.'

'So how much, Arnie? What's the offer?'

'About four thousand bucks a month.'

The numbers registered quickly because there were so few of them. 'The quarterback makes twenty thousand? What does a lineman make?'

'Who cares? You're not a lineman.'

'Just curious. Why are you so testy?'

'Because I'm spending too much time on this, Rick. I've got other deals to negotiate. You know how hectic it gets in the postseason.'

'Are you unloading me, Arnie?'

'Of course not. It's just that I really think you should go abroad for a while, recharge your batteries, you know, let the ole brain heal. Give me some time stateside to assess the damage.'

The damage. Rick tried to sit up but nothing cooperated. Every bone and muscle from the waist up was damaged. If Collins hadn't missed the block, Rick wouldn't have been crushed. Linemen, love 'em and hate 'em. He wanted linemen! 'How much do the linemen make?'

'Nothing. The linemen are Italians and they play because they love football.'

The agents must starve to death over there, Rick thought to himself. He breathed deeply and tried to remember the last player he knew who played just for the love of the game. 'Twenty thousand,' Rick mumbled.

'Which is twenty more than you're currently making,' Arnie reminded him, rather cruelly.

'Thanks, Arnie. I can always count on you.'

'Look, kid, take a year off. Go see Europe. Give me some time.'

'How good is the football?'

'Who cares? You'll be the star. All of the quarterbacks are Americans, but they're small-college types who didn't get near the draft. The Panthers are thrilled that you're even considering the deal.'

Someone was thrilled to get him. What a pleasant idea. But what would he tell his family and friends?

What friends? He had heard from exactly two old buddies in the past week.

After a pause, Arnie cleared his throat and said, 'There's something else.'

From the tone, it could not be good. 'I'm listening.'

'What time did you leave the hospital today?'

'I don't remember. Maybe around nine.'

'Well, you must've passed him in the hallway.'

'Who?'

'An investigator. Your cheerleader friend is back, Rick, quite pregnant, and now she's got lawyers, some real sleazeballs who want to make some noise, get their mugs in the paper. They're calling here with all sorts of demands.'

'Which cheerleader?' Rick asked as new waves of pain swept through his shoulders and neck.

'Tiffany something or other.'

'There's no way, Arnie. She slept with half the Browns. Why is she coming after me?'

'Did you sleep with her?'

'Of course, but it was my turn. If she's gonna have a million-dollar baby, why is she accusing me?'

An excellent question from the lowest-paid member of the team. Arnie had made the same point when arguing with Tiffany's lawyers.

'Is it possible that you might be the daddy?'

'Absolutely not. I was careful. You had to be.'

'Well, she can't go public until she serves you with the papers, and if she can't find you, then she can't serve you.'

Rick knew all this. He'd been served before. 'I'll hide in Florida for a while. They can't find me down there.'

'Don't bet on it. These lawyers are pretty aggressive. They want some publicity. There are ways to track people.' A pause, then the clincher. 'But, pal, they can't serve you in Italy.'

'I've never been to Italy.'

'Then it's time to go.'

'Let me sleep on it.'

'Sure.'

Rick dozed off quickly and slept hard for ten minutes when a nightmare jolted him from his nap. Credit cards leave a trail. Gas stations, motels, truck stops – every place was connected to a vast web of electronic information that zipped around the world in a split second, and surely some geek with a high-powered computer could tap in here and there and for a nice fee pick up the trail and send in the bloodhounds with a copy of Tiffany's paternity suit. More headlines. More legal troubles.

He grabbed his unpacked bag and fled the motel. He drove another hour, very much under the influence, and found a dump with cheap rooms for cash, by the hour or by the night. He fell onto the dusty bed and was soon sound asleep, snoring loudly and dreaming of leaning towers and Roman ruins.

Chapter 4

Coach Russo read the *Gazzetta di Parma* while he waited patiently on a hard plastic chair inside the Parma train station. He hated to admit that he was a little nervous. He and his new quarterback had chatted once by phone, while he, the quarterback, was on a golf course somewhere in Florida, and the conversation left something to be desired. Dockery was reluctant to play for Parma, though the idea of living abroad for a few months was certainly appealing. Dockery seemed reluctant to play anywhere. The 'Greatest Goat' theme had spread, and he was still the butt of many jokes. He was a football player and needed to play, yet he wasn't sure he wanted to see another football.

Dockery said he didn't speak a word of Italian but had studied Spanish in the tenth grade. Great, thought Russo. No problem.

Sam had never coached a pro quarterback. His last one had played sparingly at the

University of Delaware. How would Dockery fit? The team was excited to have such a talent, but would they accept him? Would his attitude poison the locker room? Would he be coachable?

The Eurostar from Milan coasted into the station, on time as always. Doors snapped open, passengers spilled out. It was mid-March and most were clad in dark heavy coats, still bundled from the winter and waiting for warmer weather. Then there was Dockery, fresh from south Florida with a ridiculous tan and dressed for summer drinks at the country club – cream-colored linen sports coat, lemon shirt with a tropical motif, white slacks that stopped at bronze sockless ankles, thin crocodile loafers more maroon than brown. He was wrestling with two perfectly matched and monstrous pieces of luggage on wheels, and his task was made almost impossible because he had slung over his back a bulky set of golf clubs.

The quarterback had arrived.

Sam watched the struggle and knew instantly that Dockery had never been on a train before. He finally walked over and said, 'Rick. I'm Sam Russo.'

A half smile as he jolted things upward and managed to slide the golf clubs up his back. 'Hey, Coach,' he said.

'Welcome to Parma. Let me give you a hand.' Sam grabbed one suitcase, and they began rolling through the station.

'Thanks. It's pretty cold here.'

'Colder than Florida. How was your flight?'

'Fine.'

'Play a lot of golf, do you?'

'Sure. When does it get warm?'

'A month or so.'

'Lot of golf courses around here?'

'No, I've never seen one.' They were outside now, stopping at Sam's boxy little Honda.

'This is it?' Rick asked as he glanced around and noticed all of the other very small cars.

'Throw those in the backseat,' Sam said. He popped the trunk and manhandled a suitcase into the tight space. There was no room for the other. It went into the rear seat, on top of the clubs. 'Good thing I didn't pack more,' Rick mumbled. They got in. At six feet two, Rick's knees hit the dashboard. His seat refused to slide back because of the golf clubs.

'Pretty small cars over here, huh?' he observed.

'You got it. Gas is a buck twenty a liter.'

'How much a gallon?'

'They don't use gallons. They use liters.' Sam shifted gears, and they moved away from the station.

'Okay, about how much a gallon?' Rick went on.

'Well, a liter is roughly a quart.'

Rick pondered this as he gazed blankly out his window at the buildings along Strada Garibaldi. 'Okay. How many quarts in a gallon?'

'Where'd you go to college?'

'Where'd you go?'

'Bucknell.'

'Never heard of it. They play football?'

'Sure, small stuff. Nothing like the Big Ten. Four quarts in a gallon, so a gallon here is about five bucks.'

'These buildings are really old,' Rick said.

'They don't call it the old country for nothing. What was your major in college?'

'Phys ed. Cheerleaders.'

'Study much history?'

'Hated history. Why?'

'Parma goes back two thousand years and has an interesting history.'

'Parma,' Rick said as he exhaled and managed to slide down an inch or two, as if the very mention of the place meant defeat. He fished through a coat pocket and found his cell phone but didn't open it. 'What the hell am I doing in Parma, Italy?' he asked, though it was more of a statement.

Sam figured no response was best, so he decided to become a guide. 'This is the downtown, the oldest section. First time in Italy?'

'Yep. What's that?'

'It's called Palazzo della Pilotta, started four hundred years ago, never finished, then bombed to hell and back by the Allies in 1944.'

'We bombed Parma?'

'We bombed everything, even Rome, but we laid off the Vatican. The Italians, as you might recall, had a leader named Mussolini, who cut a

38

deal with Hitler. Not a good move, though the Italians never warmed up to the notion of war. They're much better at food, wine, sports cars, fashion, sex.'

'Maybe I'll like this place.'

'You will. And they love opera. To the right there is the Teatro Regio, the famous opera house. Ever see an opera?'

'Oh yeah, sure, we were raised on the stuff in Iowa. Spent most of my childhood at the opera. Are you kidding? Why would I go to an opera?'

'There's the duomo,' Sam said.

'The what?'

'Duomo, cathedral. Think of dome, you know, like Superdome, Carrier Dome.'

Rick did not respond, but instead went silent for a moment as if the memory of domes and stadiums and their related games made him uncomfortable. They were in the center of Parma with pedestrians scurrying about and cars bumper to bumper.

Sam finally continued: 'Most Italian cities are sort of configured around a central square, called a piazza. This is Piazza Garibaldi, lots of shops and cafés and foot traffic. The Italians spend a lot of time sitting at the outdoor cafés sipping espresso and reading. Not a bad habit.'

'I don't do coffee.'

'It's time to start.'

'What do these Italians think of Americans?'

'They like us, I guess, not that they dwell on the subject. If they stop and think about it, they probably dislike our government, but generally they couldn't care less. They are crazy about our culture.'

'Even football?'

'To some degree. There's a great little bar over there. You want something to drink?'

'No, it's too early.'

'Not alcohol. A bar here is like a small pub or coffee shop, a gathering place.'

'I'll pass.'

'Anyway, the center of the city is where the action is. Your apartment is just a few streets over.'

'Can't wait. Mind if I make a call?'

'*Prego*.'

'What?'

'*Prego*. It means go right ahead.'

Rick punched the numbers while Sam worked his car through the late-afternoon traffic. When Rick glanced out his window, Sam quickly pushed a button on the radio and low-volume opera rose in the background. Whoever Rick needed to chat with was unavailable; no voice mail was left by the quarterback; phone slapped shut; returned to pocket.

Probably his agent, thought Sam. Maybe a girlfriend.

'You got a girl?' Sam asked.

'No one in particular. Lots of NFL groupies, but they're dumb as rocks. You?'

'Married for eleven years, no kids.'

They crossed a bridge called the Ponte Verdi.

'This is the Parma River. It divides the city.'

'Lovely.'

'Ahead of us is the Parco Ducale, the largest park in the city. It's quite beautiful. Italians are big on parks and landscaping and such.'

'It's pretty.'

'Glad you approve. It's a great place to walk, take a girl, read a book, lie in the sun.'

'Never spent much time in parks.'

What a surprise.

They looped around, recrossed the river, and were soon darting through narrow one-way streets. 'You've now seen most of downtown Parma,' Sam said.

'Nice.'

A few blocks south of the park they turned onto a winding street, Via Linati. 'There,' Sam said, pointing to a long row of four-story buildings, each painted a different color. 'The second one, sort of a gold color, apartment's on the third floor. It's a nice part of town. Signor Bruncardo, the gent who owns the team, also owns a few buildings. That's why you get to live downtown. It's more expensive here.'

'And these guys really play for free?' Rick said, mulling something that had stuck from a prior conversation.

'The Americans get paid – you and two others – only three this year. No one makes as much as you. Yes, the Italians play for the sport of it. And the postgame pizza.' A pause, then he added, 'You're gonna love these guys.' It was his first effort at bolstering team spirit. If the quarterback wasn't happy, then there would be many problems.

He somehow wedged his Honda into a space half its size, and they loaded up the luggage and golf clubs. There was no elevator, but the stairwell was wider than normal. The apartment was furnished and had three rooms – a bedroom, a den, a small kitchen. Because his new quarterback was coming from the NFL, Signor Bruncardo had sprung for new paint, rugs, curtains, and den furniture. There was even some splashy contemporary art on the walls.

'Not bad,' Rick said, and Russo was relieved. He knew the realities of urban real estate in Italy – most of the apartments were small and old and expensive. If the quarterback was disappointed, then Signor Bruncardo would be, too. Things would get complicated.

'On the market, it would be two thousand euros a month,' Sam said, trying to impress.

Rick was carefully placing his golf clubs on the sofa. 'Nice place,' he said. He couldn't count the number of apartments he'd passed through in the last six years. The constant moving, often in a hurry, had deadened any appreciation of square footage, decor, and furnishings.

'Why don't you change clothes and I'll meet you downstairs,' Sam said.

Rick glanced down at his white slacks and brown ankles and almost said, 'Oh, I'm fine.'

42

But then he took the hint and said, 'Sure, give me five minutes.'

'There's a café two blocks down on the right,' Sam said. 'I'll be at a table outside having a coffee.'

'Sure, Coach.'

Sam ordered coffee and opened his newspaper. It was damp and the sun had dipped behind the buildings. The Americans always went through a brief period of culture shock. The language, cars, narrow streets, smaller lodgings, the confinement of the cities. It was overwhelming, especially to the middle- and lower-class guys who'd traveled little. In his five years as coach of the Parma Panthers, Sam had met exactly one American player who'd ever been to Italy before joining the team.

Two of Italy's national treasures usually warmed them up – food and women. Coach Russo did not meddle with the latter, but he knew the power of Italian cooking. Mr. Dockery was facing a four-hour dinner and had no idea what was coming.

Ten minutes later he arrived, cell phone in hand of course, and looked much better. Navy blazer, faded jeans, dark socks, and shoes.

'Coffee?' Sam asked.

'Just a Coke.'

Sam talked to the waiter.

'So you speak the lingo, huh?' Rick said, stuffing the phone in a pocket.

'I've lived here for five years. My wife is Italian. I told you that.'

'Do the other Yanks pick up the language?'

'A few words, especially items on a menu.'

'Just curious as to how I'm supposed to call plays in the huddle?'

'We do it in English. Sometimes the Italians get the plays; sometimes they don't.'

'Just like in college,' Rick said, and they both laughed. He gulped his Coke, then said, 'Me, I'm not bothering with the language. Too much trouble. When I played in Canada, there was a lot of French. Didn't slow us down. Everyone spoke English, too.'

'Not everyone speaks English here, I can assure you of that.'

'Yes, but everyone speaks American Express and greenbacks.'

'Maybe. It's not a bad idea to study the language. Life's easier and your teammates will love you.'

'Love? Did you say love? I haven't loved a teammate since I was in college.'

'This is like college, a big fraternity with guys who like to put on the gear, brawl for a couple of hours, then go drink beer. If they accept you, and I'm sure they will, then they'll kill for you.'

'Do they know about, uh, you know, my last game?'

'I haven't asked them, but I'm sure some do. They love football and watch a lot of games. But don't worry, Rick. They're delighted you're here. These guys have never won the Italian Super Bowl, and they're convinced this is the year.'

Three signorinas walked by and required their attention. When they were out of sight, Rick gazed at the street and seemed lost in another world. Sam liked him and felt sorry for him. He had endured an avalanche of public ridicule never before seen in professional football, and here he was in Parma, alone and confused. And running. Parma was where he belonged, at least for now.

'You wanna go see the field?' Sam asked.

'Sure, Coach.'

As they walked away, Sam pointed down another street. 'There's a men's store down there, great clothes. You should check it out.'

'I brought plenty.'

'Like I said, you should check it out. Italians are very stylish and they'll watch you carefully, both men and women. You can never be overdressed here.'

'Language, clothes, anything else, coach?'

'Yes, a bit of advice. Try to enjoy yourself here. It's a wonderful old town and you're here for such a short time.'

'Sure, Coach.'

Chapter 5

The Stadio Lanfranchi is in the northwest corner of Parma, still in the city proper but away from the ancient buildings and narrow streets. It's a rugby pitch, home to two professional teams and leased to the Panthers for football. It has canopy-covered grandstands on both sides, a press box, and a playing surface of natural grass that is well maintained in spite of the heavy traffic.

Soccer is played at the much larger Stadio Tardini, a mile away in the southeast section of the city, and there larger crowds gather to celebrate Italy's modern-day reason to exist. There's not much to cheer about, though. The lowly Parma team barely clings to its place in the prestigious Series A of Italian soccer. The team still draws its faithful, though – about thirty thousand long-suffering fans show up with Cubs-like devotion year after year, game after game.

That's about twenty-nine thousand more than

generally show up for Panthers games at Stadio Lanfranchi. It has seating for three thousand, but rarely sells out. Actually, there's nothing to sell. Admission is free.

Rick Dockery walked slowly across midfield as long shadows fell, hands crammed in jeans pockets, the aimless stroll of a man in another world. Occasionally, he stopped and pressed hard with a loafer to check the turf. He had not stepped onto a field, or a pitch or whatever the hell it was, since that last day in Cleveland.

Sam sat five rows up on the home side, watching his quarterback and wondering what he was thinking.

Rick was thinking about a training camp one summer not too long ago, a brief but brutal ordeal with one of the pro teams, he couldn't remember exactly which. Camp that summer had been at a small college with a field similar to the one he was now inspecting. A Division III school, a tiny college with the obligatory rustic dorms and cafeteria and cramped locker rooms, the type of place some NFL teams choose to make training as tough and austere as possible.

And he was thinking about high school. Back at Davenport South he had played every game in front of more people, home and away. He lost in the state finals his junior year in front of eleven thousand, small maybe by Texas standards but still a heckuva crowd for Iowa high school football.

At the moment, though, Davenport South was

far away, as were many things that once seemed important. He stopped in the end zone and studied the goalposts, odd ones. Two tall posts, painted blue and yellow, anchored in the ground and wrapped with green padding that advertised Heineken. Rugby.

He climbed the steps and sat next to his coach, who said, 'Whatta you think?'

'Nice field, but you're missing a few yards.'

'Ten to be exact. The goalposts are 110 yards apart, but we need 20 for the two end zones. So we play on what's left, 90 yards. Most of the fields we play on are meant for rugby, so we have to make do.'

Rick grunted and smiled. 'Whatever.'

'It's a long way from Browns Stadium in Cleveland,' Sam said.

'Thank God for that. I never liked Cleveland, the city, the fans, the team, and I hated the stadium. Right there on Lake Erie, bitter winds, ground as hard as concrete.'

'What was your favorite stop?'

Rick grunted out a laugh and said, 'Stop. That's a good word. I stopped here and there, but never found a place. Dallas, I guess. I prefer warmer weather.'

The sun was almost gone and the air was growing cooler. Rick stuck his hands into the pockets of his tight jeans and said, 'So tell me about football in Italy. How did it happen?'

'The first teams popped up about twenty years ago and it spread like crazy, mainly here in the north. The Super Bowl in 1990 drew twenty thousand, a lot less last year. Then it declined for some reason; now it's growing again. There are nine teams in the A Division, twenty-five or so in the B Division, and flag football for the kids.'

Another pause as Rick rearranged his hands. The two months in Florida had given him a dark tan but a thin skin. His tan was already fading. 'How many fans watch the Panthers?'

'Depends. We don't sell tickets, so no one really counts. Maybe a thousand. When Bergamo rolls in, the place is packed.'

'Bergamo?'

'The Bergamo Lions, perennial champs.'

Rick found this amusing. 'Lions and Panthers. Do they all have NFL names?'

'No. We also have the Bologna Warriors, Rome Gladiators, Naples Bandits, Milan Rhinos, Lazio Marines, as well as the Ancona Dolphins, and Bolzano Giants.'

Rick chuckled at the names.

'What's so funny?' Sam asked.

'Nothing. Where am I?'

'It's normal. The shock wears off fast, though. Once you put on the gear and start hitting you'll feel at home.'

I don't hit, Rick wanted to say, but thought better of it. 'So Bergamo is the team to beat?'

'Oh yes. They've won eight straight Super Bowls and sixty-one straight games.'

'The Italian Super Bowl. Can't believe I missed it.'

'A lot of people missed it. On the sports pages we go last, after swimming and motorbiking. The Super Bowl is televised, though. On one of the lesser channels.'

Because he was still horrified at the thought of his friends learning that he was playing intramural ball in Italy, the prospect of no press and no televised games was quite appealing. Rick was not looking for glory in Parma, just a small paycheck while he and Arnie waited for a miracle back home. He didn't want anyone to know where he was.

'How often do we practice?'

'We get the field Monday, Wednesday, and Friday, eight o'clock at night. These guys have real jobs.'

'What kinds of jobs?'

'Everything. Airline pilot, engineer, several truck drivers, property agent, contractors, one guy owns a cheese shop, another runs a bar, a dentist, two or three work in gyms. Two stone-masons, a couple of auto mechanics.'

Rick considered this for a while. His thoughts were slow, the shock was wearing off. 'What type of offense?'

'We keep things basic. Power I, lots of motion and misdirection. Our quarterback last year couldn't throw, so it really limited our attack.'

'Your quarterback couldn't throw?'

'Well, he could, but not very well.'

'We got a runner?'

'Oh yes. Slidell Turner. Tough little black kid

from Colorado State, drafted late by the Colts four years ago, got cut, just too small.'

'How small?'

'Five eight, 180. Too small for the NFL, but perfect for the Panthers. They have trouble catching him here.'

'What the hell is a black kid from Colorado State doing here in Parma, Italy?'

'Playing football, waiting for the phone call. Same as you.'

'Do I have a receiver?'

'Yes, Fabrizio, one of the Italians. Great set of hands, great feet, great big ego. Thinks he's the greatest Italian footballer of all time. High maintenance, but not a bad boy.'

'Can he catch me?'

'I doubt it. It'll take a lot of practice. Just don't kill him the first day.'

Rick jumped to his feet and said, 'I'm cold. Let's make a move.'

'You wanna see the team room?'

'Sure, why not?'

There was a clubhouse just beyond the north end zone, and as they walked toward it, a train roared by, a stone's throw away. Inside, the long flat building was adorned with dozens of posters advertising the corporate sponsors. Rugby occupied most of it, but the Panthers had a small room packed with lockers and equipment.

'Whatta you think?' Sam asked.

'It's a locker room,' Rick said. He tried not to make comparisons, but for a moment couldn't help but remember the lavish digs in the newer NFL stadiums. Carpet, wood-paneled lockers big enough for small cars, leather recliners built for linemen, private stalls in a shower room bigger than this. Oh well. He told himself he could endure anything for five months.

'This is yours,' Sam said, pointing. Rick walked to his locker, an old metal cage, empty except for a white Panther helmet hanging from a hook. He had requested the number 8, and it was stenciled on the back of his helmet. Size seven and a half. Slidell Turner's locker was to the right, and the name to the left was Trey Colby.

'Who's this?' Rick asked.

'Colby is our free safety. Played at Ole Miss. Rooms with Slidell, the only two black guys on the team. We have only three Americans this year. Last year it was five, but they changed the rules again.'

On a table in the center there were neat stacks of game jerseys and pants. Rick inspected them carefully. 'Good stuff,' he declared.

'Glad you approve.'

'You mentioned dinner. I'm not sure which meal my body needs, but food would be welcome.'

'I have just the place. It's an old trattoria owned by two brothers. Carlo runs the kitchen and does the cooking. Nino handles the front and makes sure everyone is well fed. Nino is also your center, and don't be surprised when you meet him. Your center in high school was probably bigger, but he's tough on the field, and his idea of a good time is knocking people around for two hours once a week. He's also the offensive translator. You call the plays in English, then Nino does a quick version in Italian, then you break huddle. As you walk to the line, you pray that Nino got the translation right. Most of the Italians can understand the basics in English, and they're quick to go with their first impulse. Often they don't wait for Nino. On some plays the entire team breaks in different directions and you have no idea what's going on.'

'So what do I do?'

'Run like hell.'

'This should be fun.'

'It can be. But these guys take it serious, especially in the heat of the battle. They love to hit, both before the whistle and after. They cuss and fight, then they hug and go drink together. A player by the name of Paolo might join us for dinner. His English is very good. And there might be one or two others. They're anxious to meet you. Nino will take care of the food and wine, so don't worry with the menu. It will be delicious, trust me.'

Chapter 6

They drove near the university and parked on one of the endless narrow streets. It was dark now, and packs of students drifted by in noisy conversations. Rick was subdued, so Sam handled the dialogue. 'A trattoria, by definition, is an unassuming family-owned place with great local dishes and wines, generous portions, not too expensive. Are you listening to me?'

'Yes.' They were walking quickly along a sidewalk. 'Are you going to feed me or talk me to death?'

'I'm trying to ease you into Italian culture.'

'Just find me a pizza.'

'Where was I?'

'A trattoria.'

'Yes, as opposed to a restaurant, which is usually more elegant and expensive. Then there's the osteria, which traditionally was a dining room in an inn but now can mean almost anything. And the bar, which we've covered.

And the *enoteca*, which usually doubles as a wine shop and offers snacks and smaller dishes. I think that covers it all.'

'So no one goes hungry in Italy.'

'Are you kidding?'

A small sign for Café Montana hung over the door. Through the front window they could see a long room with empty tables, all covered with starched and pressed white cloths and adorned with blue plates, linens, and massive wine goblets.

'We're a bit early,' Sam said. 'The place gets busy around eight. But Nino is waiting.'

'Montana?' Rick said.

'Yes, after Joe. The quarterback.'

'No.'

'Dead serious. These guys love their football. Carlo played years ago but ruined a knee. Now he just cooks. Legend has it that he holds all kinds of records for personal fouls.'

They stepped inside, and whatever Carlo was preparing back in the kitchen hit them hard. The aroma of garlic and rich meat sauces and frying pork hung like smoke over the front room, and Rick was ready to eat. A fire was burning in a wall pit halfway back.

From a side door, Nino bounded into the room and began kissing Sam. A mighty embrace, then a manly, noisy peck somewhere near the right cheek, same for the left, then he grabbed Rick's right hand with both of his and said, 'Rick, my quarterback, welcome to Parma.' Rick shook hands firmly but was prepared to step backward if the kissing continued. It did not.

The accent was thick, but the words were clear. Rick was more like Reek.

'My pleasure,' Rick said.

'I am center,' Nino announced proudly. 'But be careful with your hands. My wife, she is jealous.' At which Nino and Sam doubled over in horse laughter, and Rick awkwardly followed suit.

Nino was less than six feet tall, thick and fit, probably around 210 pounds. As he laughed at his own humor, Rick quickly sized him up and realized it could be a very long season. A five-foot-ten center?

Nor was he a youngster. Nino had wavy dark hair with the first shades of gray at the temples. He was in his mid-thirties. But there was a strong chin and a definite glow of wildness, a man who loved to brawl.

I'll have to scramble for my life, Rick thought to himself.

Carlo rumbled in from the kitchen in his starched white apron and chef's hat. Now, here is the center. Six feet two, at least 250 pounds, broad shoulders. But a slight limp. He greeted Rick warmly, a quick embrace, no kissing. His English was far below Nino's, and after a few words he ditched it and switched to Italian, leaving Rick to tread water.

Sam was quick to step in. 'He says welcome to Parma and to their restaurant. They have never been so excited to have a real American Super Bowl hero playing for the Panthers. And he hopes you will eat and drink many times at their little café.'

'Thank you,' Rick said to Carlo. Their hands were still entangled. Carlo resumed his chatter and Sam was ready. 'He says the owner of the team is his friend and often eats at Café Montana. And that all of Parma is thrilled to have the great Rick Dockery wearing the black and silver.' Pause.

Rick said thanks again, smiled as warmly as possible, and repeated to himself the words 'Super Bowl.' Carlo finally released him and began yelling at the kitchen.

As Nino led them to their table, Rick whispered to Sam, 'Super Bowl. Where did that come from?'

'I don't know. Maybe I didn't get the translation right.'

'Great. You said you're fluent.'

'Most of the time.'

'All of Parma? The great Rick Dockery? What have you been telling these people?'

'The Italians exaggerate everything.'

Their table was near the fireplace. Nino and Carlo both pulled out chairs for their guests, and before Rick settled into his seat, three young waiters in perfect whites descended upon them. One had a large platter of food. One had a magnum of sparkling wine. One had a basket of breads and two bottles – olive oil and vinegar.

Nino snapped his fingers and pointed, and Carlo barked at one of the waiters, who returned fire, and off they went to the kitchen, arguing every step of the way.

Rick stared at the platter. In the center was a large chunk of straw-colored hard cheese, and surrounding it in precise loops were what appeared to be cold cuts. Deep, rich cured meats, unlike anything Rick had ever seen. As Sam and Nino chattered in Italian, a waiter quickly uncorked the wine and filled three glasses. He then stood at attention, starched towel over his arm.

Nino passed around the glasses, then held his high. 'A toast, to the great Reek Dockery, and to a Super Bowl win for the Parma Panthers.' Sam and Rick took a sip while Nino drained half of his. 'Is Malvasia Secco,' he said. 'From a winemaker close by. Everything tonight is from Emilia. The olive oil, the balsamic vinegar, wine, and food, everything from right here,' he said proudly, thumping his chest with an impressive fist. 'The best food in the world.'

Sam leaned over. 'This is the Parma province of Emilia-Romagna, one of the regions.'

Rick nodded and took another sip. On the flight over he had flipped through a guidebook and knew where he was, sort of. There are twenty regions in Italy, and according to his quick review almost all claimed to have the greatest food and wine in the country.

Now for the food.

Nino took another gulp, then leaned in, all ten fingertips touching, the professor set to deliver a lecture he'd given many times. With a casual wave at the cheese he said, 'Of course you know the greatest cheese of all. Parmigiano-Reggiano. You say Parmesan. The king of cheese, and made right here. Only real parmigiano comes from our little town. This one is made by my uncle four kilometers from where you are sitting. The best.'

He kissed the tips of his fingers, then gracefully shaved off a few slices, leaving them on the platter as the lecture continued. 'Next,' he said, pointing to the first loop, 'is the world-famous prosciutto. You say Parma ham. Made only here, from special pigs raised on barley and oats and the milk left over from making the parmigiano. Our prosciutto is never cooked,' he said gravely, wagging a finger for a second in disapproval. 'But cured with salt, fresh air, and lots of love. Eighteen months it's cured.'

He deftly took a small slice of brown bread, dipped it in olive oil, then layered it with a slice of prosciutto and a shaving of parmigiano. When it was perfect, he handed it to Rick and said, 'A little sandwich.' Rick took it in one large bite, then closed his eyes and savored the moment.

For someone who still enjoyed McDonald's, the tastes were astounding. The flavors coated every taste bud in his mouth and made him chew as slowly as possible. Sam was slicing more for himself, and Nino was pouring wine. 'Is good?' Nino asked Rick.

'Oh yes.'

Nino thrust another bite at his quarterback, then continued, pointing, 'And then we have *culatello*, from the pig's leg, pulled off the bone, only the best parts, then covered in salt, white wine, garlic, lots of herbs, and rubbed by hand for many hours before stuffed into a pig's bladder and cured for fourteen months. The summer air dries it, the wet winters keep it tender.' As he spoke, both hands were in constant motion – pointing, drinking, slicing more cheese, carefully mixing the balsamic vinegar into the bowl of olive oil. 'These are the best pigs, for the *culatello*,' he said, with another frown. 'Small black pigs with a few red patches, carefully selected and fed only natural foods. Never locked up, no. These pigs roam free and eat acorns and chestnuts.' He referred to the creatures with such deference it was difficult to believe they were about to eat one.

Rick was craving a bite of *culatello*, a meat he'd never before encountered. Finally, with a pause in the narrative, Nino handed over another small slice of bread, layered with a thick round of *culatello* and topped with parmigiano.

'Is good?' he asked, as Rick chomped away and held his hand out for more.

The wineglasses were refilled.

'The olive oil is from a farm just down the road,' Nino was saying. 'And the balsamic vinegar is from Modena, forty kilometers to the east. Home of Pavarotti, you know. The best balsamic vinegar comes from Modena. But we have better food in Parma.'

The final loop, at the edge of the platter, was Felino salami, made practically on the premises, aged for twelve months, and without a doubt the best salami in all of Italy. After serving it to Sam and Rick, Nino suddenly dashed to the front, where others were arriving. Finally alone, Rick took a knife and began carving off huge chunks of the parmigiano. He covered his plate with the meats, cheese, and breads, and ate like a refugee.

'Might want to pace yourself,' Sam cautioned. 'This is just the antipasto, the warm-up.'

'Helluva warm-up.'

'Are you in shape?'

'More or less. I'm at 225, about 10 over. I'll burn it off.'

'Not tonight, you won't.'

Two large young men, Paolo and Giorgio, joined them. Nino presented them to their quarterback while insulting them in Italian, and when all the embracing and greetings were out of the way, they plunked down and stared at the antipasto. Sam explained that they were linemen who could play both sides of the ball if necessary. Rick was encouraged because they were in their mid-twenties, well over six feet tall, thick-chested, and seemingly capable of throwing people around.

Glasses were filled, cheese sliced, prosciutto attacked with a vengeance.

'When did you arrive?' Paolo asked with only a trace of an accent.

'This afternoon,' Rick said.

'Are you excited?'

Rick managed to say, 'Sure,' with some conviction. Excited about the next course, excited about meeting Italian cheerleaders.

Sam explained that Paolo had a degree from Texas A&M and worked for his family's company, one that made small tractors and farm implements.

'So you're an Aggie,' Rick said.

'Yes,' Paolo said proudly. 'I love Texas. That's where I found football.'

Giorgio just smiled as he ate and listened to the conversation. Sam said that he was studying English, then whispered that looks were deceiving because Giorgio couldn't block a doorway. Great.

Carlo was back, directing waiters and rearranging the table. Nino produced another bottle, which, surprisingly, came from just around the corner. It was a Lambrusco, a sparkling red, and Nino knew the winemaker. There are many fine Lambruscos throughout Emilia-Romagna, he explained, but this was the best. And the perfect complement to the *tortellini in brodo* that his brother was serving at the moment. Nino took a step back, and Carlo began a rapid recitation in Italian.

Sam translated softly, but quickly. 'This is tortellini in meat stock, a famous dish here. The little round pasta balls are stuffed with braised beef, prosciutto, and parmigiano; the filling varies from town to town, but of course Parma has the best recipe. The pasta was handmade this afternoon by Carlo himself. Legend has it that the guy who created tortellini modeled it after the belly button of a beautiful naked woman. All sorts of such legends here involving food, wine, and sex. The broth is beef, garlic, butter, and a few other things.' Rick's nose was a few inches above his bowl, inhaling the rich aromas.

Carlo took a bow, then added something with caution. Sam said, 'He says these are small servings because more of the first course is on the way.'

Rick's first ever tortellini almost made him cry. Swimming in broth, the pasta and its filling jolted his senses and caused him to blurt, 'This is the best thing I've ever tasted.' Carlo smiled and began his retreat to the kitchen.

Rick washed the first tortellini down with Lambrusco, and attacked the others swimming in the deep bowl. Small servings? Paolo and Giorgio had gone silent and were deeply involved with their tortellini. Only Sam showed some restraint.

Nino seated a young couple nearby, then rushed forth with the next bottle, a fabulous dry red Sangiovese from a vineyard near Bologna that he personally visited once a month to monitor the progress of the grapes. 'The next course is a little more heavy,' he said. 'So the wine needs to be more strong.' He uncorked it with a flair, sniffed the bottle, rolled his eyes in approval, then began pouring. 'We are in for a treat,' he said as he filled five glasses, giving himself a slightly more generous serving. Another toast, more of a curse directed at the Bergamo Lions, and they tasted the wine.

Rick had always been a beer man. This headlong dive into the world of Italian wines was bewildering, but also very tasty.

One waiter was gathering the remains of the tortellini while another whisked down fresh plates. Carlo marched from the kitchen with two waiters in tow and directed traffic.

'This is my favorite,' Carlo began in English, then switched to a friendlier tongue. 'It's a stuffed pasta roll,' Sam was saying as they gawked at the delicacy before them. 'It is stuffed with veal, pork, chicken livers, sausage, ricotta cheese, and spinach, and layered with fresh pasta.'

Everyone but Rick said, '*Grazie*,' and Carlo took another bow and disappeared. The restaurant was almost full and becoming noisy. Rick, while never missing a bite, was curious about the people around him. They seemed to be locals, enjoying a typical meal at the neighborhood café. Back home, food like this would cause a stampede. Here, they took it for granted.

'You get a lot of tourists here?' he asked.

'Not many,' Sam said. 'All the Americans go to Florence, Venice, and Rome. A few in the summer. More Europeans than anyone else.'

'What's to see in Parma?' Rick asked. The Parma section of his guidebook had been rather scant.

'The Panthers!' Paolo said with a laugh.

Sam laughed, too, then sipped his wine and thought for a moment. 'It's a lovely little town of a hundred and fifty thousand. Great food and wine, great people who work hard and live well. But it doesn't attract a lot of attention. And that's good. You agree, Paolo?'

'Yes. We do not want Parma to change.'

Rick worked a mouthful and tried to isolate the veal, but it was impossible. The meats, cheese, and spinach blended together into one delicious taste. He was certainly no longer hungry, nor was he full. They had been there for an hour and a half, a very long dinner by his old standards, but just warming up in Parma. On cue from the other three, he began to eat slowly, very slowly. The Italians around him talked more than they ate, and a mild roar engulfed the trattoria. Dining was certainly about great food, but it was also a social event.

Nino dropped by every few minutes with a quick 'Is good?' for Rick. Great, wonderful, delicious, unbelievable.

For the second course, Carlo took a break from the pasta. The plates were covered – small portions still – with *cotolette alla parmigiana*, another famous dish from Parma and one of the chef's all-time favorites. 'Veal cutlets, Parma

65

style,' Sam translated. 'The veal cutlets are beaten with a small bat, then dipped in eggs, fried in a skillet, then baked in the oven with a mix of parmigiano cheese and stock until the cheese melts. Carlo's wife's uncle raised the veal himself and delivered it this afternoon.' As Carlo narrated and Sam interpreted, Nino was busy with the next wine, a dry red from the Parma region. Fresh glasses, even larger, were presented, and Nino swirled and sniffed and gulped. Another orgasmic roll of the eyes and it was declared sensational. A very close friend made the wine, perhaps Nino's favorite of all.

Sam whispered, 'Parma is famous for its food, but not its wine.'

Rick sipped the wine and smiled at the veal and vowed that he would, for the rest of the meal anyway, eat slower than the Italians. Sam watched him closely, certain that the culture shock was vanishing in a flood of food and wine.

'You eat like this often?' Rick asked him.

'Not every day, but this is not unusual,' Sam replied casually. 'This is typical food for Parma.'

Paolo and Giorgio were slicing their veal, and Rick slowly attacked his. The cutlets lasted half an hour, and when the plates were clean, they were removed with a flourish. A long pause followed as Nino and the waiters worked the other tables.

Dessert was not an option, because Carlo had baked his special, *torta nera*, or black pie, and because Nino had secured a very special wine for the occasion, a dry sparkling white from the province. He was saying that the black pie, created in Parma, was chocolate with almonds and coffee, and since it was so fresh from the oven, Carlo had added just a touch of vanilla ice cream on the side. Nino had a minute to spare, so he pulled up a chair and joined his teammates and coach for the final course, unless they were in the mood for some cheese and a digestif.

They were not. The restaurant was still half-full when Sam and Rick began offering their thanks and trying to say good-bye. Embraces, pats on backs, powerful handshakes, promises to come again, more welcomes to Parma, many thanks for the unforgettable dinner – the ritual took forever.

Paolo and Giorgio decided to stay behind and have a bite of cheese and finish off the wine.

'I'm not driving,' Sam said. 'We can walk. Your apartment is not far, and I'll catch a cab from there.'

'I gained ten pounds,' Rick said, pushing his stomach forward and following a step behind his coach.

'Welcome to Parma.'

Chapter 7

The buzzer had the high-pitched whine of a cheap scooter with a missing exhaust pipe. It arrived in long bursts, and since Rick had never heard it before, he at first had no idea what it meant, or where it was coming from. Things were foggy anyway. After the marathon at Montana's, he and Sam, for reasons that were not clear then or now, had stopped at a pub for a couple of beers. Rick vaguely remembered entering his apartment around midnight, but from then on, nothing.

He was on his sofa, which was too short for a man his size to comfortably sleep on, and as he listened to the mysterious buzzer, he tried to remember why he had chosen the den instead of the bedroom. He could not recall a good reason.

'All right!' he yelled at the door when the knocking began. 'I'm coming.'

He was barefoot, but wearing jeans and a T-shirt. He studied his brown toes for a long time and contemplated his spinning head. Another screech from the buzzer. 'All right!' he yelled again. Unsteady, he walked to the door and yanked it open.

He was met with a pleasant '*Buongiorno*' from a short, stocky man with an enormous gray mustache and rumpled brown trench coat. Beside him was a smartly uniformed young policeman who nodded his greetings but said nothing.

'Good morning,' Rick said with as much respect as he could muster.

'Signor Dockery?'

'Yes.'

'I am police.' From somewhere deep in the trench coat he produced documentation, waved it under Rick's nose, then returned it to its hiding place with a move so casual the message was 'Don't ask any questions.' It could've been a parking ticket or a receipt from the cleaners.

'Signor Romo, Parma police,' he said through the mustache, though it barely moved.

Rick looked at Romo, then at the cop in the uniform, then back at Romo. 'Okay,' he managed to say.

'We have complaints. You must come with us.'

Rick grimaced and tried to say something, but a thick wave of nausea rumbled down low, and he thought about bolting. It passed. His palms were sweaty, his knees rubbery. 'Complaints?' he said in disbelief.

'Yes.' Romo nodded gravely, as if he had already made up his mind and Rick was guilty of something far worse than whatever the complaint was. 'Come with us.'

'Uh, to where?'

'Come with us. Now.'

Complaints? The pub had been virtually empty last night, and he and Sam, to the best of his memory, had spoken to no one but the bartender. Over beers, they had talked football and nothing else. Pleasant conversation, no cursing or fighting with the other drinkers. The walk through the old town to his apartment had been thoroughly uneventful. Perhaps the avalanche of pasta and wine had made him snore too loudly, but that couldn't be a crime, could it?

'Who complained?' Rick asked.

'The judge will explain. We must go. Please, your shoes.'

'Are you arresting me?'

'No, maybe later. Let's go. The judge is waiting.' For effect, Romo turned and rattled some serious Italian at the young cop, who managed to deepen his frown and shake his head as if things could not possibly be worse.

They obviously weren't leaving without Signor Dockery. The nearest shoes were the maroon loafers, which he found in the kitchen, and as he put them on and looked for a jacket, he told himself it had to be a misunderstanding. He quickly brushed his teeth and tried to gargle away the layers of garlic and stale wine. One look in the small mirror was enough; he certainly looked guilty of something. Red puffy eyes, three days' growth, wild hair. He tousled his hair, to no effect, then grabbed his wallet, U.S. cash, apartment key, and cell phone. Maybe he should call Sam.

Romo and his assistant were waiting patiently in the hallway, both smoking, neither with handcuffs. They also seemed to lack any real desire to catch criminals. Romo had watched too many detective shows, and every movement was bored and rehearsed. He nodded down the hall and said, 'I follow.' He dropped the cigarette in a hall ashtray, then stuck both hands deep in the pockets of his trench coat. The cop in the uniform led the perpetrator away, and Romo protected from the rear. Down three flights, onto the sidewalk. It was almost 9:00 a.m., a bright spring day.

Another cop was waiting by a well-dressed Fiat sedan, complete with an array of lights and the word *Polizia* painted in orange on every fender. The second cop was working on a cigarette and studying the rear ends of two ladies who had just passed him. He gave Rick a look of utter disregard, then took another puff.

'Let's walk,' Romo said. 'Is not far. You need air, I think.'

Indeed I do, Rick thought. He decided to cooperate, score some points with these guys, and help them discover the truth, whatever that was. Romo nodded down the street and walked beside Rick as they followed the first cop.

'Can I make a phone call?' Rick asked.

'Of course. A lawyer?'

'No.'

Sam's phone went straight to voice mail. Rick thought about Arnie, but little good that would do. Arnie had grown increasingly hard to catch by phone.

And so they walked, along the Strada Farini, past the small shops with their doors and windows open, past the sidewalk cafés where people sat almost motionless with their newspapers and little espressos. Rick's head was clearing, his stomach had settled. One of those small strong coffees might be welcome.

Romo lit another cigarette, blew out a small cloud of smoke, then said, 'You like Parma?'

'I don't think so.'

'No?'

'No. This is my first full day here, and I'm under arrest for something I did not do. Kinda hard to like the place.'

'There's no arrest,' Romo said as he lumbered heavily from side to side, as if both knees were about to fold. Every third or fourth step his shoulder nudged Rick's right arm as he lurched again.

'Then what do you call it?' Rick asked.

'Our system is different here. No arrest.'

Oh well, that certainly explains things. Rick bit his tongue and let it pass. Arguing would get him nowhere. He had done nothing wrong, and the truth would soon settle matters. This was not, after all, some Third World dictatorship where they randomly rounded up people for a few months of torture. This was Italy, part of Europe, the heart of Western civilization. Opera, the Vatican, the Renaissance, da Vinci, Armani, Lamborghini. It was all right there in his guidebook.

Rick had seen worse. His only prior arrest had been in college, during the spring of his freshman year when he found himself a willing member of a drunken gang determined to crash an off-campus fraternity party. Fights and broken bones ensued; the police showed up in force. Several of the hooligans were subdued, handcuffed, knocked around by the cops, and finally thrown in the rear of a police wagon, where they were poked a few times by nightsticks, for good measure. At the jail, they slept on cold concrete floors in the drunk tank. Four of those arrested were members of the Hawkeye football team, and their adventures through the legal system were sensationally reported by several newspapers.

In addition to the humiliation, Rick got thirty days suspended, a fine of four hundred dollars, a scathing tongue-lashing from his father, and the promise from his coach that another infraction, however minor, would cost him his scholarship and send him to either jail or junior college.

Rick managed the next five years without so much as a speeding ticket.

They changed streets and turned abruptly into a quiet cobblestoned alley. An officer in a different uniform stood benignly by an unmarked opening. Nods and quick words were exchanged, and Rick was led through the door, up a flight of faded marble steps to the second floor, and into a hallway that obviously housed government offices. The decor was drab; the walls needed paint; portraits of long-forgotten civil servants hung in a sad row. Romo selected a harsh wooden bench and said, 'Please have a seat.'

Rick obeyed and tried Sam's number once more. Same voice mail.

Romo disappeared into one of the offices. There was no name on the door, nothing to indicate where the accused was or whom he was about to see. There was certainly no courtroom nearby, none of the usual hustle and noise of frantic lawyers and worried families and cops bantering back and forth. A typewriter rattled in the distance. Desk phones rang and voices could be heard.

The cop in the uniform drifted away and struck up a conversation with a young lady at a desk forty feet down the hall. He soon forgot about Rick, who was quite alone and unwatched and could have nonchalantly disappeared. But why bother?

Ten minutes passed, and the cop in the uniform finally left without saying a word. Romo was gone, too.

The door opened and a pleasant woman smiled and said, 'Mr. Dockery? Yes? Please.' She was offering him an entrance into the office. Rick walked inside. It was a crowded front room with two desks and two secretaries, both of whom were smiling at Rick as if they knew something he didn't. One in particular was very cute, and Rick instinctively tried to think of something to say. But what if she spoke no English?

'A moment please,' the first lady said, and Rick stood awkwardly as the other two pretended to return to work. Romo had evidently found the side door and was no doubt back on the street pestering someone else.

Rick turned and noticed the large, dark double wooden doors, and beside them was an impressive bronze plaque that announced the eminence of Giuseppe Lazzarino, *Giudice*. Rick walked closer, then even closer, then pointed to the word *Giudice* and asked, 'What is this?'

'Judge,' the first lady said.

Both doors suddenly flew open and Rick came face-to-face with the judge. 'Reek Dockery!' he shouted, thrusting a right hand forward while grabbing a shoulder with his left, as though they had not seen each other in years. Indeed they had not.

'I am Giuseppe Lazzarino, a Panther. I am fullback.' He pumped and squeezed and flashed his large white teeth.

'Nice to meet you,' Rick said, trying to inch backward.

'Welcome to Parma, my friend,' Lazzarino said. 'Please come in.' He was already pulling on

75

Rick's right hand as he continued to shake it. Once inside the large office, he released Rick, closed both doors, and said again, 'Welcome.'

'Thanks,' Rick said, feeling slightly assaulted. 'Are you a judge?'

'Call me Franco,' he demanded, waving at a leather sofa in one corner. It was evident that Franco was too young to be a seasoned judge and too old to be a useful fullback. His large round head was shaved slick; the only hair on his head was an odd thin patch on his chin. Mid-thirties, like Nino, but over six feet tall, solid and fit. He fell into a chair, pulled it close to Rick on the sofa, and said, 'Yes, I am judge, but, more importantly, I am fullback. Franco is my nickname. Franco is my hero.'

Then Rick looked around, and understood. Franco was everywhere. A life-size cutout of Franco Harris running the ball during a very muddy game. A photo of Franco and other Steelers holding a Super Bowl trophy triumphantly over their heads. A framed white jersey, number 32, apparently signed by the great man himself. A small Franco Harris doll with an oversize head on the judge's immense desk. And displayed prominently in the center of the Ego Wall, two large color photographs, one of Franco Harris in full Steeler game gear, minus the helmet, and the other of Franco the judge here, in a Panther uniform, no helmet, and wearing number 32 and trying his best to imitate his hero.

'I love Franco Harris, the greatest Italian football player,' Franco was saying, his eyes practically moist, his voice a bit gravelly. 'Just look at him.' He waved his hands triumphantly around the office, which was practically a shrine to Franco Harris.

'Franco was Italian?' Rick asked slowly. Though never a Steelers fan, and too young to recall the glory days of Pittsburgh's dynasty, Rick was nonetheless a fair student of the game. He was certain that Franco Harris was a black guy who played at Penn State, then led the Steelers to a number of Super Bowls back in the 1970s. He was dominant, a Pro Bowler, and later inducted into the Hall of Fame. Every football fan knew Franco Harris.

'His mother was Italian. His father was an American soldier. You like the Steelers? I love the Steelers.'

'Well, no, actually—'

'Why haven't you played for the Steelers?'

'They haven't called yet.'

Franco was on the edge of his seat, hyper with the presence of his new quarterback. 'Let's have coffee,' he said, jumping to his feet, and before Rick could answer, he was at the door, barking instructions to one of the girls. He was stylish – snug black suit, long pointed Italian loafers, size 14 at least.

'We really want a Super Bowl trophy here in Parma,' he said as he grabbed something from his desk. 'Look.' He pointed the remote control to a flat-screen TV in a corner, and suddenly there was more Franco – pounding through the line as tacklers bounced off, leaping over the pile for a touchdown, stiff-arming a Cleveland Brown (yes!) and ripping off another touchdown, taking a handoff from Bradshaw, and bowling over two massive linemen. It was Franco's greatest hits, long, punishing runs that were enjoyable to watch. The judge, thoroughly mesmerized, jerked and cut and pumped his fists with each great move.

How many times has he seen this? Rick asked himself.

The last play was the most famous – the Immaculate Reception – Franco's inadvertent catch of a deflected pass and his miracle gallop to the end zone in a 1972 play-off game against Oakland. The play had created more debate, review, analysis, and fights than any in the history of the NFL, and the judge had memorized every frame.

The secretary arrived with the coffee, and Rick managed a bad 'Grazie.'

Then it was back to the video. Part two was interesting but also a bit depressing. Franco the judge had added his own greatest hits, a few sluggish runs through and around linemen and linebackers even slower than himself. He beamed at Rick as they watched the Panthers in action, Rick's first glimpse of his future.

'You like?' Franco asked.

'Nice,' Rick said, a word that seemed to satisfy many inquiries in Parma.

The final play was a screen pass that Franco took from an emaciated quarterback. He tucked the ball into his gut, bent over like an infantryman, and began looking for the first defender to hit. A couple bounced off, Franco spun free, kicked up his legs, and was off to the races. Two cornerbacks made halfhearted attempts to stick their helmets into his churning legs, but they bounced off like flies. Franco was soaring down the sideline, straining mightily in his best Franco Harris imitation.

'Is this in slow motion?' Rick asked, a half effort at humor.

Franco's mouth fell open. He was wounded.

'Just kidding,' Rick said quickly. 'A joke.'

Franco managed to fake a laugh. As he crossed the goal line, he spiked the ball, and the screen went blank.

'For seven years I play fullback,' Franco said as he resumed his perch on the edge of his seat. 'And we never beat Bergamo. This year, with our great quarterback, we will win the Super Bowl. Yes?'

'Of course. So where did you learn football?'

'Some friends.'

They both took a sip of coffee and waited through an awkward pause. 'What kind of judge are you?' Rick finally asked.

Franco rubbed his chin and considered this at great length, as though he'd never before thought about what he did. 'I do lots of things,' he finally said with a smile. His phone rang on the desk, and though he didn't answer it, he did look at his watch.

'We are so glad to have you here in Parma, my friend Rick. My quarterback.'

'Thanks.'

'I will see you at practice tonight.'

'Of course.'

Franco was on his feet now, his other duties calling him. Rick was not exactly expecting to be fined or otherwise punished, but Romo's 'complaints' needed to be addressed, didn't they?

Evidently not. Franco swept Rick from his office with the mandatory embraces and handshakes and promises to help in any way, and Rick was soon in the hall, then down the stairs and into the alley, all alone, a free man.

Chapter 8

Sam passed the time in the empty café with the Panther playbook, a thick binder with a thousand Xs and Os, a hundred offensive plays, and a dozen defensive schemes. Thick, but not nearly as thick as the ones handed out by college teams, and a mere memo compared with the tomes used in the NFL. And too thick, according to the Italians. It was often mumbled, in the tedium of a long chalkboard session, that there was little wonder soccer was so popular throughout the rest of the world. It was so easy to learn, to play, and to understand.

And these are just the basics, Sam was always tempted to say.

Rick arrived promptly at 11:30, and the café was still empty. Only a couple of Americans would arrange a lunch at such an odd hour. Lunch, but only salads and water.

Rick had showered and shaved and looked far less criminal. With great animation, he relayed the story of his encounter with Detective Romo, his 'non-arrest,' and the meeting with Judge Franco. Sam was highly entertained and assured Rick that no other American had received such a special welcome from Franco. Sam had seen the video. Yes, Franco was as slow in the flesh as he was on the film, but he was a punishing blocker and would run through a brick wall, or at least give it his best shot.

Sam explained that to the best of his limited knowledge, Italian judges are different from their American counterparts. Franco had broad authority to initiate investigations and proceedings, and he also presided over trials. After a thirty-second summary of Italian law, Sam had exhausted his knowledge on the subject, and it was back to football.

They picked through the lettuce and played with the tomatoes, but neither had much of an appetite. After an hour, they left on foot to handle some business. The first item was the opening of a checking account. Sam chose his bank, primarily because a certain assistant manager could thrash through enough English to resolve matters. Sam pressed Rick to do it himself, and helped only when things were at an impasse. It took an hour, and Rick was frustrated and more than a little intimidated. Sam would not always be around to translate.

With a quick tour of Rick's neighborhood and the center of Parma, they found a small grocery with fruits and vegetables stacked along the sidewalk. Sam was explaining that Italians prefer to buy their food fresh each day and avoid stock-piling groceries in cans and bottles. The butcher was next door to the fish market. Bakeries were on every corner. 'The Kroger concept doesn't work over here,' Sam said. 'Housewives plan their day around shopping for fresh food.' Rick gamely tagged along, somewhat engaged in the sightseeing but not interested in the notion of cooking. Why bother? There were so many places to eat. The wine and cheese shop held little interest, at least until Rick spotted a very attractive young lady stocking reds. Sam pointed out two men's stores, and again dropped rather pointed hints about ditching the Florida garb and upgrading to the local fashions. They also found a cleaners, a bar with great cappuccino, a bookstore where every book was in Italian, and a pizzeria with a menu in four languages.

Then it was time for the car. Somewhere in Signor Bruncardo's little empire a well-used but clean and shiny Fiat Punto had become avail-able, and for the next five months it belonged to the quarterback. Rick walked around it, inspected it carefully without uttering a word, but couldn't help but think that at least four of them would fit into the SUV he'd been driving until three days ago.

He folded himself into the driver's seat and inspected the dash. 'It'll do,' he finally said to Sam, who was standing a few feet away on the sidewalk.

He touched the stick shift and realized it was not rigid. It moved, too much. Then his left foot got caught on something that was not a brake pedal. A clutch?

'Manual, huh?' he said.

'All cars here are manual. Not a problem, is it?'

'Of course not.' He could not remember the last time his left foot had depressed a clutch. A friend in high school had a Mazda with a stick shift, and Rick had practiced once or twice. That was at least ten years ago. He jumped out, slammed the door, and almost said, Got anything with an automatic? But he didn't. He could not show concern with something as simple as a car with a clutch.

'It's either this or a scooter,' Sam said.

Give me the scooter, Rick wanted to say.

Sam left him there, with the Fiat he was afraid to drive. They agreed to meet in a couple of hours in the locker room. The playbook had to be addressed as soon as possible. The Italians might not learn all the plays, but the quarterback was required to.

Rick walked around the block, thinking of all the playbooks he'd suffered through in his nomadic career. Arnie would call with a new deal. Rick would take off to his newest team, terribly excited. A quick hello at the front office; quick tour of the stadium, locker room, and so on. Then all enthusiasm faded the instant some assistant coach marched in with the massive playbook and dropped it in front of him. 'Memorize it by tomorrow' was always the command.

Sure, Coach. A thousand plays. No problem.

How many playbooks? How many assistant coaches? How many teams? How many stops along the way in a frustrating career that had now led him to a small town in northern Italy? He drank a beer at a sidewalk café and couldn't shake the lonely feeling that this was not where he was supposed to be.

He shuffled through the wine shop, terrified a clerk might ask him if there was anything in particular he needed. The cute girl stocking the reds was gone.

And then he was back, staring at the five-speed Fiat, clutch and all. He didn't even like the color, a deep copper he'd never seen. It was in a row of similar cars parked tightly together, less than a foot between bumpers, on a one-way street with a fair amount of traffic. Any effort to drive away would require him to ease forward and back, forward and back, at least a half dozen times as he inched the front wheels into the street. Perfect coordination of the clutch, stick, and accelerator would be essential.

It would be a challenge in an automatic. Why did these people park so close together? The key was in his pocket.

Maybe later. He walked to his apartment and took a nap.

*   *   *

Rick changed quickly into the Panther practice uniform – black shirt, silver shorts, white socks. Each player bought his own shoes, and Rick had hauled over three pairs of the game-day Nikes the Browns had so freely dispensed. Most NFL players had shoe contracts. Rick had never been offered one.

He was alone in the locker room, flipping through the playbook, when Sly Turner bounced in, all smiles and wearing a bright orange Denver Broncos sweatshirt. They introduced themselves, shook hands politely, and before long Rick said, 'You wearing that for a reason?'

'Yep, love my Broncos,' Sly said, still smiling. 'Grew up near Denver, went to Colorado State.'

'That's nice. I hear I'm a popular guy in Denver.'

'We love you, man.'

'Always needed to be loved. Are we gonna be pals, Sly?'

'Sure, just give me the ball twenty times a game.'

'Done.' Rick removed a shoe from his locker, slowly put it on his right foot, and began lacing it. 'You get drafted?'

'Seventh round by the Colts, four years ago. Last player cut. One year in Canada, two years in arena ball.' The smile was gone and Sly was undressing. He looked much shorter than five feet eight, but he was solid muscle.

'And here last year, right?'

'Right. It ain't that bad. Kinda fun, if you keep

86

your sense of humor. The guys on the team are wonderful. If not for them, I'd never come back.'

'Why are you here?'

'Same reason you're here. Too young to give up the dream. Plus, I got a wife and kid now and I need the money.'

'The money?'

'Sad, ain't it? A professional football player making ten thousand bucks for five months' work. But, like I said, I ain't ready to quit.' He finally pulled off the orange sweatshirt and replaced it with a Panther practice jersey.

'Let's go loosen up,' Rick said, and they left the locker room and walked onto the field.

'My arm's pretty stiff,' Rick said as he made a weak throw.

'You're lucky you're not crippled,' Sly said.

'Thanks.'

'What a hit. I was at my brother's, yelling at the TV. Game was over, then Marroon goes out with an injury. Eleven minutes to go, everything was hopeless, then—'

Rick held the ball for a second. 'Sly, really, I'd rather not replay it. Okay?'

'Sure. Sorry.'

'Is your family here?' Rick asked, quickly changing the subject.

'No, back in Denver. My wife's a nurse, good job. She told me I got one more year of football, then the dream is over. You got a wife?'

'No, not even close.'

'You'll like it here.'

'Tell me about it.' Rick walked back five yards and straightened his passes.

'Well, it's a very different culture. The women are beautiful, but much more reserved. It's a very chauvinistic society. The men don't marry until they're thirty; they live at home with their mothers, who wait on them hand and foot, and when they get married, they expect their wives to do the same. The women are reluctant to get married. They need to work, so the women are having fewer kids. The birthrate here is declining rapidly.'

'I wasn't exactly thinking about marriage and birthrates, Sly. I'm more curious about the nightlife, you know what I mean?'

'Yeah, lots of girls, and pretty ones, but the language thing is a problem.'

'What about the cheerleaders?'

'What about them?'

'Are they cute, easy, available?'

'I wouldn't know. We don't have any.'

Rick held the ball, froze, looked hard at his tailback. 'No cheerleaders?'

'Nope.'

'But my agent . . .' He stopped before he embarrassed himself. So his agent had promised something that couldn't happen. What else was new?

Sly was laughing, a loud infectious laugh that said, 'Joke's on you, clown.'

'You came over here for the cheerleaders?' he said, high-pitched and mocking.

Rick fired a bullet, which Sly easily caught with his fingertips, then kept laughing. 'Sounds like my agent. Tells the truth about half the time.'

Rick finally laughed at himself as he backed up another five yards. 'What's the game like here?' he asked.

'Absolutely delightful, because they can't catch me. I averaged two hundred yards a game last year. You'll have a great time, if you can remember to throw to our players instead of the other team.'

'Cheap shot.' Rick zipped another bullet; again it was easily caught by Sly, who in return lobbed it back. The unwritten rule held firm – never throw a hard pass to a quarterback.

Jogging up from the locker room was the other black Panther, Trey Colby, a tall, gangly kid too skinny for football. He had an easy smile, and in less than a minute said to Rick, 'Are you okay, man?'

'Doing well, thanks.'

'I mean, the last time I saw you, you were on a stretcher and—'

'I'm fine, Trey. Let's talk about something else.'

Sly was enjoying the moment. 'He'd rather not talk about it. I've already tried,' he said.

For an hour they played catch and talked about players they knew back home.

Chapter 9

The Italians were in a festive mood. For the first practice they arrived early and loud. They bickered over who got which locker, complained about the wall decor, yelled at the equipment boy for a multitude of offenses, and vowed all manner of revenge against Bergamo. They continually insulted and ridiculed one another as they slowly changed into their practice shorts and jerseys. The locker room was cramped and rowdy and felt more like a fraternity house.

Rick absorbed it all. There were about forty of them, ranging from kids who looked like teenagers to a few aging warriors pushing forty. There were some solid bodies; in fact most seemed to be in excellent shape. Sly said they lifted in the off-season and pushed each other in the weight room. But the contrasts were startling, and Rick, as much as he tried not to, couldn't avoid a few silent comparisons. First, with the exception of Sly and Trey, all faces were white. Every NFL team he'd 'visited' along the way had been at least 70 percent black. Even at Iowa, hell, even in Canada, the teams were 50–50. And though there were some big boys in the room, there were no 300-pounders. The Browns had eight players at 310 or more, and only two under 200. A few of the Panthers would stretch to hit 175.

Trey said they were excited about their new quarterback, but cautious about approaching him. To help matters, Judge Franco assumed a position on Rick's right, and Nino took charge of the left. They made lengthy, even rambling introductions as the players took turns greeting Rick. Each little intro required at least two insults, often with Franco and Nino tag-teaming against their fellow Italian. Rick was embraced and gripped and fawned over until he was almost embarrassed. He was surprised by the amount of English used. Every Panther was learning the language at some level.

Sly and Trey were close by, laughing at him but also reuniting with their old teammates. Both had already vowed that this would be their last year in Italy. Few Americans returned for a third season.

Coach Russo called things to order and welcomed everyone back. His Italian was slow and thoughtful. The players were sprawled on the floor, on benches, in chairs, even in lockers. Though he kept trying not to, Rick couldn't help but flash back. He remembered the locker room at Davenport South High School. It was at least four times larger than the one he was now in.

'You understand this?' he whispered to Sly.

'Sure,' he said with a grin.

'Then what's he saying?'

'Says the team was unable to find a decent quarterback in the off-season so we're screwed again.'

'Quiet!' Sam yelled at the Americans, and the Italians were amused.

If you only knew, thought Rick. He'd once seen a semi-famous NFL coach cut a rookie for chatting in a team meeting during camp. Cut him on the spot, almost made him cry. Some of the most memorable tongue-lashings, dog-cussings, verbal bloodlettings Rick had seen in football had happened not in the heat of battle but in the seemingly safe confines of the locker room.

'*Mi dispiace*,' Sly said loudly, causing even more chuckles.

Sam continued. 'What was that?' Rick whispered.

'Means I'm sorry,' Sly hissed with his jaws clenched. 'Now will you shut up.'

Rick had mentioned to Sam earlier that he needed just a few words with the team. When Sam finished his welcoming remarks, he introduced Rick and handled the translation. Rick stood, nodded to his new teammates, and said, 'I'm very happy to be here, and looking forward to the season.' Sam threw up a hand – halt – translation. The Italians smiled.

'I'd like to clear up one thing.' Halt, more Italian.

'I've played in the NFL, but not very much, and I have never played in the Super Bowl.' Sam frowned and rendered. He would explain later that the Italians take a dim view of modesty and self-deprecation.

'In fact, I've never started a game as a professional.' Another frown, slower Italian, and Rick wondered if Sam wasn't doctoring his little speech. There were no smiles among the Italians.

Rick looked at Nino and continued, 'Just wanted to clear that up. It is my goal to win my first Super Bowl here in Italy.' Sam's voice grew much stronger, and when he finished, the room erupted into applause. Rick sat down and got a bruising bear hug from Franco, who had slightly outmaneuvered Nino as the bodyguard.

Sam outlined the practice plan, and the speeches were over. With a rousing cheer, they hustled from the locker room and over to the practice field, where they fanned out into a somewhat organized pattern and began stretching. At this point, a thick-necked gentleman with a shaved head and bulging biceps took over. He was Alex Olivetto, a former player, now an assistant coach, and a real Italian. He strutted up and down the lines of players barking orders like an angry field marshal, and there was no back talk.

'He's psycho,' Sly said when Alex was far away.

Rick was at the end of a line, next to Sly and

behind Trey, copying the stretches and exercises of his teammates. Alex went from the basics – jumping jacks, push-ups, sit-ups, lunges – to a grueling session of running in place with an occasional drop to the ground, then back up. After fifteen minutes, Rick was heaving and trying to forget last night's dinner. He glanced to his left and noticed that Nino had worked up a good sweat.

After thirty minutes, Rick was sorely tempted to pull Sam aside and explain a few things. He was the quarterback, you know, and quarter-backs, at the professional level, are not subjected to the same drills and boot camp banalities required of the regular players. But Sam was far away, at the other end of the field. Then Rick realized he was being watched. As the warm-up dragged on, he caught more glances from his teammates, just checking to see if a real pro quarterback could grind it out with them. Was he a member of the team, or a prima donna just passing through?

Rick kicked it up a notch to impress them.

Usually, wind sprints were put off until the end of practice, but not so with Alex. After forty-five minutes of bruising exercises, the team members gathered at the goal line, and in groups of six sprinted forty yards downfield, where Alex was waiting with a very active whistle and a nasty insult for whoever brought up the rear. Rick ran with the backs. Sly easily raced away, and Franco easily thundered in last. Rick was in the middle, and as he sprinted, he remembered the glory days at Davenport South when he ran wild and scored almost as many touchdowns with his feet as with his arm. The running slowed considerably in college; he was simply not a running quarterback. Running was almost prohibited in the pros; it was an excellent way to get a leg broken.

The Italians chattered at each other, offering encouragement as the sprints dragged on. After five they were breathing heavily and Alex was just warming up.

'Can you puke?' Sly asked between breaths.

'Why?'

'Because he runs us until someone pukes.'

'Go ahead.'

'I wish I could.'

After ten forties, Rick was asking himself what, exactly, he had been expecting in Parma. His hamstrings were on fire, his calves ached, he was straining and gasping and soaked with sweat, though the temperature was hardly warm. He'd have a talk with Sam and get some things straight. This wasn't high school ball. He was a pro!

Nino bolted for the sideline, ripped off his helmet, and delivered. The team yelled its encouragement, and Alex gave three quick bursts on the whistle. After a water break, Sam stepped forward with instructions. He would take the backs and receivers. Nino had the offensive linemen. Alex had the linebackers and defensive linemen. Trey was in charge of the secondary. They scattered around the field.

'This is Fabrizio,' Sam said, introducing the rather slim receiver to Rick. 'Our wideout, great hands.' They acknowledged each other. High-maintenance, high-strung, God's gift to Italian football. Sam had briefed Rick on Fabrizio and suggested that he take it easy on the kid for the first couple of days. There had been no small number of receivers in the NFL who'd had trouble with Rick's bullets, at least in practice. In games, the bullets, though beautiful, had too often sailed high and wide. A few had been caught by fans five rows up.

The backup quarterback was a twenty-year-old Italian named Alberto something or other. Rick threw soft sideline routes to one group, Alberto to the other. According to Sam, Alberto preferred to run the ball because he had a rather weak arm. Weak it was, Rick noticed after a couple of passes. He threw like a shot-putter, and his passes fluttered through the air like wounded birds.

'Was he the backup last year?' Rick asked when Sam got close enough.

'Yes, but didn't play much.'

Fabrizio was a natural athlete, quick and graceful with soft hands. He worked hard to appear nonchalant, as if anything Rick fired to him was just another easy catch. He big-leagued a few catches, snared them with too much cocky indifference, then committed a sin that would have cost him dearly in the NFL. On a lack-adaisical quick-out, he snatched the ball with one hand simply to show off. The pass was on target and did not need a one-arm grab. Rick simmered, but Sam was all over it. 'Let it go,' he said. 'He doesn't know any better.'

Rick's arm was still slightly sore, and though he was in no hurry to impress anyone, he was tempted to gun one into Fabrizio's chest and watch him drop like a rock. Relax, he said to himself, he's just a kid having fun.

Then Sam barked at Fabrizio for running sloppy patterns, and the kid sulked like a baby. More patterns, longer throws, then Sam brought the offense together for a review of the basics. Nino squatted over the ball, and to prevent jammed fingers, Rick suggested they practice a few snaps, slowly. Nino agreed that this was an excellent idea, but when Rick's hands touched his backside, he flinched. Not a radical jerk of the rear, nothing that would cause a referee to flag him for illegal procedure or offside, but a distinguishable tightening of the gluteus maximus much like a schoolkid about to receive licks from a thick wooden paddle. Perhaps it was just a case of new-quarterback jitters, Rick told himself. For the next snap, Nino hovered over the ball, Rick bent slightly forward, eased his hands just under the center's rump, as he had done since junior high school, and upon contact Nino's glutes instinctively tightened again.

The snaps were slow and soft, and Rick knew

immediately that hours were needed to improve Nino's technique. A full step would be wasted waiting on the ball while tailbacks broke for their holes and receivers ran to their spots.

On the third snap, Rick's fingers grazed Nino's zone ever so slightly, and evidently such a soft touch was far worse than an outright slap with the hands. Both cheeks arched painfully at the delicate contact. Rick glanced at Sam and quickly said, 'Can you tell him to relax his ass?'

Sam turned away to keep from laughing.

'Is problem?' Nino asked.

'Never mind,' Rick said. Sam blew his whistle, called a play in English, then Italian. It was a simple tailback off-tackle to the right, Sly taking the handoff with Franco plowing through the hole first like a bulldozer.

'The cadence?' Rick asked as the linemen settled into place.

'Down, set, hut,' Sam replied. 'In English.'

Nino, who evidently held the unofficial position of offensive line coach, inspected the guards and tackles before squatting over the ball and preparing his glutes. Rick touched them as he yelled, 'Down!' They flinched and Rick hurriedly added, 'Set,' then, 'Hut.'

Franco grunted like a bear as he lunged from his three-point stance and lurched to the right. The line moved forward, bodies jolting upright, voices growling as if the hated Bergamo Lions were over there, and Rick waited an eternity for the ball to arrive from his center. He was half a step back when he finally grabbed it, turned, and thrust it at Sly, who had already run up the back of Franco.

Sam blew his whistle, yelled something in Italian, then, 'Do it again.' And again and again.

After ten snaps, Alberto stepped in to run the offense, and Rick found some water. He sat on his helmet and was soon drifting away to other teams, other fields. The drudgery of practice was the same everywhere, he decided. From Iowa to Canada to Parma and all those stops in between, the worst part of the game, in whatever language, was the numbing tedium of physical conditioning and the repetition of running play after play.

It was late when Alex assumed authority again, and with his quick shrill whistle the forty-yard sprints began with a fury. The jokes and insults were gone. No one laughed or yelled as they ran down the field, slower with each whistle, but not so slow that Alex might get upset. After each sprint, they trotted back to the goal line, rested for a few seconds, then off again.

Rick vowed to have a serious little chat with the head coach tomorrow. Real quarterbacks do not run wind sprints, he kept telling himself as he urged himself to get sick.

★ ★ ★

The Panthers had a delightful post-practice ritual – a late dinner of pizza and beer at Polipo's, a small restaurant on Via La Spezia on the edge of the city. By 11:30, most of the team had arrived, fresh from showers and anxious to officially kick off another season. Gianni, the owner, put them in a back corner so they wouldn't be too disruptive. They gathered around two long tables and all talked at once. Just minutes after they settled in, two waiters brought pitchers of beer and mugs, quickly followed by more waiters with the largest pizzas Rick had ever seen. He was at one end, with Sam on one side and Sly on the other. Nino rose to make a toast, first in rapid Italian, and everyone looked at Rick, then in slightly slower English. Welcome to our little town, Mr. Reek, we hope you find a home here and bring us a Super Bowl. An odd round of hollering followed, and they drained their glasses.

Sam explained that Signor Bruncardo picked up the tab for these rather boisterous dinners, and treated the team at least once a week after practice. Pizza and pasta, some of the best spaghetti in town, without all the fuss and ceremony that Nino so fondly dispensed at Montana's. Cheap food, but delicious. Judge Franco stood with a fresh glass and launched into a windy speech about something.

'More of the same,' Sam mumbled in English. 'A toast to a great season, brotherhood, no injuries, et cetera. And of course to the great new quarterback.' It was obvious Franco would not allow himself to be outdone by Nino. After they drank and cheered some more, Sam said, 'Those two jockey for attention. They're permanent co-captains.'

'Picked by the team?'

'I suppose, but I've never seen an election, and this is my sixth season. It's their team, basically. They keep the boys motivated in the off-season. They're always recruiting new locals to take up the sport, especially ex–soccer players who've lost a step. They'll convert a rugby player every now and then. They yell and scream before the game, and some of their halftime tongue-lashings are beautiful. In the heat of battle, you want them in your foxhole.'

The beer flowed and the pizza disappeared. Nino called for order and introduced two new members of the team. Karl was a Danish math professor who'd settled in Parma with his Italian wife and taught at the university. He wasn't sure what position he might play but was anxious to select one. Pietro was a baby-faced fireplug, short and thick, a linebacker. Rick had noticed his quick feet in practice.

Franco led them in some mournful chant that not even Sam understood, then they burst into laughter and grabbed the beer pitchers. Waves of clamorous Italian rattled around the room, and after a few beers Rick was content to just sit and absorb the scene.

He was an extra in a foreign film.

★ ★ ★

Shortly before midnight, Rick plugged in his laptop and e-mailed Arnie:

In Parma, arrived late yesterday, first practice today – food and wine are worth the visit – no cheerleaders Arnie, you promised me beautiful cheerleaders – no agents here so you'd hate the place – no golf anywhere, yet – any word from Tiffany and her lawyers – I remember Jason Cosgrove talking about her in the shower, with details, and he made eight mill last year – sic the lawyers on him – I ain't the daddy. Even the little kids speak Italian over here – why am I in Parma? – could be worse I guess, could be in Cleveland. Later, RD

While Rick was asleep, Arnie returned the message:

Rick: Great to hear from you, delighted you're there and enjoying yourself. Treat it as an adventure. Not much happening here. No word from the lawyers, I'll suggest Cosgrove as the sperm donor. She's seven months along now. I know you hate the arena game but a GM called today and said he might get you fifty grand for next season. I said no. What about it?

Chapter 10

Waking at such a dreadful hour could only be accomplished with the aid of an alarm clock set at high volume. The steady, piercing beep penetrated the darkness and finally found its mark. Rick, who seldom used an alarm and had developed the pleasant routine of waking whenever his body was tired of sleep, flopped around under the sheets until he found an off switch. In the shock of the moment he thought of Officer Romo and was horrified of another non-arrest. Then he shook off the cobwebs and wild thoughts. As his heart rate began a gradual decline and he propped himself up on the pillows, he finally remembered why he'd set the alarm in the first place. He had a plan, and darkness was a crucial element.

Since his off-season regimen had been nothing but golf, both legs felt broken to bits and his abs ached as if he'd been punched repeatedly. His arms, shoulders, back, even ankles and toes, were sore to the touch. He cursed Alex and Sam and the entire Panther organization, if it could be called that. He cursed football, and Arnie, and, beginning with the Browns, every team in reverse order that had given him the pink slip. As he conjured up vile thoughts about the game, he tried carefully to stretch a muscle or two, but the muscles were simply too sore.

Fortunately, he had laid off the beer at Polipo's, or at least he had stopped at a reasonable limit. His head was clearing with no signs of a hangover.

If he could hurry and complete his mission as planned, he might be back under the covers in an hour or so. He passed on a shower – the pressure was startlingly weak and the hot water only passably lukewarm – and, forcing each movement with a grim determination, was outside on the street in less than ten minutes. Walking loosened the joints and circulated the blood, and after two blocks he was moving briskly and feeling much better.

The Fiat was five minutes away. He stood on the sidewalk staring at it. The narrow street was lined on both sides by compact cars parked bumper to bumper, leaving between them a single lane of traffic headed north, to the center of Parma. The street was dark, quiet, empty of traffic. Behind the Fiat was a lime green Smart car, a model slightly larger than a decent-sized go-kart, and its front bumper was about ten inches from Signor Bruncardo's Fiat. To the front was a white

Citroën, not much larger than the Smart car and wedged in just as tightly. Dislodging the Fiat would be a challenge even for a driver with years of stick-shift experience.

A quick glance right and left to make sure no one was stirring on Via Antini, then Rick unlocked the car and crawled in as sharp pains shot through his joints. He wiggled the stick to make sure it was in neutral, tried to unfold his legs, checked the parking brake, then started the engine. Lights on, gauges up, plenty of fuel, where was the heater? He adjusted mirrors, the seat, the seat belt, and for a good five minutes went through the preflight as the Fiat warmed itself. Not a single car, scooter, or bike passed him on the street.

Once the windshield was defrosted, there was no reason for further delays. His rising heart rate angered him, but he tried to ignore it. This was just a car with a clutch, and not even his car at that. He released the parking brake, held his breath, and nothing happened. Via Antini happens to be quite flat.

Foot on clutch, ease into first, a touch of accelerator, turn the wheel hard to the right, so far so good. A check of the mirror, no traffic, let's go. Rick eased off the clutch and gave it some gas, but gave it too much. The engine growled, he let off the clutch, and the Fiat lurched forward and bumped the Citroën just as he slammed the brake. Red gauge lights lit up the dash, and it took a few seconds to realize the car had died. He quickly turned the key while shifting into reverse and pressing the clutch and pulling on the parking brake and cursing under his breath while glancing over his shoulder at the street. No one was coming. No one was watching. The trip in reverse was as rough as the one forward, and when he tapped the Smart car, he hit the brake again and the engine died. Now he cursed loudly, no effort to keep the language under control. He took a deep breath and decided not to inspect the damage; there really wasn't any, he decided. Just a little nudge. Damned guy deserved it for parking on top of the Fiat. His hands moved quickly – steering, ignition, stick, parking brake. Why was he using the brake? His feet were all over the place, tap-dancing wildly from clutch to brake to gas. He roared forward again, barely nicking the Citroën before stopping, but this time the engine did not die. Progress. The Fiat was halfway in the street; still no traffic. Quickly into reverse again, but a bit too quickly and he lurched back, his head snapping and sore muscles aching. He hit the Smart car much harder the second time, and the Fiat was dead. His language was out of control as he again glanced around, looking for spectators.

She just appeared. He hadn't noticed her walking down the sidewalk. She stood there as if she'd been standing for hours, her body draped in a long wool overcoat, her head wrapped in a yellow shawl. An old woman with an old dog on a leash, out for the morning stroll, and now stopped dead by the violent pinball action of a copper-colored Fiat driven by an idiot.

Their eyes met. Her scowl and heavily wrinkled face conveyed exactly what she was thinking. Rick's wild desperation was quite evident. He stopped cursing for a second. The dog was staring, too, some type of frail terrier with a look as perplexed as the master's.

It took a second for Rick to realize she was not the owner of either of the cars he was pounding; of course she wasn't. She was a pedestrian, and before she could call the cops, if she were so inclined, he'd be gone. He hoped. Anyway, he started to say something like 'What the hell are you looking at?' But then, she wouldn't understand, and she would probably realize he was an American. A sudden patriotism sealed his lips.

With the front of the car jutting into the street, he had no time for a stare-down. He jerked his head arrogantly back to the matters at hand, re-shifting and restarting and urging himself to work the gas and the clutch with perfect co-ordination so the Fiat could finally roll away and be gone, leaving his audience behind. He pressed the gas hard, the engine strained again, and he slowly released the clutch as he turned the wheel hard and barely missed the Citroën. Free at last, he was rolling now, along Via Antini, the Fiat still in first and straining mightily. He made the mistake of one last triumphant look at the woman and the dog. He saw her brown teeth;

she was laughing at him. The dog was barking and pulling on the leash, also amused.

Rick had memorized the streets along his escape route, no small feat since many were narrow, one-way, and often confusing. He worked his way south, shifting only when necessary, and soon hit Viale Berenini, a major street with a few cars and delivery trucks moving about. He stopped at a red light, shifted into first, and prayed no one would stop behind him. He waited for the green, then lurched forward without killing the engine. Atta boy. He was surviving.

He crossed the Parma River on the Ponte Italia, and a quick glance revealed quiet waters below. He was away from downtown now, and there was even less traffic. The target was Viale Vittoria, a wide, sweeping four-lane avenue that circled the west side of Parma. Very flat and almost deserted in the predawn darkness. Perfect for practice.

For an hour, as day broke over the city, Rick drove up and down the wonderfully level street. The clutch was dragging a bit halfway down, and this slight problem captured his attention. However, after an hour of diligent work he was gaining confidence, and he and the Fiat were becoming one. Sleep was no longer an option; he was far too impressed with his new talent.

In a wide median, he practiced parking within the yellow lines, back and forth, back and forth until he grew bored. He was quite confident now, and he noticed a bar near Piazza Santa Croce. Why not? He was feeling more Italian by the minute, and he needed caffeine. He parked again, turned off the engine, and enjoyed a brisk walk. The streets were busy now, the city had come to life.

The bar was full and noisy, and his first inclination was to make a quick exit and return to the safety of his Fiat. But no, he had signed on for five months, and he would not spend that time on the run. He walked to a bar, caught the attention of a barista, and said, 'Espresso.'

The barista nodded to a corner where a plump lady sat behind a cash register. The barista had no interest in making an espresso for Rick, who retreated a step and again thought about fleeing. A well-dressed businessman entered in a rush, holding at least two newspapers and a briefcase, and walked directly to the cashier. '*Buongiorno*,' he said, and she offered the same. 'Caffè,' he said as he pulled out a five–euro note. She took it, made change, and handed him a receipt. He took the receipt directly to the counter and laid it where one of the baristas could plainly see it. A barista finally took it, they exchanged '*buongiornos*,' and everything worked fine. Within seconds a small cup and saucer landed on the counter, and the businessman, already deep in front-page news, added sugar, stirred, then demolished the drink in one long gulp.

So that's how you do it.

Rick walked to the cashier, mumbled a

passable '*Buongiorno*,' and flung over a five-euro note of his own before the lady could respond. She made change and handed him a magical receipt.

As he stood at the counter and sipped his coffee, he absorbed the frenzy of the bar. Most of the people were on their way to work, and they seemed to know one another. Some talked non-stop, while others were buried in newspapers. The baristas worked feverishly, but never wasted a step. They bantered in rapid Italian and were quick to return quips from their customers. Away from the counters there were tables where waiters in white aprons delivered coffee and bottled water and all manner of pastries. Rick was suddenly hungry, in spite of the truckload of carbs he had consumed just a few hours earlier at Polipo's. A shelf of sweet rolls caught his attention, and he desperately wanted one covered with chocolate and cream. But how to get it? He wouldn't dare open his mouth, not with so many people within earshot. Perhaps the cashier in the corner would be sympathetic to an American who could only point.

He left the bar hungry. He walked along Viale Vittoria, then ventured down a side street, looking for nothing but enjoying the sights. Another bar beckoned. He walked in with confidence, went straight to the cashier, another hefty old woman, and said, '*Buongiorno*, cappuccino please.' She couldn't have cared less where he was from, and her indifference encouraged him.

110

He pointed to a thick pastry on a rack by the counter and said, 'And one of these.' She nodded again as he handed over a ten-euro note, certainly enough to cover coffee and a croissant. The bar was less crowded than the other one, and Rick savored the *cornetto* and cappuccino.

It was called Bar Bruno, and whoever Bruno was, he certainly loved his soccer. The walls were covered with team posters and action shots and schedules that dated back thirty years. There was a banner from the World Cup victory in 1982. Above the cashier Bruno had nailed a collection of enlarged black and whites – Bruno with Chinaglia, Bruno hugging Baggio.

Rick assumed that he would be hard-pressed to find a bar or café in Parma with a single photo of the Panthers. Oh well. This ain't Pittsburgh.

The Fiat was exactly where he'd left it. The jolts of caffeine had raised his confidence. He eased perfectly into reverse, then pulled away smoothly as if he'd worked a clutch for years.

The challenge of central Parma was daunting, but he had no choice. Sooner or later he had to go home, and take his Fiat with him. At first glance, the police car did not alarm him. It was following at a benign pace. Rick stopped at a red light and waited patiently while mentally working the clutch and accelerator. The light turned green, the clutch slipped, the Fiat lunged, then died. Frantically, he re-shifted as he turned the key and cursed and kept one eye on the police. The black-and-white cruiser was on his rear bumper, and the two young cops were frowning.

What the hell? Something wrong back there?

His second attempt was worse than the first, and when the Fiat died another quick death, the police suddenly laid on the horn.

Finally the engine caught. He hit the gas and barely released the clutch, and the Fiat rolled forward, roaring in such a low gear but hardly moving. The police followed tightly, probably amused at the bucking and lunging ahead of them. After a block, they turned on the blue lights.

Rick managed to pull over in a loading zone in front of a row of shops. He turned the ignition off, pulled hard on the parking brake, then instinctively reached for the glove box. He had given no thought to Italian laws governing vehicle registration or driving privileges, nor had he assumed that the Panthers and specifically Signor Bruncardo would handle such matters. He had assumed nothing, thought of nothing, worried about nothing. He was a professional athlete who was once a high school and college star, and from that lofty perch small details had never mattered.

The glove box was empty.

A cop was tapping on his window, and he rolled it down. No power windows.

The cop said something, and Rick caught the word 'documenti.' He snatched his wallet and thrust out his Iowa driver's license. Iowa? He hadn't lived in Iowa in six years, but then, he hadn't established a home anywhere else. As the cop frowned at the plastic card, Rick sunk a few inches lower as he remembered a phone call from his mother before Christmas. She had just received a notice from the state. His license had expired.

'*Americano?*' the officer said. His tone was accusatory. His name badge declared him to be Aski.

'Yes,' Rick replied, though he could've handled a quick '*Sì.*' He did not, because even the slightest use of Italian prompted the speaker on the other end to assume the foreigner was fluent.

Aski opened the door and motioned for Rick to get out. The other officer, Dini, strutted up with a sneer, and they launched into a quick round of Italian. From their looks, Rick thought he might be beaten on the spot. They were in their early twenties, tall, and built like weight lifters. They could play defense for the Panthers. An elderly couple stopped on the sidewalk to witness the drama from ten feet away.

'Speak Italian?' Dini asked.

'No, sorry.'

Both rolled their eyes. A moron.

They separated and began a dramatic inspection of the crime scene. They studied the front license plates, then the rear. The glove box was opened, carefully, as if it might just hold a bomb. Then the trunk. Rick grew bored with it and leaned against the left front fender. They huddled, consulted, and radioed headquarters, then the inevitable paperwork began with both officers scribbling furiously.

Rick was very curious about his crime. He was certain that registration laws had been broken, but he would plead not guilty to any moving violation. He thought about calling Sam, but his cell phone was next to his bed. When he saw the tow truck, he almost laughed.

After the Fiat disappeared, Rick was put into the rear seat of the police car and driven away. No handcuffs, no threats, everything nice and civilized. As they crossed the river, he remembered something in his wallet. He pulled out a business card he had taken from Franco's office and handed it to Dini in the front seat. 'My friend,' he said.

Giuseppe Lazzarino, *Giudice*.

Both cops seemed to know Judge Lazzarino quite well. Their tone, demeanor, and body language changed. Both talked at once in muffled voices, as if they didn't want their prisoner to hear. Aski sighed heavily as Dini's shoulders sagged. Across the river, they changed directions and for a few minutes seemed to go in circles. Aski called someone on the radio, but did not find whomever or whatever he wanted. Dini used his cell phone, but he, too, was disappointed. Rick sat low in the rear seat, laughing at himself and trying to enjoy the tour of Parma.

They parked him on the bench outside

Franco's office, the same spot Romo had selected about twenty-four hours earlier. Dini reluctantly went inside, while Aski found a spot twenty feet down the hall, as if he had nothing to do with Rick. They waited as the minutes dragged by.

Rick was curious as to whether this qualified as a real arrest, or one of the Romo variety. How was one supposed to know? One more altercation with the police, and the Panthers and Sam Russo and Signor Bruncardo and his paltry contract could all take a hike. He almost missed Cleveland.

Loud voices, then the door swung open as his fullback charged through, Dini in tow. Aski bolted to attention.

'Reek, I am so sorry,' Franco thundered as he yanked him from the bench and smothered him with a bear hug. 'I'm so sorry. There is a mistake, no?' The judge glared at Dini, who was studying his very shiny black boots and looked somewhat pale. Aski was a deer in headlights.

Rick tried to say something, but words failed him. In the doorway, Franco's cute secretary watched the encounter. Franco unloaded a few words at Aski, then a sharp question for Dini, who tried to answer but thought better of it. Back to Rick. 'Is no problem, okay?'

'Fine,' Rick said. 'It's okay.'

'The car, it is not yours?'

'Uh, no. I think Signor Bruncardo owns it.'

Franco's eyes widened and his spine stiffened. 'Bruncardo's?'

115

Both Aski and Dini partially collapsed at the news. They stayed on their feet but couldn't breathe. Franco shot some harsh Italian at them, and Rick caught at least two 'Bruncardo's.'

Two gentlemen who appeared to be lawyers – dark suits, thick briefcases, important airs – approached. For their benefit, and Rick's and his staff's, Judge Lazzarino proceeded to blister the two young cops with the fervor of an angry drill sergeant.

Rick immediately felt sorry for them. After all, they had treated him with more respect than a common street criminal could expect. When the tongue-lashing was over, Aski and Dini scattered, never to be seen again. Franco explained that the car was being retrieved that very moment and would be returned to Rick immediately. No need to tell Signor Bruncardo. More apologies. The two lawyers finally drifted into the judge's office, and the secretaries returned to work.

Franco apologized again, and to show his sincere regret at the way Rick had been welcomed in Parma, he insisted on dinner the following night at his home. His wife – very pretty, he said – was an excellent cook. He would not take no for an answer.

Rick accepted the invitation, and Franco then explained that he had an important meeting with some lawyers. They would see each other at dinner. Farewell. 'Ciao.'

116

Chapter 11

The team trainer was a wiry, wild-eyed college boy named Matteo who spoke terrible English and spoke it rapidly. After several efforts, he finally made his point – he wanted to give their great new quarterback a rubdown. He was studying something that had something else to do with a new theory of massage. Rick desperately needed a rubdown. He stretched out on one of the two training tables and told Matteo to have a go. After a few seconds, the kid was hacking at his hamstrings and Rick wanted to scream. But you can't complain during a massage – it was a rule that had never been violated in the history of professional football. Regardless of how much things might hurt, big tough footballers do not complain during rubdowns.

'Is good?' Matteo said between breaths.

'Yes, slow down.'

It didn't survive the translation, and Rick

buried his face in a towel. They were in the locker room, which doubled as the equipment room and tripled as the coaches' offices. No one else was present. Practice was four hours away. As Matteo pounded furiously, Rick managed to drift away from the assault. He wrestled with the proper approach to suggest to Coach Russo that he preferred not to suffer through the conditioning drills anymore. No more wind sprints, push-ups, or sit-ups. He was in good shape, at least good enough for what was ahead. Too much running might injure a leg, pull a muscle, or something of that nature. In most pro camps the quarterbacks handled their own stretching and warm-ups and had their own little routines while everyone else grunted it out.

However, he was also fretting about how it would look to the team. Spoiled American quarterback. Too good for drills. Too soft for a little conditioning. The Italians seemed to thrive on dirt and sweat, and full pads were three days away.

Matteo settled onto his lower back and calmed down. The massage was working. The stiff, sore muscles were relaxing. Sam appeared and took a seat on the other training table. 'I thought you were in shape,' he began pleasantly.

'I thought I was, too.' With an audience, Matteo returned to his jackhammer method.

'Pretty sore, huh?'

'A little. I don't normally run too many wind sprints.'

'Get used to it. If you slack off, the Italians will think you're just a pretty boy.'

That settled that. 'I'm not the one who puked.'

'No, but you sure looked like it.'

'Thanks.'

'Just got a call from Franco. More trouble with the police, huh? You all right?'

'As long as I got Franco, the cops can arrest me for nothing every day.' He was sweating now, from the pain, and trying to appear nonchalant.

'We'll get you a temporary license and some paperwork for the car. My mistake. Sorry about it.'

'No sweat. Franco's got some cute secretaries.'

'Wait'll you see his wife. He included us for dinner tomorrow night, me and Anna.'

'Great.'

Matteo flipped him over and began pinching his thighs. Rick almost screamed, but managed to keep a straight face. 'Can we talk about the offense?' Rick asked.

'You've gone through the playbook?'

'It's high school stuff.'

'Yes, it's very basic. We can't get too fancy here. The players have limited experience, and there's not much practice time.'

'No complaints. I just have a few ideas.'

'Let's go.'

Matteo backed away like a proud surgeon, and Rick thanked him. 'Very nice job,' he said, limping away. Sly came bouncing in with wires running from his ears, trucker's cap cocked to one side, and again wearing the Broncos sweatshirt. 'Hey, Sly, how about a great massage over here!' Rick yelled. 'Matteo's wonderful.'

They exchanged jabs – Broncos versus Browns and so on – as Sly stripped to his boxers and stretched out on the table. Matteo cracked his knuckles, then plunged in. Sly grimaced, but bit his tongue.

Two hours before practice, Rick, Sly, and Trey Colby were on the field with Coach Russo, walking through the offensive plays. To Sam's relief, his new quarterback had no interest in changing everything. Rick made suggestions here and there, tweaked some of the pass routes, and offered ideas about the running game. Sly reminded him more than once that the Panthers' running game was quite simple – just give the ball to Sly and get out of the way.

Fabrizio appeared at the far end of the field, alone and determined to keep to himself. He began an elaborate stretching routine, one designed more for show than to loosen tight muscles.

'Well, he's back for the second day,' Sly said as they watched him for a moment.

'What does that mean?' Rick asked.

'He hasn't quit yet,' Trey said.

'Quit?'

'Yeah, he has the habit of walking off,' Sam said. 'Could be a bad practice, maybe a bad game, could be nothing.'

'Why tolerate it?'

'He's by far our best receiver,' Sam said. 'Plus he plays for cheap.'

'Dude's got some hands,' Trey said.

'And he can fly,' Sly said. 'Faster than me.'

'Come on?'

'Nope. Beats me four steps in the forty.'

Nino arrived early, too, and after a round of *buongiornos* he stretched quickly, then began a long lap around the field.

'Why does his ass flinch like that?' Rick asked as they watched him jog away. Sly laughed much too loudly. Sam and Trey broke up, too, then Sly seized the opportunity to give a quick review of Nino's overactive glutes. 'He ain't bad in practice, in shorts, but when he's in full gear and we're hitting, then everything gets tight, especially the muscles that run up his rear cheeks. Nino loves to hit, and sometimes he almost forgets to snap the ball because he's thinking so hard about hitting the noseguard. And when he's poised to hit, all bent over like that, then the glutes start quivering, and when you touch 'em, he damn near jumps out of his skin.'

'Perhaps we can run the shotgun,' Rick said, and they laughed even harder.

'Sure,' said Trey. 'But Nino's not too accurate. You'll be chasing the ball all over the field.'

'We've tried it,' Sam said. 'It's a disaster.'

'We gotta speed up his snaps,' Sly said.

'Sometimes I'm already in the hole before the quarterback gets the ball. He's chasing me around, I'm looking for the damned ball. Nino's off growling at some poor sucker.'

Nino was back, and he brought Fabrizio with him. Rick suggested they work from the shotgun, do a few patterns. His snaps were okay, not too errant, but awfully slow. Other Panthers arrived, and footballs were soon flying around the field as the Italians practiced their punting and passing.

Sam walked close to Rick and said, 'Hour and a half before practice, and they can't wait to start. Pretty refreshing, huh?'

'I've never seen it before.'

'They love the game.'

* * *

Franco and his small family lived on the top floor of a palazzo overlooking the Piazza della Steccata in the heart of the city. Everything was old – the worn marble staircase on the way up, the wooden floors, the tastefully cracked plaster walls, the portraits of ancient royals, the vaulted ceilings with lead chandeliers, the oversize leather sofas and chairs.

His wife, however, looked remarkably young. She was Antonella, a beautiful dark-haired woman who attracted second looks and outright stares. Even her heavily accented English left Rick wanting to hear more.

Their son was Ivano, age six, and their

daughter was Susanna, age three. The children were allowed to hang around for the first half hour before heading off to bed. A nanny of some sort lurked in the background.

Sam's wife, Anna, was also attractive, and as Rick sipped his Prosecco, he devoted his attention to the two ladies. He'd found a quick girlfriend in Florida, after fleeing Cleveland, but was content to vanish without a word to her when it was time to leave for Italy. He had seen beautiful women in Parma, but they all spoke a different language. There were no cheerleaders, and he had cursed Arnie many times for that lie. Rick was longing for female companionship, even the accented variety over a cocktail with the wives of friends. But the husbands stayed close, and at times Rick was lost in a world of Italian as the other four laughed at Franco's punch lines. A tiny gray-haired woman in an apron passed through occasionally with a platter of appetizers – cured meats, parmigiano cheese, olives – then she disappeared into the narrow kitchen where dinner was being prepared.

The surprise was the dinner table, a slab of black marble resting on two massive urns on the patio, a small flower-lined terrace overlooking the center of town. The table was crowded with candles and silver and flowers and fine china and liters of red wine. The night air was clear and still, chilly only when a slight wind blew. From a hidden speaker, an opera could barely be heard.

Rick was given the best seat, the one with a

clear view of the top of the duomo. Franco poured generous glasses of red wine, then offered a toast to their new friend. 'A Super Bowl for Parma,' he said, almost lustfully, in closing.

Where am I? Rick asked himself. Usually in March he was hanging out in Florida, bumming a room off a friend, playing golf, lifting weights, running, trying to stay in shape while Arnie worked the phones in a desperate search for a team in need of an arm. There was always hope. The next call could mean the next contract. The next team could mean the big break. Each spring brought a fresh dream that he'd finally find his place – a team with a great offensive line, a brilliant coordinator, talented receivers, everything. His passes would be on target. Defenses would crumble. The Super Bowl. Pro Bowl. Fat contract. Endorsements. Fame. Lots of cheerleaders.

It all seemed possible every March.

Where am I?

The first course, or the antipasto, was thickly sliced cantaloupe covered with thin slices of prosciutto. Franco poured more wine as he explained that this dish was very common throughout the Emilia-Romagna region, something Rick had heard more than once. But, of course, only the best prosciutto comes from Parma. Even Sam rolled his eyes at Rick.

After a few hearty bites, Franco asked, 'So, Rick, do you like opera?'

To give an honest 'Hell no' would be to insult everyone within a hundred miles at least, so Rick

124

played it safe. 'We don't listen to a lot of it back home,' he said.

'Is very big here,' Franco said. Antonella smiled at Rick as she nibbled on a tiny bit of melon.

'We take you sometime, yes? We have Teatro Regio, the most beautiful opera house in the world,' Franco said.

'Parmesans are crazy about opera,' Anna said. She was sitting next to Rick, with Antonella directly across, and Franco, the judge, at the head of the table.

'And where are you from?' Rick asked Anna, anxious to change subjects.

'Parma. My uncle was a great baritone.'

'Teatro Regio is more magnificent than La Scala in Milan,' Franco was announcing to no one in particular, so Sam decided to quibble. 'No way,' he said. 'La Scala is the greatest.'

Franco's eyes widened as if he might attack. The rebuke sent him directly into Italian, and for a moment everyone listened in an uneasy silence. He finally composed himself and said, in English, 'When did you go to La Scala?'

'Never,' Sam said. 'Just saw some photos.'

Franco laughed loudly as Antonella left for the next course. 'I take you to the opera,' Franco said to Rick, who just smiled and tried to think of something worse.

The next course, the *primo piatto*, was *anolini*, a small round pasta stuffed with parmigiano and beef and smothered in porcini mushrooms.

Antonella explained that it was a very famous dish from Parma, and her description was in the most beautifully accented English Rick had ever heard. He really didn't care how the pasta tasted. Just keep talking about it.

Franco and Sam were discussing opera, in English. Anna and Antonella were discussing children, in English. Finally Rick said, 'Please, speak Italian. It's much prettier.' And they did. Rick savored the food and wine and view. The dome of the cathedral was majestic in its lights, and the center of Parma was alive with traffic and pedestrians.

The *anolini* yielded to the *secondo piatto*, the main course, a roasted stuffed capon. Franco, several glasses deep into the wine, graphically described a capon as a male chicken who gets castrated – 'Whack!' – when only two months old. 'Adds to the flavor,' Antonella said, leaving the impression, at least to Rick, that the rejected parts might actually be in the stuffing. After two tentative bites, though, it didn't matter. Testicles or not, the capon was delicious.

He ate slowly, very amused at the Italians and their love of conversation at the table. At times they focused on him and wanted to know about his life, then they would drift back to their musical language and forget about him. Even Sam, from Baltimore and Bucknell, seemed more at ease chatting with the women in Italian. For the first time in his new home, Rick admitted to himself that learning a few words was not a bad idea. In fact, it was a great idea if he had any hope of scoring points with the girls.

After the capon, there was cheese and another wine, then dessert and coffee. Rick finally made a graceful departure a few minutes after midnight. He strolled through the night, back to his apartment, and fell asleep on his bed without undressing.

Chapter 12

On a beautiful Saturday in April, a perfect spring day in the Po valley, the Bandits from Naples left home at 7:00 a.m. on a train headed north for the season's opening game. They arrived in Parma just before 2:00 p.m. Kickoff was at 3:00. The return train would leave at 11:40, and the team would arrive in Naples around 7:00 a.m. on Sunday, twenty-four hours after leaving.

Once in Parma, the Bandits, thirty of them, took a bus to Stadio Lanfranchi and hauled their gear to a cramped dressing room just down the hall from the Panthers. They changed quickly and scattered around the field, stretching and following the usual pregame rituals.

★   ★   ★

Two hours before kickoff all forty-two Panthers were in their locker room, most burning nervous energy and anxious to hit someone. Signor

Bruncardo surprised them with new game jerseys – black with shiny silver numbers and the word 'Panthers' across the chest.

Nino smoked a pregame cigarette. Franco chatted with Sly and Trey. Pietro, the middle linebacker who was improving by the day, was meditating with his iPod. Matteo scurried around, rubbing muscles, taping ankles, repairing equipment.

A typical pregame, thought Rick. Smaller locker room, smaller players, smaller stakes, but some things about the game were always the same. He was ready to play. Sam addressed the team, offered a few observations, then turned them loose.

When Rick stepped onto the field ninety minutes before kickoff, the stands were empty. Sam had predicted a big crowd – 'maybe a thousand.' The weather was great, and the day before the *Gazzetta di Parma* ran an impressive story about the Panthers' first game and especially about their new NFL quarterback. Rick's handsome face, in color, had been splashed across half a page. Signor Bruncardo had pulled some strings and thrown some weight around, according to Sam.

Walking onto a field in an NFL stadium, or even one in the Big Ten, was always a nerve-racking experience. The pregame jitters were so bad in the locker room that the players fled as soon as they were allowed. Outside, engulfed by enormous decks of seats and thousands of fans, and cameras and bands and cheerleaders and the seemingly endless mob of people who somehow had access to the field, players spent the first few moments adjusting to the barely controlled chaos.

Walking onto the grass of Stadio Lanfranchi, Rick couldn't help but chuckle at the latest stop in his career. A frat boy limbering up for a flag football game would've been more nervous.

After a few minutes of stretching and calisthenics, led by Alex Olivetto, Sam gathered the offense on the five-yard line and began running plays. He and Rick had selected twelve that they would run the entire game, six on the ground and six in the air. The Bandits were notoriously weak in the secondary – not a single American back there – and the year before the Panthers' quarterback had thrown for two hundred yards.

Of the six running plays, five went to Sly. Franco's only touch would be a dive play on short yardage, and only when the game was won. Though he loved to hit, he also had the habit of fumbling. All six pass plays went to Fabrizio.

After an hour of warm-ups, both teams retreated to their dressing rooms. Sam huddled the Panthers for a rousing speech, and Coach Olivetto pumped them up with a ferocious assault on the city of Naples.

Rick didn't understand a word, but the Italians certainly did. They were ready for war.

* * *

130

The Bandits' kicker was another ex–soccer player with a big foot, and his opening drive sailed through the end zone. As Rick trotted onto the field for the first series, he tried to remember the last game he started. It was in Toronto, a hundred years ago.

The home stands were packed now, and the fans knew how to make noise. They waved large hand-painted banners and yelled in unison. Their racket had the Panthers looking for blood. Nino especially was out of his mind.

They huddled, and Rick called, 'Twenty-six smash.' Nino translated, and they headed for the line. In an I formation, with Franco four yards behind him at fullback and Sly seven yards deep, Rick quickly scanned the defense and saw nothing that worried him. The smash was a deep handoff to the right side that allowed the tailback flexibility to read the blocking and pick a hole. The Bandits had five down linemen and two linebackers, both smaller than Rick. Nino's glutes were in full panic, and Rick had long since decided to go with a quick snap, especially on the first drive. He did a quick 'Down.' A beat. Hands under center, a hard slap because a feather touch sent the center into illegal motion, then, 'Set.' A beat. Then, 'Hut.'

For a split second, everything moved but the ball. The line fired forward, everyone growling and grunting, and Rick waited. When he finally got the ball, he did a quick pump to freeze the safety, then turned for the handoff. Franco lurched by, hissing at the linebacker he planned to maul. Sly got the ball deep in the backfield, faked toward the line, then cut wide for six yards before going out of bounds.

'Twenty-seven smash,' Rick called. Same play, but to the left. Gain of eleven, and the fans reacted with whistles and horns. Rick had never heard so much noise from a thousand fans. Sly ran right, then left, right, then left, and the offense crossed midfield. It stalled at the Bandits' 40, and with a third and four Rick decided to toss one to Fabrizio. Sly was panting and needed a break.

'I right flex Z, 64 curl H swing,' Rick said in the huddle. Nino hissed out the translation. A curl to Fabrizio. His linemen were sweating now, and very happy. They were stuffing the ball into the heart of the defense, driving at will. After six plays, Rick was almost bored and looking forward to showing off his arm. After all, they weren't paying him twenty grand for nothing.

The Bandits guessed right and sent everyone but the two safeties. Rick saw it coming and wanted to check off, but he also didn't want to risk a busted play. Audibles were tricky enough in English. He dropped back three steps, hurried his pass, and fired a bullet to the spot Fabrizio was supposed to be curling into. A linebacker from the blind side hit Rick hard in the square of his back and they went down together. The pass was perfect, but for a ten-yarder it had too much velocity. Fabrizio went up, got both hands near it, then took it hard in the chest. The ball shot upward and was an easy interception for the strong-side safety.

Here we go again, Rick thought as he walked to the sideline. His first pass in Italy was an exact replica of his last one in Cleveland. The crowd was silent. The Bandits were celebrating. Fabrizio was limping to the bench, gasping for breath.

'Way too hard,' Sam said, leaving no doubt about blame.

Rick removed his helmet and knelt on the sideline. The quarterback for Naples, a small kid from Bowling Green, completed his first five passes and in less than three minutes had the Bandits in the end zone.

Fabrizio stayed on the bench, pouting and rubbing his chest as though ribs were cracked. The backup wide receiver was a fireman named Claudio, and Claudio caught about half of his passes in pregame warm-up and even fewer in practice. The Panthers' second drive began at their 21. Two handoffs to Sly picked up fifteen yards. He was fun to watch, from the safety of the backfield. He was quick and made wonderful cuts.

'When do I get the ball?' Franco asked in the huddle. Second and four, so why not? 'Take it now,' Rick said, and called, 'Thirty-two dive.'

'Thirty-two dive?' Nino asked in disbelief. Franco cursed him in Italian and Nino cursed back, and as they broke huddle, half the offense was grumbling about something.

Franco took the ball on a quick dive to the right, did not fumble, but instead showed an astounding ability to stay on his feet. A tackle hit him and he spun loose. A linebacker chopped his knees, but he kept his legs churning. A safety came up fast and Franco delivered a stiff-arm that would have impressed the great Franco Harris. He rumbled on, across midfield, bodies bouncing off, a cornerback riding him like a bull, and finally a tackle caught up with the mayhem and slapped his ankles together. Gain of twenty-four yards. As Franco strutted back to the huddle, he said something to Nino, who of course took full credit for the gain because it all came down to blocking.

Fabrizio jogged to the huddle, one of his famous quick recoveries. Rick decided to deal with him immediately. He called a play-action pass, with Fabrizio on a post pattern, and it worked beautifully. On first down, the defense collapsed on Sly. The strong safety bit hard, and Fabrizio was by him with ease. The pass was long and soft and perfectly on target, and when Fabrizio took it at a full sprint at the 15, he was all alone.

More fireworks. More chants. Rick grabbed a cup of water and enjoyed the racket. He savored his first touchdown pass in four years. It felt good, regardless of where he was.

★　★　★

By halftime, he had two more touchdowns, and the Panthers were up 28–14. In the locker room, Sam bitched about the penalties – the offense had jumped four times – and he bitched about the zone coverage that had allowed 180 yards passing. Alex Olivetto carped at the defensive line because there was no pass rush, not a single sack. There was a lot of yelling and finger-pointing, and Rick just wanted everyone to relax.

A loss to Naples would ruin the season. With only eight games on the schedule, and with Bergamo poised to again run the table, there was no room for a bad day.

After twenty minutes of impressive abuse, the Panthers hustled back to the field. Rick felt like he'd suffered through another NFL halftime.

The Bandits tied the game with four minutes left in the third quarter, and the Parma sideline took on an intensity Rick had not seen in years. He was telling everyone, 'Relax, just relax,' but he wasn't sure he was understood. The players were looking to him, their great new quarterback.

After three quarters, it was obvious to both Sam and Rick that they needed more plays. The defense keyed on Sly every snap and double-covered Fabrizio. Sam was getting outfoxed by the very young Naples coach, a former assistant at Ball State. However, the offense was soon to discover a new weapon. On a third and four, Rick dropped back to pass but saw the left corner coming on a blitz. There was no one to block, so he faked a pass and watched the corner go sailing by. Then he dropped the ball, and for the next three seconds, an eternity, worked feverishly to pick it up. When it was retrieved, he had no choice but to run. And run he did, just like in the old days at Davenport South. He scooted around the pile, where the linebackers were preoccupied, and was immediately in the secondary. The crowd erupted, and Rick Dockery was off to the races. He faked out a corner, cut across to the center, just like Gale Sayers in the old footage, a real broken-field ace. The last person he expected help from was Fabrizio, but the kid came through. He managed to roll under the weak-side safety just long enough to allow Rick to sprint past, all the way to the promised land. When he crossed the goal line, he flipped the ball to the official, and couldn't help but laugh at himself. He had just galloped seventy-two yards for a touchdown, the longest of his career. Not even in high school had he scored from so far away.

At the bench, he was grabbed by his team-mates and offered all manner of congratulations, little of which he understood. Sly, through a wide smile, said, 'That took forever.'

Five minutes later, the running quarterback struck again. Suddenly anxious to show off his moves, he scrambled out of the pocket and seemed ready for another jaunt downfield. The entire secondary broke coverage, and at the last second, two feet from the line of scrimmage,

Rick zipped a bullet thirty yards across the middle to Fabrizio, who galloped untouched into the end zone.

Game over. Trey Colby picked off two passes late in the fourth quarter, and the Panthers won 48–28.

* * *

They gathered at Polipo's for all the beer and pizza they wanted, at Signor Bruncardo's expense. The night went long, with bawdy drinking songs and dirty jokes. The Americans – Rick, Sly, Trey, and Sam – sat together at one end of a long table, and laughed at the Italians until the laughter was painful.

At 1:00 a.m., Rick e-mailed his parents:

Mom and Dad: Had our first game today, beat Naples (Bandits) by 3 touchdowns. 18 for 22, 310 yards, 4 td's, one pick; also rushed for 98 yards, one td; kinda reminded me of the old high school days. Having fun. Love, Rick

And to Arnie:

Undefeated here in Parma; first game, 5 td's, 4 by air, one by ground. A real stud. No, I will not, under any circumstances, play arena football. Have you talked to Tampa Bay?

Chapter 13

The Bruncardo palazzo was a grand eighteenth-century edifice on Viale Mariotti, overlooking the river and a few blocks from the duomo. Rick made the walk in ten minutes. His Fiat was tucked away on a side street in a fine parking space, one he was reluctant to relinquish.

It was late Sunday afternoon, the day after the great victory over the Bandits, and though he had no plans for the evening, he certainly didn't want to do what he was about to do. As he strolled up and down Viale Mariotti, trying to analyze the palazzo without looking stupid and searching desperately for its front door, he asked himself once again how he had been boxed into this corner.

Sam. Sam had applied the pressure, with help from Franco.

He finally found the doorbell, and an ancient butler appeared without a smile and reluctantly allowed him to enter. The butler, dressed in black with tails, quickly scanned Rick for proper attire and appeared not to approve. Rick thought he looked rather nice. Ink-colored navy jacket, dark slacks, real socks, black loafers, white shirt, and tie, all purchased from one of the stores Sam had suggested. He almost felt like an Italian. He followed the old goat through a great hall with high frescoed ceilings and shiny marble floors. They stopped at a long parlor, and Signora Bruncardo came rushing forth. She spoke sultry English. Her name was Silvia. She was attractive, heavily made-up, nicely nipped and tucked, very thin, and her thinness was accented by a sparkling black gown that was as tight as skin. She was about forty-five, twenty years younger than her husband, Rodolfo Bruncardo, who soon appeared and shook hands with his quarterback. Rick had the immediate impression that he kept her on a short leash, and for good reason. She had the look. Anytime, anywhere.

With a thick accent, Rodolfo said in English that he was so sorry for not having met Rick sooner. But business had kept him out of town, and so on. He was a very busy man with lots of deals. Silvia watched with large brown eyes that were easy to dwell on. Mercifully, Sam appeared with Anna, and the conversation became easier. They talked about yesterday's win and, more important, the article on the Sunday sports page. NFL star Rick Dockery had led the Panthers to a smashing win in their home opener, and the color photo was of Rick crossing the goal line with his first rushing touchdown in a decade.

Rick said all the right things. He loved Parma.
The apartment and car were wonderful. The
team was a blast. Couldn't wait to win the Super
Bowl. Franco and Antonella entered the room
and the embracing rituals were carried out. A
waiter stopped by with glasses of chilled
Prosecco.

It was a small party – the Bruncardos, Sam
and Anna, Franco and Antonella, and Rick.
After drinks and appetizers, they left on foot, the
ladies in gowns and high heels and minks, the
men in dark suits, everybody speaking Italian at
once. Rick smoldered quietly, cursing Sam and
Franco and old man Bruncardo for the absurdity
of the evening.

He'd found a book in English on the region of
Emilia-Romagna, and though most of it was
about food and wine, there was a generous
section on opera. Very slow reading.

* * *

The Teatro Regio was built in the early nine-
teenth century by one of Napoleon's former
wives, Maria Luisa, who preferred life in Parma
because it kept her far away from the emperor.
Five levels of private boxes look down on the
audience, the orchestra, and the expansive stage.
Parmesans consider it the finest opera house in
the world, and they also consider opera their
birthright. They are acute listeners and fierce

critics, and a performer who leaves with applause is prepared to face the world. A faulty performance or a missed note often leads to noisy disapproval.

The Bruncardo box was on the second level, stage left, excellent seats, and as the party settled in, Rick was awed by the ornate interior and the seriousness of the evening. The well-dressed crowd below them buzzed with nervous anticipation. Someone waved. It was Karl Korberg, the large Dane who taught at the university and was trying to play left offensive tackle. He had missed no fewer than five clean blocks against the Bandits. Karl was wearing a fashionable tuxedo, and his Italian wife looked splendid. Rick admired the ladies from above.

Sam stayed at his elbow, anxious to help the novice through his first performance. 'These people are crazy about opera,' he whispered. 'They're fanatics.'

'And you?' Rick whispered back.

'This is the place to be. Believe it or not, in Parma opera is more popular than soccer.'

'And more popular than the Panthers?'

Sam laughed and nodded at a stunning brunette passing just under them.

'How long will this last?' Rick asked, gawking.

'Couple of hours.'

'Can't we just skip out at intermission and go have dinner?'

'Sorry. And dinner will be superb.'

'I have no doubt.'

Signor Bruncardo handed over a program. 'I found one in English,' he said.

'Thanks.'

'You might want to give it a glance,' Sam said. 'Opera is sometimes hard to follow, at least from a plot angle.'

'I thought it was just a bunch of fat people singing at full blast.'

'How much opera did you see in Iowa?'

The lights dimmed slightly and the crowd settled down. Rick and Anna were given the two tiny velvet seats at the front of the box, very near the ledge, with perfect views of the stage. Tucked in closely behind them were the rest.

Anna pulled out a pencil-like flashlight and pointed it at Rick's program. She said softly, 'This is a performance of *Otello*, a very famous opera written by Giuseppe Verdi, a local, from Busseto.'

'Is he here?'

'No,' she said with a smile. 'Verdi died a hundred years ago. He was the world's greatest composer when he lived. Have you read much Shakespeare?'

'Oh sure.'

'Good.' The lights went dimmer. Anna flipped through the program, then aimed the light at page four. 'This is the summary of the story. Give it a quick look. The opera is in Italian, of course, and it might be a bit hard to follow.'

Rick took the light, glanced at his watch, and

did as he was told. As he read, the crowd, quite noisy in anticipation, settled down and everyone found a seat. When the theater was dark, the conductor marched out and received a rousing ovation. The orchestra came to attention, then began playing.

The curtain rose slowly to a silent, still audience. The stage was elaborately decorated. The setting was the island of Cyprus, a crowd was waiting for a ship, and on the ship was Otello, their governor, who'd been off fighting somewhere, with great success. Otello was suddenly on the stage singing something like 'Celebrate, Celebrate,' and the entire town joined in the chorus.

Rick read quickly while trying not to miss the spectacle before him. The costumes were elaborate; the makeup thick and dramatic; the voices truly sensational. He tried to remember the last time he had watched live theater. There'd been a girlfriend at Davenport South who starred in the senior play ten years earlier. A long time ago.

Otello's young wife, Desdemona, appeared in Scene 3, and the spectacle took a different turn. Desdemona was stunning – long dark hair, perfect features, deep brown eyes that Rick could see clearly from eighty feet. She was petite and thin, and fortunately her costume was tight and revealed marvelous curves.

He scanned the program and found her name – Gabriella Ballini, soprano.

Not surprisingly, Desdemona soon attracted the attention of another man, Roderigo, and all manner of backstabbing and scheming began. Near the end of Act 1, Otello and Desdemona sang a duet, a high-powered romantic back-and-forth that sounded fine to Rick and those in the Bruncardo box, but others were bothered by it. Up in the fifth level, the cheap seats, several spectators actually booed.

Rick had been booed many times, in many places, and the booing had been easy to shake off, no doubt helped by the sheer magnitude of football stadiums. A few thousand fans booing was just part of the game. But in a tightly packed theater with only a thousand seats, five or six rowdy fans booing heartily sounded like a hundred. What cruelty! Rick was shocked by it, and as the curtain dropped on Act 1, he watched Desdemona standing stoically with her head held high, as if she were deaf.

'Why did they boo?' Rick whispered to Anna as the lights came on.

'The people here are very critical. She has been struggling.'

'Struggling? She sounded great.' And looked great, too. How could they boo someone so gorgeous?

'They think she missed a couple of notes. They are pigs. Let's go.'

They were on their feet as the entire audience stood for a stretch. 'So far, you like?' Anna asked.

'Oh yes,' Rick said, and he was being truthful. The production was so elaborate. He had never heard such voices. But he was baffled by the boo birds in the top level. Anna explained: 'There are only about one hundred seats available to the public, and they are up there,' she said, waving at the top. 'Very tough fans up there. They are serious about opera and quick to show their enthusiasm but also their displeasure. This Desdemona was a controversial selection, and she has not won over the crowd.'

They were outside the box, taking a glass of Prosecco and saying hello to people Rick would never see again. The first act lasted for forty minutes, and the break after it lasted for twenty. Rick began to wonder how late dinner might be.

In Act 2, Otello began to suspect his wife was fooling around with a man named Cassio, and this caused great conflict, which, of course, was played out in dazzling song. The bad guys convinced Otello that Desdemona was being unfaithful, and Otello, with a hair-trigger temper, finally vowed to kill his wife.

Curtains, another twenty-minute break between acts. Is this really going to last for four hours? Rick asked himself. But then, he was anxious to see more of Desdemona. More booing, and he might scurry up to the fifth floor and punch someone.

In Act 3, she made several appearances without provoking any boos. Subplots spun in all directions as Otello continued to listen to the bad guys and became more convinced that he must kill his beautiful wife. After nine or ten scenes, the act was over, and it was time for another recess.

Act 4 took place in Desdemona's bedroom. She got murdered by her husband, who soon realized that she was faithful after all. Distraught, out of his mind, but still able to sing magnificently, Otello produced an impressive dagger and gutted himself. He fell onto his wife's corpse, kissed her three times, then died in a most colorful fashion. Rick managed to follow most of this, but his eyes rarely left Gabriella Ballini.

Four hours after he first sat down, Rick stood with the audience and applauded politely at the curtain call. When Desdemona appeared, the booing returned with a fury, which provoked angry responses from many of those on the floor and in the private boxes. Fists were pumped, gestures made, the crowd turned on the disgruntled fans way up there in the cheap seats. They booed even louder, and poor Gabriella Ballini was forced to take a bow with a painful smile as if she heard nothing.

Rick admired her courage, and adored her beauty.

He thought Philadelphia fans were tough.

★ ★ ★

The palazzo's dining room was larger than Rick's entire apartment. A half dozen other friends joined them for the post-performance feast, and the guests were still wrung out from *Otello*. They chatted excitedly, all at the same time, all in rapid-fire Italian. Even Sam, the only other American, seemed as animated as the others.

Rick tried to smile and act as though he was as emotionally charged as the natives. A friendly servant kept his wineglass full, and before the first course was finished, he was quite mellow. His thoughts were on Gabriella, the beautiful little soprano who had not been appreciated.

She must be devastated, ruined, suicidal. To sing so perfectly and emotionally, and not be appreciated. Hell, he had deserved all the booing he'd received. But not Gabriella.

There were two more performances, then the season was over. Rick, deep in the wine and thinking of nothing but the girl, thought the unthinkable. He would somehow get a ticket and sneak into another performance of *Otello*.

Chapter 14

Monday's practice was a halfhearted effort at watching game tapes while the beer flowed. Sam ran through the film, growling and bitching, but no one was in the mood for serious football. Their next opponent, the Rhinos of Milan, had been easily thumped the day before by the Gladiators of Rome, a team that rarely contended for the Super Bowl. So, contrary to what Coach Russo wanted, the mood was set for an easy week and an easy win. Disaster was looming. At 9:30, Sam sent them home.

Rick parked far from his apartment, then hiked across the center of town to a trattoria called Il Tribunale, just off Strada Farini and very near the courthouse where the cops liked to take him. Pietro was waiting, along with his new wife, Ivana, who was very pregnant.

The Italian players had quickly adopted their American teammates. Sly said it happened every year. They were honored to have real

148

professionals playing on their team, and they wanted to make sure Parma was hospitable enough. Food and wine were the keys to the city. One by one, the Panthers invited the Americans to dinner. Some were long meals in fine apartments, like Franco's, others were family feasts with parents and aunts and uncles. Silvio, a rustic young man with a violent streak who played linebacker and often used his fists when tackling, lived on a farm ten kilometers from town. His dinner, on a Friday night, in the renovated ruins of an old castle, lasted four hours, included twenty-one blood relatives, none of whom spoke a word of English, and ended with Rick sprawled safely on a bunk in a cold attic. A rooster woke him.

Later he learned that Sly and Trey had been driven away by a drunk uncle who couldn't find Parma.

This was Pietro's dinner. He had explained that he and Ivana were waiting on a newer, larger apartment, and the one they were presently in was simply not suitable for entertaining. He apologized, but he was also quite fond of Il Tribunale, his favorite restaurant in Parma. He worked for a company that sold fertilizer and seeds, and his boss wanted him to expand their business into Germany and France. Thus, he was studying English with a passion and practiced on Rick every day.

Ivana was not studying English, had never studied it, and showed no interest in learning it

149

now. She was rather plain, and plump, but then she was expecting. She smiled a lot and whispered when necessary to her husband.

After ten minutes, Sly and Trey strolled in and collected a few of the customary second looks from the other diners. It was still unusual to see black faces in Parma. They settled around the tiny table and listened as Pietro practiced his English. A thick wedge of parmigiano arrived, just to munch on while food was contemplated, and soon there were platters of antipasti. They ordered baked lasagna, ravioli stuffed with herbs and squash, ravioli smothered in a cream sauce, fettuccini with mushrooms, fettuccini with a rabbit sauce, and *anolini*.

After a glass of red wine, Rick glanced around the small dining room, and his eyes locked onto a beautiful young lady sitting about twenty feet away. She was at a table with a well-dressed young man, and whatever they were discussing was not pleasant. Like most Italian women, she was a brunette, though, as Sly had explained several times, there was no shortage of blondes in northern Italy. Her dark eyes were beautiful, and although they radiated mischief, they were, at that moment, not at all happy. She was thin and petite, fashionably dressed, and . . .

'What are you looking at?' Sly asked.

'That girl over there,' Rick said before he could stop himself.

All five at their table turned for a look, but the young lady did not acknowledge them. She was deep in a troubled conversation with her man.

'I've seen her before,' Rick said.

'Where?' Trey asked.

'At the opera, last night.'

'You went to the opera?' Sly asked, ready to pounce.

'Of course I went to the opera. Didn't see you there.'

'You were at opera?' Pietro asked, with admiration.

'Sure, *Otello*. It was spectacular. That lady over there played the role of Desdemona. Her name is Gabriella Ballini.'

Ivana understood enough of this to glance a second time. She then spoke to her husband, who did a quick translation. 'Yes, that's her.' Pietro was very proud of his quarterback.

'Is she famous?' Rick asked.

'Not really,' Pietro said. 'She's a soprano, good but not great.' He then ran this by his wife, who added a few comments. Pietro translated: 'Ivana says she's having a rough time.'

Small salads with tomatoes arrived, and the conversation returned to football and playing in America. Rick managed to contribute while keeping an eye on Gabriella. He did not see a wedding band or engagement ring. She did not seem to enjoy the company of her date, but they knew each other very well because the conversation was serious. They never touched – in fact things were rather frosty.

Halfway through a monstrous plate of

fettuccini and mushrooms, Rick saw a tear drop from Gabriella's left eye and run down her cheek. Her companion didn't wipe it for her; he seemed not to care. She barely touched her food.

Poor Gabriella. Her life was certainly a mess. On Sunday night she gets booed by the beasts at Teatro Regio, and tonight she's having an ugly spat with her man.

Rick couldn't keep his eyes away from her.

★ ★ ★

He was learning. The best parking places opened up between 5:00 and 7:00 p.m., when those who worked in the center of the city left for home. Rick often drove the streets in the early evenings, waiting to pounce on a fresh opening. Parking was a rough sport, and he was very close to either buying or leasing a scooter.

After 10:00 p.m., it was almost impossible to find a space anywhere near his apartment, and it was not unusual to park a dozen blocks away.

Though towing was rare, it did happen. Judge Franco and Signor Bruncardo could pull strings, but Rick preferred to avoid the hassle. After practice Monday, he had been forced to park north of the center, a good fifteen minutes by foot from his apartment. And he'd parked in a restricted space reserved for deliveries. After dinner at Il Tribunale, he hustled back to the Fiat, found it safe and un-towed, and began the frustrating task of finding a spot closer to home.

It was almost midnight when he crossed Piazza Garibaldi and began prowling for a gap between two cars. Nothing. The pasta was settling in, as was the wine. A long night's sleep wasn't far away. He cruised up and down the narrow streets, all of which were lined with tiny cars parked bumper to bumper. Near Piazza Santafiora, he found an ancient passageway he had not seen before. There was an opening to his right, a very tight squeeze, but why not? He pulled even with the parked car in front, and noticed a couple of pedestrians hurrying along the sidewalk. He shifted into reverse, released the clutch, turned hard to the right, and sort of staggered back into the space, hitting the curb with the right rear wheel. It was a lousy miss, another effort was required. He saw headlights approaching but did not worry. The Italians, especially those who lived in the center, were remarkably patient. Parking was a chore for all of them.

As Rick pulled back into the street, he had the quick thought of moving on. The space was very tight, and it could take some time and effort to maneuver into it. He'd try once more. Shifting and turning and trying to ignore the headlights that were now very close behind him, he somehow allowed his foot to slip off the clutch. The car lunged, then died. The other driver then sat on the horn, a very loud shrill horn from under the hood of a shiny burgundy BMW. A tough guy's car. A man in a hurry. A bully unafraid to

153

hide behind locked doors and honk at someone struggling. Rick froze, and for a split second thought again about racing off to another street. Then something snapped. He yanked open his door, flipped the bird at the BMW, and started for it. The horn continued. Rick walked to the driver's window, yelling something about getting out. The horn continued. Behind the wheel was a forty-year-old asshole in a dark suit with a dark overcoat and dark leather driving gloves. He would not look at Rick, but chose instead to press the horn and stare straight ahead.

'Get out of the car!' Rick yelled. The horn continued. Now there was another car behind the BMW, and another was approaching. There was no way around the Fiat, and its driver wasn't ready to drive. The horn continued.

'Get out of the car!' Rick yelled again. He thought of Judge Franco. God bless him.

The car behind the BMW began honking, too, and for good measure Rick flipped the bird in its direction, too.

How, exactly, was this going to end?

The driver of the second car, a woman, rolled down her window and yelled something unpleasant. Rick yelled back. More horns, more yelling, more cars approaching on a street that had been completely silent one minute earlier.

Rick heard a car door slam, and turned to watch a young woman start his Fiat, shift it quickly into reverse, and thrust it perfectly into the parking space. One easy effort, with no bumps or scrapes, second or third tries. It seemed physically impossible. The Fiat came to rest with twelve inches between it and the car in front, and the same for the car in the rear.

The BMW roared by, as did the other cars. When they passed, the Fiat's driver's door opened, and the young woman jumped out – open-toe pumps, really nice legs – and began walking away. Rick watched for a second, his heart still laboring from the encounter, his blood pumping, his fists clenched.

'Hey!' Rick yelled.

She did not flinch, did not hesitate.

'Hey! Thanks!'

She kept walking, fading into the night. Rick watched her without moving, mesmerized by the miracle at hand. There was something familiar about her figure, her elegance, her hair, and then it hit him. 'Gabriella!' he yelled. What was there to lose? If it wasn't her, then she wouldn't stop, would she?

But she stopped.

He walked toward her and they met under a streetlamp. He wasn't sure what to say, so he started to say something stupid like '*Grazie*.' But she said, 'Who are you?'

English. Nice English. 'My name is Rick. I'm American. Thanks for, uh, that.' He was pointing awkwardly in the general direction of his car. Her eyes were large and soft and still sad.

'How do you know my name?' she asked.

155

'I saw you onstage last night. You were magnificent.'

A moment of surprise, then a smile. The smile was the clincher – perfect teeth, dimples, and her eyes sparkled. 'Thank you.'

But he had the impression she did not smile often.

'Anyway, I just wanted to say, uh, hello.'

'Hello.'

'You live around here?' he asked.

'I'm close.'

'Got time for a drink?'

Another smile. 'Sure.'

* * *

The pub was owned by a man from Wales, and it attracted Anglos who ventured into Parma. Fortunately, it was Monday and the place was quiet. They found a table near the front window. Rick ordered a beer and Gabriella ordered a Campari and ice, a drink he had never heard of.

'Your English is beautiful,' he said. At that moment, everything about her was beautiful.

'I lived in London for six years, after university,' she said. He guessed she was about twenty-five, but perhaps she was closer to thirty.

'What were you doing in London?'

'I studied at the London College of Music, then I worked with the Royal Opera.'

'Are you from Parma?'

'No. Florence. And you, Mr. . . . .'

'Dockery. It's an Irish name.'

'Are you from Parma?'

They both laughed to relieve some tension. 'No, I grew up in Iowa, in the Midwest. Have you been to the U.S.?'

'Twice, on tour. I've seen most of the major cities.'

'So have I. A little tour of my own.'

Rick had deliberately picked a round table that was small. They were sitting close together, drinks in front of them, knees not too far apart, both working hard to appear relaxed.

'What kind of tour?'

'I play professional football. My career is not working out so well, and now I'm in Parma this season, playing for the Panthers.' He had a hunch that her career might be a bit off track, too, so he felt comfortable being completely honest. Her eyes encouraged honesty.

'The Panthers?'

'Yes, there is a professional football league here in Italy. Few people know about it, mainly teams here in the North – Bologna, Milan, Bergamo, a few others.'

'I've never heard of it.'

'American football is not very popular here. As you know, this is soccer country.'

'Oh yes.' She seemed less than enthused about soccer. She sipped the reddish liquid in her glass. 'How long have you been here?'

'Three weeks. And you?'

'Since December. The season ends in a week,

and I'll go back to Florence.' She looked away sadly, as if Florence was not where she wanted to be. Rick sipped his beer and looked blankly at an old dartboard on the wall.

'I saw you at dinner tonight,' he said. 'At Il Tribunale. You were with someone.'

A quick fake grin, then, 'Yes, that's Carletto, my boyfriend.'

Another pause as Rick decided not to pursue this. If she wanted to talk about her boyfriend, it was up to her.

'He lives in Florence, too,' she said. 'We've been together for seven years.'

'That's a long time.'

'Yes. Do you have someone?'

'No. I've never had a serious girlfriend. Lots of girls, but nothing serious.'

'Why not?'

'Hard to say. I've enjoyed being a bachelor. It's a natural when you're a professional athlete.'

'Where did you learn to drive?' she blurted, and they laughed.

'I've never had a car with a clutch,' he said.

'Evidently you have.'

'Driving is different here, so is parking.'

'You are superb at parking and singing.'

'Thank you.' A beautiful smile, a pause, a sip from the glass. 'You're an opera fan?'

I am now, Rick almost said. 'Last night was my first, and I enjoyed it, especially when you were onstage, which wasn't often enough.'

'You must come again.'

'When?'

'We perform Wednesday, and then Sunday is our last of the season.'

'We play in Milan on Sunday.'

'I can get you a ticket for Wednesday.'

'It's a deal.'

The pub closed at 2:00 a.m. Rick offered to walk her home, and she easily agreed. Her hotel suite was furnished by the opera company. It was near the river, a few blocks from the Teatro Regio.

They said good night with a nod, a smile, a promise to meet the next day.

* * *

They met for lunch, and over large salads and crepes they talked for two hours. Her schedule was not that different from his – a long night's sleep, coffee and breakfast late in the morning, an hour or two at the gym, then an hour or two of work. When they were not performing, the cast was expected to gather and grind through another practice. Same as football. Rick got the clear impression that a struggling soprano earned more than a struggling itinerant quarterback, but not by much.

Carletto was never mentioned.

They talked about their careers. She had begun singing as a young teenager in Florence, where her mother still lived. Her father was dead. At seventeen, she began winning awards

159

and receiving auditions. Her voice developed early, and there were big dreams. She worked hard in London and won role after role, but then nature set in, genetics became a factor, and she was struggling with the realization that her career – her voice – had reached its pinnacle.

Rick had been booed so many times it didn't faze him. But to get booed on an opera stage seemed unusually cruel. He wanted an explanation, but he did not bring up the issue. Instead, he asked questions about *Otello*. If he was going to watch it again the following night, he wanted to understand everything. *Otello* was dissected for a long time as the lunch went on. There was no hurry.

After coffee, they went for a walk and found a gelato stand. When they finally said good-bye, Rick went straight to the gym, where he sweated like a madman for two hours and thought of nothing but Gabriella.

Chapter 15

Due to a rugby conflict, Wednesday's practice began at 6:00 p.m, and was much worse than Monday's. In a cold, light rain the Panthers slogged through thirty minutes of uninspired calisthenics and sprints, and when they were over, it was too wet for anything else. The team hurried back to the locker room, where Alex arranged the video and Coach Russo tried to get serious about the Milan Rhinos, an expansion team that had played the year before in the B division. For this reason alone, the Panthers had no trouble dismissing them as a viable opponent. There were jokes and cheap shots and plenty of laughs as Sam rolled the video. Finally, he switched discs and went back to their game against Naples. He began with a sequence of missed blocks by the offensive line, and before long Nino was bickering with Franco. Paolo, the Texas Aggie and left tackle, took offense at something said by Silvio, a linebacker, and the

161

mood turned nasty. The cheap shots grew more pointed and spread around the locker room. The squabbling took on sharper tones. Alex, handling the Italian now, offered scathing critiques of just about everyone in a black jersey.

Rick sat low in his locker, enjoying the bitch session but also aware of what Sam was doing. Sam wanted trouble, infighting, emotions. Often an ugly practice or a nasty film session can be productive. The team was flat and over-confident.

When the lights came on, Sam told everyone to go home. There was little chatter as they showered and changed. Rick sneaked away from the stadium and hurried to his apartment. He changed into his finest Italian threads, and at 8:00 p.m. sharp was seated in the fifth row from the orchestra in Teatro Regio. He knew *Otello* now, inside and out. Gabriella had explained everything.

He endured Act 1, no Desdemona until the third scene, when she eased onto the stage and began groveling at the feet of her husband, the crazy Otello. Rick watched her carefully, and with perfect timing, as Otello wailed on about something, she glanced at the fifth row to make sure he was there. Then she began to sing, back and forth with Otello as the first act came to a close.

Rick waited for a second, maybe two, then began applauding. The hefty signora to his right was at first startled, then slowly put her hands together and followed his lead. Her husband did the same, and the light applause spread. Those inclined to boo were preempted, and suddenly the crowd en masse decided that Desdemona deserved better than what she had been receiving. Emboldened, and not one to give much of a damn anyway, Rick served up a hearty 'Bravo!' A gentleman two rows back, no doubt as struck by Desdemona's beauty as Rick, did the same. A few other enlightened souls agreed, and as the curtain fell, Gabriella stood at center stage, eyes closed, but with a slightly noticeable smile.

At 1:00 a.m., they were in the Welsh pub again, having drinks and talking opera and football. The final performance of *Otello* would be the following Sunday, when the Panthers were in Milan slugging it out with the Rhinos. She wanted to see a game, and Rick convinced her to stay in Parma another week.

* * *

With Paolo the Aggie as their guide, the three Americans caught the 10:05 train for Milan Friday night, not long after the last practice of the week. The rest of the Panthers were at Polipo's for the weekly pizza party.

The drink cart stopped at their seats, and Rick bought four beers, the first round, the first of many. Sly said he drank little, said his wife did not approve, but at that moment his wife was in

163

Denver, very far away. She would become even more removed as the night progressed. Trey said he preferred bourbon, but could certainly handle a beer. Paolo seemed ready to drink a keg.

An hour later they were in the sprawling lights of Milan's perimeter. Paolo claimed to know the city well, and the country boy was visibly excited about a weekend in town.

The train stopped inside the cavernous Milano Centrale, Europe's largest train station, a place that had thoroughly intimidated Rick a month earlier when he passed through. They squeezed into a cab and headed for the hotel. Paolo had handled the details. They had decided on a decent hotel, not too expensive, in a section of town known for its nightlife. No cultural excursion into the heart of old Milan. No interest in history or art. Sly in particular had seen enough cathedrals and baptisteries and cobble-stoned streets. They checked into the Hotel Johnny in the northwest section of Milan. It was a family-run *albergo*, with a little charm and little rooms. Double rooms – with Sly and Trey in one and Rick and Paolo in the other. The narrow beds were not far apart, and Rick wondered, as he quickly unpacked, just how cozy things might get if both roommates got lucky with the girls.

Food was a priority, at least for Paolo, though the Americans could have grabbed a sandwich on the run. He selected a place called Quattro Mori because of its fish, said he needed a break from the endless pasta and meat in Parma. They ate freshly caught pike from Lake Garda and fried perch from Lake Como, but the winner was a baked tench stuffed with bread crumbs, Parmesan cheese, and parsley. Paolo, of course, preferred a slow proper meal with wine, followed by dessert and coffee. The Americans were ready for the bars.

The first was an establishment known as a discopub, a genuine Irish pub with a long happy hour followed by wall-to-wall dancing. They arrived around 2:00 a.m., and the pub was rocking with a screeching British punk band and hundreds of young men and women gyrating wildly with the music. They drained a few beers and approached a few ladies. The language thing was quite a barrier.

The second was a pricier club with a ten-euro cover charge, but Paolo knew someone who knew someone else, and the cover was waived. They found a table on the second level and watched the band and dance floor below. A bottle of Danish vodka arrived, with four glasses of ice, and the evening took a different turn. Rick flashed a credit card and paid for the drinks. Sly and Trey were on tight budgets, as was Paolo, though he tried not to show it. Rick, the quarterback at twenty grand a year, was happy enough to play the big shot. Paolo disappeared and returned with three women, three very attractive Italian girls willing to at least say hello to the Americans. One spoke broken English, but after a few minutes of awkward chitchat they resorted to Italian with Paolo, and the Americans were gently pushed to the sidelines.

'How do you pick up girls if they can't speak English?' Rick asked Sly.

'My wife speaks English.'

Then Trey led one of the girls away to the dance floor. 'These European girls,' Sly said, 'always checking out the black dudes.'

'Must be awful.'

After an hour, the Italians moved on. The vodka was gone.

The party began some time after 4:00 a.m. when they stepped into a packed Bavarian beer hall with a reggae band onstage. English was the dominant tongue – lots of American students and twentysomethings. On the way back from the bar with four steins of beer, Rick found himself cornered by a group of ladies from the South, according to their drawls.

'Dallas,' one said. They were travel agents, all in their mid-thirties and probably married, though no wedding rings were visible. Rick sat the beers on their table and offered them up. To hell with his teammates. There was no brother-hood. Within seconds he was dancing with Beverly, a slightly overweight redhead with beautiful skin, and when Beverly danced it was full contact. The floor was crowded, bodies bumped into bodies, and to keep close Beverly kept her hands on Rick. She hugged and hunched and groped, and between songs suggested they retire to a corner where they could be alone, away from her competition. She was a clinger, and a determined one.

There was no sign of the other Panthers.

But Rick guided her back to her table, where her fellow travel agents were assaulting all manner of men. He danced with one named Lisa from Houston whose ex-husband ran off with his law partner, and so on. She was a bore, and of the two he preferred Beverly.

Paolo popped in to check on his quarterback, and with his accented English thrilled the ladies with an amazing string of lies. He and Rick were famous rugby players from Rome who traveled the world with their team, earning millions and living life in grand style. Rick rarely lied to pick up women; it simply wasn't necessary. But it was humorous to watch the Italian work the crowd.

Sly and Trey were gone, Paolo told Rick as he moved to another table. Left with two blondes who spoke the language, albeit with a funny accent. Probably Irish, he thought.

After the third dance, maybe the fourth, Beverly finally convinced him to leave, through a side door to avoid her friends. They walked a few blocks, completely lost, then found a cab. They groped for ten minutes in the backseat until it stopped at the Regency. Her room was on the fifth floor. As Rick pulled the curtains, he saw the first hint of dawn.

★ ★ ★

167

He managed to open one eye in the early afternoon, and with it he saw red toenails and realized Bev was still asleep. He closed it and drifted away. His head felt worse the second time he awoke. She was not in the bed but in the shower, and for a few minutes he thought about his escape.

Though the disentanglement and clumsy good-bye would be over quickly, he still hated it. He always had. Was cheap sex really worth the lies on the run? 'Hey, you were great, gotta go now.' 'Sure, I'll give you a call.'

How many times had he opened his eyes, tried to remember the girl's name, tried to remember where he found her, tried to recall the details of the actual deed, the momentous occasion that got them into bed to begin with?

The shower was running. His clothes were in a pile by the door.

He suddenly felt older, not necessarily more mature, but certainly tired of the role of the bed-hopping bachelor with the golden arm. All the women had been throwaways, from the cute cheerleaders in college to this stranger in a foreign city.

The football-stud act was over. It ended in Cleveland with his last real game.

He thought of Gabriella, then tried not to. How odd that he felt guilty lying under thin sheets listening to the water run over the body of a woman whose last name he never heard.

He quickly dressed and waited. The water

stopped, and Bev walked out in a hotel bathrobe. 'So you're awake,' she said with a forced smile.

'Finally,' he said, standing and anxious to get it over with. He hoped she didn't stall and want drinks and dinner and another night of it. 'I need to go.'

'So long,' she said, then abruptly returned to the bathroom and shut the door. He heard the lock click.

How wonderful. In the hallway, he decided that she was indeed married, and she probably felt a lot guiltier than he did.

Over beer and pizza, the four amigos nursed their hangovers and compared stories. Rick, to his surprise, found such frat boy talk silly. 'Ever hear of the forty-eight-hour rule?' he asked. And before anyone could answer, he said, 'It's pretty common in pro football. No booze forty-eight hours before kickoff.'

'Kickoff is in about twenty hours,' Trey said.

'So much for that rule,' Sly said, gulping his beer.

'I say we take it easy tonight,' Rick said.

The other three nodded but did not commit. They found a half-empty discopub and threw darts for an hour as the place filled and a band tuned up in one corner. Suddenly the pub was flooded with German college students, most of them female and all of them ready for a hard night. The darts were forgotten when the dancing began.

A lot of things were forgotten.

American football was less popular in Milan than in Parma. Someone said there were 100,000 Yanks living in Milan, and evidently most hated football. A couple hundred fans showed up for the kickoff.

The Rhinos' home was an old soccer field with a few sections of bleachers. The team had labored for years in Series B before being promoted this season. They were no match for the mighty Panthers, which made it hard to explain their twenty-point lead at halftime.

The first half was Sam's worst nightmare. As he anticipated, the team was flat and lackadaisical, and no amount of screaming could motivate them. After four carries, Sly was on the sideline gasping and heaving. Franco fumbled the ball away on his first and only carry. His ace quarterback seemed a bit slow, and his passes were uncatchable. Two were batted around long enough for the Rhinos' safety to grab them. Rick fumbled one handoff, and refused to run the ball. His feet felt like bricks.

As they jogged off the field at halftime, Sam went after his quarterback. 'You hungover?' he demanded, rather loudly, or at least loud enough for the rest of the team to hear. 'How long you been in Milan? All weekend? You been drunk all weekend? You look like shit and you play like shit, you know that!'

'Thanks, Coach,' Rick said, still jogging. Sam

stayed beside him step for step, and the Italians got out of the way.

'You're supposed to be the leader, right?'

'Thanks, Coach.'

'And you show up all red-eyed and hungover and you can't hit a barn with a pass. You make me sick, you know that?'

'Thanks, Coach.'

Inside the locker room, Alex Olivetto took over in Italian and it was not pretty. Many of the Panthers glared at Rick and Sly, who was gritting his teeth and fighting nausea. Trey had made no great errors in the first half, but he'd certainly done nothing spectacular. Paolo, so far, had been able to survive by hiding in the mass of humanity at the line of scrimmage.

A flashback. The hospital room in Cleveland, watching ESPN highlights and wanting to reach up to the IV bag and turn the valve so that the Vicodin could flow freely into his bloodstream and put him out of his misery.

Where were the chemicals when he needed them? And why, exactly, did he love this game?

When Alex grew tired, Franco asked the coaches to leave the room, which they gladly did. The judge then addressed his teammates. Without raising his voice, he pleaded for a greater effort. There was plenty of time. The Rhinos were an inferior bunch.

All of this was in Italian, but Rick got the message.

The comeback began in dramatic fashion, and

was over before it really started. On the second play of the second half, Sly darted through the line and raced sixty-five yards for an easy touchdown. But by the time he reached the end zone, he was done for the day. He barely made it back to the sideline before crouching behind the bench and disgorging the entire weekend's worth of hell-raising. Rick heard it but preferred not to look.

There was a flag, and after some discussion the play was called back. Nino had yanked a linebacker's face mask, then placed a knee in his groin. Nino was ejected, and though this fired up the Panthers, it also infuriated the Rhinos. The cursing and taunting reached a nasty level, and Rick picked the wrong time to bootleg and run. He gained fifteen yards and, to prove his determination, lowered his helmet instead of stepping out of bounds. He was slaughtered by half the Rhinos' defense. He staggered back to the huddle and called a pass play to Fabrizio. The new center, a forty-year-old named Sandro, bobbled the snap, the ball shot loose from the line, and Rick managed to fall on it. A large and angry tackle drilled him into the ground for good measure. On third and fourteen, he fired a pass at Fabrizio. The bullet was much too hard and hit the kid in the helmet, which he promptly removed and threw angrily at Rick as they left the field.

Fabrizio then left the field, too. He was last seen jogging toward the locker room.

With no running game and no passing game, Rick's offense was left with few options. Franco punched the ball into the middle of the pileup over and over, quite heroically.

Late in the fourth quarter, trailing 34–0, Rick sat alone on the bench and watched the defense struggle valiantly to save face. Pietro and Silvio, the two psycho linebackers, hit like wild men and screamed at their defense to kill whoever had the ball.

If Rick had ever felt worse late in a football game, he could not remember when. He got himself benched on the last possession. 'Take a break,' Sam hissed at him, and Alberto jogged to the huddle. The drive took ten plays, all on the ground, and consumed four minutes. Franco pounded into the middle, and Andreo, Sly's replacement, swept right and left with little speed, few moves, but a gritty determination. Playing for nothing but pride, the Panthers finally scored with ten seconds to go when Franco lurched his way into the end zone. The extra point was blocked.

The bus ride home was slow and painful. Rick was given a seat by himself and suffered alone. The coaches sat in the front and seethed. Someone with a cell phone got the news that Bergamo had beaten Naples 42–7, in Naples, and this made a bad day even worse.

Chapter 16

Mercifully, the *Gazzetta di Parma* did not mention the game. Sam read the sports page early Monday morning and for once was happy to be lost in the land of soccer. He flipped through the paper while parked on the curb outside the Hotel Palace Maria Luigia waiting for Hank and Claudelle Withers from Topeka. He'd spent last Saturday showing them the highlights of the Po valley, and now they wanted a full day seeing more.

He wished he could've spent Sunday with them as well, and skipped Milan.

His cell phone rang. 'Hello.'

'Sam, it's Rick.'

Sam skipped a beat, thought some terrible things, then said, 'What's up?'

'Where are you?'

'I'm a guide today. Why?'

'You gotta minute?'

'No, as I said, I'm working now.'

'Where are you?'

'Outside the Hotel Palace Maria Luigia.'

'Be there in five minutes.'

Minutes later Rick turned the corner, running hard and sweating as if he'd been at it for an hour. Sam slowly removed himself from the car and leaned against a fender.

Rick pulled alongside, stopped on the sidewalk, took a couple of deep breaths, and said, 'Nice car.' He pretended to admire the black Mercedes.

Sam had little to say, so he said, 'It's a rental.'

Another deep breath, a step closer. 'Sorry about yesterday,' Rick said, eyeball-to-eyeball with his coach.

'It might be a party for you,' Sam growled. 'But it's my job.'

'You have the right to be pissed.'

'Oh thank you.'

'It won't happen again.'

'Damned right it won't. You show up again in bad shape and I'll bench your ass. I'd rather lose with Alberto and a little dignity than lose with some prima donna with a hangover. You were pretty disgusting.'

'Go ahead. Unload. I got it coming.'

'You lost more than a game yesterday. You lost your team.'

'They weren't exactly ready to play.'

'True, but don't pass the buck. You're the key, whether you like it or not. They feed off you, or at least they did.'

Rick watched a few cars pass, then backed away. 'I'm sorry, Sam. It won't happen again.'

'We'll see.'

Hank and Claudelle emerged from the hotel and said good morning to their guide. 'Later,' Sam hissed at Rick, then got in the car.

* * *

Gabriella's Sunday had been as disastrous as Rick's. In the final performance of *Otello*, she had been flat and uninspired, according to her own critique, and, evidently, according to the audience as well. She reluctantly explained things over a light lunch, and though Rick wanted to know if they had actually booed her again, he did not ask. She was cheerless and preoccupied, and Rick tried to lighten her mood by describing his pathetic game in Milan. Misery loves company, and he was certain his performance was much worse than hers.

It didn't work. Halfway through the meal she informed him, sadly, that she was leaving in a few hours for Florence. She needed to go home, to get away from Parma and the pressure of the stage.

'You promised to stay another week,' he said, trying not to sound desperate.

'No, I must go.'

'I thought you wanted to see a football game.'

'I did, but now I don't. I'm sorry, Rick.'

He stopped eating and tried to appear

176

supportive, and nonchalant. But he was an easy read.

'I'm sorry,' she said, but he doubted her sincerity.

'Is it Carletto?'

'No.'

'I think it is.'

'Carletto is always there, somewhere. He's not going away. We've been together too long.'

Exactly, much too long. Dump the creep and let's have some fun. Rick bit his tongue and decided not to beg. They had been together for seven years, and their relationship was certainly complicated. Wedging into the middle of it, or even working the edges, would get him burned. He inched his plate away and folded his hands. Her eyes were wet, but she was not crying.

She was a wreck. She had reached the point onstage where her career was teetering on the brink. Rick suspected Carletto offered more threats than support, though how could he ever know for sure?

And so it ended like most of the other quick romances he'd botched along the way. A hug on the sidewalk, an awkward kiss, a tear or two from her, good-byes, promises to call, and, finally, a fleeting wave of the hand. As he watched her disappear down the street, though, he longed to race after her and beg like a fool. He prayed she would stop, and quickly turn around, and come running back.

He walked a few blocks, trying to knock off

the numbness, and when that didn't work, he changed into running gear and jogged to Stadio Lanfranchi.

* * *

The locker room was empty, except for Matteo the trainer, who did not offer a massage. He was sufficiently pleasant, but something was missing from his usual jovial self. Matteo wanted to study sports medicine in the United States and for this reason gave Rick loads of unwanted attention. Today the kid was preoccupied and soon disappeared.

Rick stretched out on the training table, closed his eyes, and thought about the girl. Then he thought about Sam, and his plan to catch him early before practice and, tail wagging, try once more to repair the damage. He thought about the Italians and almost dreaded the cold shoulders. But as a race, they were not prone to keep their feelings bottled up, and he figured that after a few testy encounters and harsh words they would all hug and be pals again.

'Hey, buddy,' someone whispered and jolted him from his zone. It was Sly, wearing jeans and a jacket and headed somewhere.

Rick sat up and dangled his feet off the table. 'What's up?'

'You seen Sam?'

'He's not here yet. Where you going?'

Sly leaned on the other training table, folded

his arms, frowned, and in a low voice said, 'Home, Ricky, I'm headed home.'

'You're quitting?'

'Call it whatever. We all quit at some point.'

'You can't just walk out, Sly, after two games. Come on!'

'I'm packed and the train leaves in an hour. My lovely wife will be waiting at the airport in Denver when I get there tomorrow. I gotta go, Ricky. It's over. I'm tired of chasing a dream that'll never happen.'

'I think I understand that, Sly, but you're walking out in the middle of a season. You're leaving me with a backfield in which no one runs the forty in under five seconds, except me, and I'm not supposed to run.'

Sly was nodding, his eyes glancing around. He obviously hoped to sneak in, have a few words with Sam, then sneak out. Rick wanted to choke him because the thought of handing off to Judge Franco twenty times a game was not appealing.

'I got no choice, Rick,' he said, even softer, even sadder. 'My wife called this morning, pregnant and very surprised to be pregnant. She's fed up. She wants a real husband, at home. And what am I doing over here anyway? Chasing girls in Milan like I'm still in college? We're kidding ourselves.'

'You committed to play this season. You're leaving us with no running game, Sly. That's not fair.'

'Nothing's fair.'

The decision was made, and bickering wouldn't change anything. As Yanks, they'd been forced together in a foreign land. They had survived together and had fun doing so, but they would never be close friends.

'They'll find somebody else,' Sly said, standing straight, ready to bolt. 'They pick up players all the time.'

'During the season?'

'Sure. You watch. Sam'll have a tailback by Sunday.'

Rick relaxed a little.

'You coming home in July?' Sly asked.

'Sure.'

'You gonna try out somewhere?'

'I don't know.'

'You get to Denver, give me a call, okay?'

'Sure.'

A quick manly hug, and Sly was gone. Rick watched him dart through the side door, and he knew he would never see him again. And Sly would never again see Rick, or Sam, or any of the Italians. He would vanish from Italy and never return.

An hour later, Rick broke the news to Sam, who'd had a very long day with Hank and Claudelle. Sam actually threw a magazine against the wall while unloading the expected stream of profanities, and when he settled down, he said, 'You know any running backs?'

'Yes, a great one. Franco.'

'Ha-ha. Americans, preferably college players who run real fast.'

'Not right offhand.'

'Can you call your agent?'

'I could, but he hasn't been real prompt returning my calls. I think he has unofficially dumped me.'

'You're on a roll.'

'I'm having a very good day, Sam.'

Chapter 17

At 8:00 Monday evening, the Panthers began arriving at the field. The mood was quiet and gloomy. They were embarrassed by the loss, and the news that half the offense had just fled town did not help their spirits. Rick sat on a stool in front of his locker, his back to everyone, his head buried in the playbook. He could feel the stares and the resentment, and he knew he had been terribly wrong. Maybe it was just a club sport, but winning meant something. Commitment meant even more.

He slowly flipped the pages, looking blankly at the Xs and Os. Whoever created them assumed the offense had a tailback who could run and a receiver who could catch. Rick could deliver the ball, but if there was no one on the other end, the stats simply recorded another incompletion.

Fabrizio had not been seen. His locker was empty.

Sam got their attention and had a few

measured words for the team. No sense yelling. His players felt bad enough. Yesterday's game was over, and there was another in six days. He delivered the news about Sly, though the gossip had made the rounds.

Their next opponent was Bologna, traditionally a strong team that usually played in the Super Bowl. Sam talked about the Warriors and made them sound rather fierce. They had easily won their first two games with a punishing ground attack led by a tailback named Montrose, who had once played at Rutgers. Montrose was new to the league, and his legend was growing by the week. Yesterday, against the Rome Gladiators, he carried the ball twenty-eight times for over three hundred yards and four touchdowns.

Pietro vowed, loudly, to break his leg, and this was well received by the team.

After a halfhearted pep talk, the team filed out of the locker room and jogged onto the field. The day after a game, most of the players were stiff and sore. Alex worked them gently through some light stretching and exercises, then they divided into offense and defense.

Rick's suggestion for a new offense was to move Trey from free safety to wide receiver, and throw him the ball thirty times a game. Trey had speed, great hands, quickness, and he'd played wideout in high school. Sam was cool to the idea, primarily because it came from Rick and at the moment he was barely talking to his quarterback.

183

Halfway through the workout, though, Sam issued an open call for anyone who might consider playing receiver. Rick and Alberto tossed easy passes to a dozen prospects for half an hour, after which Sam called Trey over and made the switch. His presence on offense left a huge gap on defense.

'If we can't stop them, maybe we can outscore them,' Sam mumbled as he scratched his cap.

'Let's go watch film,' he said, and then blew his whistle.

Monday night film meant cold beer and some laughs, exactly what the team needed. Bottles of Peroni, the national favorite, were handed out, and the mood lightened considerably. Sam chose to ignore the Rhinos tape and dwell on Bologna. On defense, the Warriors were big across the front and had a strong safety who had played two years of arena ball and hit really hard. A head-hunter.

Just what I need, thought Rick as he pulled a long gulp of beer. Another concussion. Montrose looked a step or two slow, the Rome defenders much slower, and Pietro and Silvio soon dismissed him as a threat. 'We shall crush him,' Pietro said in plain English.

The beer flowed until after eleven, when Sam turned off the projector and dismissed them with the usual promise of a rough practice on Wednesday. Rick and Trey hung around, and when all the Italians had left, they opened another bottle with Sam.

'Mr. Bruncardo is reluctant to bring in another running back,' Sam said.

'Why?' Trey asked.

'Not sure, but I think it's money. He's really upset with the loss yesterday. If we can't compete for the Super Bowl, why burn any more cash? This is not exactly a moneymaker for him anyway.'

'Why does he do it?' Rick asked.

'Excellent question. They have some funny tax laws here in Italy, and he gets big write-offs for owning a sports team. Otherwise, it would not make sense.'

'The answer is Fabrizio,' Rick said.

'Forget him.'

'I'm serious. With Trey and Fabrizio we have two great receivers. No team in the league can afford two Americans in the secondary, so they can't cover us. We don't need a tailback. Franco can grunt out fifty yards a game and keep the defense honest. With Trey and Fabrizio, we play pitch and catch for four hundred yards.'

'I'm tired of that kid,' Sam said, and Fabrizio was no longer discussed.

Later, in a pub, Rick and Trey raised a glass to Sly and cursed him at the same time. Though neither would admit it, they were homesick and envied Sly for calling it quits.

★ ★ ★

Tuesday afternoon, Rick and Trey, along with

Alberto, the dutiful understudy, met Sam at the field and for three hours worked on precision routes, timing, hand signals, and a general overhaul of the offense. Nino arrived late for the party. Sam informed him they were switching to a shotgun formation for the rest of the season, and he worked frantically on his snaps. With time, they improved to the point that Rick wasn't chasing them around the backfield.

Wednesday night, in full pads, Rick spread the receivers, Trey and Claudio, and began firing passes everywhere. Slants, hooks, posts, curls – every pattern worked. He threw to Claudio often enough to keep the defense honest, and every tenth play he stuck the ball in Franco's gut for a little violence at the line. Trey was unstoppable. After an hour of sprinting up and down the field, he needed a break. The offense, almost shut out by a weak Milan team three days earlier, now seemed capable of scoring at will. The team rallied from its slumber and came alive. Nino began trash-talking the defense, and he and Pietro were soon cussing back and forth. Someone threw a punch, a quick brawl ensued, and when Sam broke it up, he was the happiest guy in Parma. He saw what every coach wanted – emotion, fire, and anger!

He made them quit at 10:30. The locker room was chaos; the air was full of dirty socks, dirty jokes, insults, threats of stealing girlfriends. Things were back to normal. The Panthers were ready for war.

* * *

The call came on Sam's cell. The man identified himself as a lawyer and had something to do with athletics and marketing. He spoke rapid Italian, and over the phone it sounded even more urgent. Sam often survived by reading lips and hand gestures.

The lawyer finally got to the point. He represented Fabrizio, and Sam at first thought the kid was in trouble. Not hardly. The lawyer was also a sports agent, with many soccer and basketball players on his roster, and he wanted to negotiate a contract for his client.

Sam's jaw dropped an inch or two. Agents? Here in Italy?

There goes the game.

'That son of a bitch walked off the field in the middle of a game,' Sam said in the rough Italian equivalent.

'He was upset. He is sorry. It's obvious you can't win without him.'

Sam bit his tongue, counted to five. Keep cool, he told himself. A contract meant money, something no Italian Panther had ever sought. There were rumors that some of the Italians in Bergamo got paid, but it was unheard-of in the rest of the league.

Play along, Sam thought. 'What kind of contract do you have in mind?' he asked, rather businesslike.

'He's a great player, you know. Probably the

187

best Italian ever, don't you think? I value him at two thousand euros a month.'

'Two thousand,' Sam repeated.

Then the usual agent's trick. 'And we are talking to other teams.'

'Good. Keep talking. We're not interested.'

'He might consider less, but not much.'

'The answer is no, pal. And tell the kid to stay away from our field. He might get a leg broke.'

★ ★ ★

Charley Cray of the *Cleveland Post* slithered into Parma late Saturday afternoon. One of his many readers had stumbled across the Panthers' Web site and was intrigued by the news that the Greatest Goat on Cray's list was hiding in Italy.

The story was simply too good to ignore.

Sunday, Cray got in a cab at his hotel and tried to explain where he wanted to go. The driver was not familiar with '*football americano*' and had no idea where the field was. Great, thought Cray. The cabbies can't even find the field. The story was growing richer by the hour.

He finally arrived at Stadio Lanfranchi thirty minutes before kickoff. He counted 145 people in the stands, 40 Panthers in black and silver, 36 Warriors in white and blue, one black face on each team. At kickoff, he estimated the crowd at 850.

Late that night, he finished his story and zipped it around the world to Cleveland, in plenty of time for the Monday morning sports special. He could not remember having so much fun. It read:

BIG CHEESE IN THE PIZZA LEAGUE

(PARMA, ITALY). In his miserable NFL career, Rick Dockery completed 16 passes for 241 yards, and that was with six different teams over four years. Today, playing for the Panthers of Parma in Italy's version of the NFL, Dockery exceeded those numbers. In the first half!

21 completions, 275 yards, 4 touchdowns, and, the most unbelievable stat of all – no interceptions.

Is this the same quarterback who single-handedly threw away the AFC title game? The same no-name signed by the Browns late last season for reasons still unknown and now considered the Greatest Goat in the history of pro football?

Yes, this is Signor Dockery. And on this lovely spring day in the Po valley he was simply masterful – throwing beautiful spirals, standing bravely in the pocket, reading the defense (word used loosely), and, believe it or not, scrambling for yardage when necessary. Rick Dockery has finally found his game. He's The Man playing with a bunch of overgrown boys.

Before a noisy crowd of fewer than a thousand, and on a rugby pitch 90 yards long, the Panthers of Parma hosted the Warriors of Bologna. Either team would be a 20-point underdog against Slippery Rock, but who cares? Under Italian rules, each team can have up to three Americans. Dockery's favorite receiver today was Trey Colby, a rather thin young man who once played at Ole Miss and could not, under any defensive scheme, manage to get himself covered by the Bologna secondary.

Colby ran wild and free. He caught three touchdowns in the first 10 minutes!

The other Panthers are rowdy young men who picked up the sport as a hobby later in life. Not a single one could start for a class 5A high school in Ohio. They are white, slow, small, and play football because they can't play soccer or rugby.

(By the way, rugby, basketball, volleyball, swimming, motorbiking, and cycling all rank far above *football americano* in this part of the world.)

But the Warriors were no pushovers. Their quarterback played at Rhodes (where? – Memphis, D-3) and their tailback once carried the ball (58 times in 3 years) for Rutgers. Ray Montrose is his name and today he ran for 200 yards and 3 touchdowns, including the game winner with a minute to go.

That's right, even here in Parma, Dockery can't escape the ghosts of his past. Up 27–7 at halftime, he once again managed to snatch defeat from the jaws of victory. But, in all fairness, it wasn't entirely his fault. On the first play of the second half, Trey Colby went high for an errant pass (surprise, surprise) and landed badly. He was hauled off the field with a compound fracture somewhere in his lower left leg. The offense sputtered, and Mr. Montrose began marching up and down the field. The Warriors put together a dramatic drive as time ran out and won 35–34.

Rick Dockery and his Panthers have lost their last two, and with only five games remaining their chances of making the play-offs look slim. There is an Italian Super Bowl in July, and evidently the Panthers thought Dockery could get them there.

They should have asked Browns fans. We would tell them to ditch this bum now and find a real quarterback, one from a junior college. And quick, before Dockery starts firing passes to the other team.

We know what this gunslinger can really do. Poor Parma Panthers.

Chapter 18

Rick and Sam waited like expectant fathers at the end of a hallway on the second floor of the hospital. It was 11:30 Sunday night, and Trey had been in surgery since just after 8:00 p.m. The play was a thirty-yard pass at midfield, near the Panthers' bench. Sam heard the crack of the fibula. Rick did not. He did, however, see the blood and the bone fragment protruding through the sock.

They said little as they killed time by reading magazines. Sam was of the opinion that they could still qualify for the play-offs if they won the remaining five games, a tough chore since Bergamo lay ahead. And Bolzano was strong again; they had just lost to Bergamo by two points. But winning seemed unlikely with so little offense left, and with no American in the secondary to stifle the passing game.

It was more pleasant to ignore football and stare at magazines.

A nurse called them and led them to the third floor to a semiprivate room where Trey was being arranged for the night. His left leg was covered in a massive plaster cast. Tubes ran from his arm and nose. 'He'll sleep all night,' another nurse said.

She went on to explain that the doctor said everything had gone fine, no complications, a fairly routine compound fracture. She found a blanket and a pillow, and Rick settled into a vinyl chair next to the bed. Sam promised to hustle back early Monday morning to check on things.

A curtain was pulled, and Rick was left alone with the last black Panther, a very sweet country kid from rural Mississippi who would now be shipped home to his mother like broken merchandise. Trey's right leg was uncovered, and Rick studied it. The ankle was very thin, much too thin to withstand the violence of SEC football. He was too skinny and had trouble keeping his weight up, though he had been voted third-team all-conference his senior year at Ole Miss.

What would he do now? What was Sly doing now? What would any of them do once they faced the reality that the game was over?

The nurse eased in around one and turned down the lights. She handed Rick a small blue pill and said, 'To sleep.' Twenty minutes later he was knocked out as cold as Trey.

* * *

Sam brought coffee and croissants. They found two chairs in the hall and huddled over their breakfast. Trey had made some racket an hour earlier, enough to arouse the nurses.

'Just had a quick meeting with Mr. Bruncardo,' Sam was saying. 'He likes to start the week with a seven o'clock ass chewing on Monday morning.'

'And today's your day.'

'Evidently. He doesn't make any money off the Panthers, but he certainly doesn't like to lose money either. Or games. A rather substantial ego.'

'That's rare for an owner.'

'He had a bad day. His minor-league soccer team lost. His volleyball team lost. And his beloved Panthers, with a real NFL quarterback, lost for the second time in a row. Plus, I think he's losing money on every team.'

'Maybe he needs to stick to real estate, or whatever else he does.'

'I didn't give him any advice. He wants to know about the rest of our season. And, he says he's not spending more money.'

'It's very simple, Sam,' Rick said, placing his coffee cup on the floor. 'In the first half yesterday we scored four touchdowns with no sweat. Why? Because I had a receiver. With my arm and a good set of hands, we are unstoppable and we won't lose again. I guarantee we can score forty points every game, hell, every half.'

'Your receiver is in there with a broken leg.'

'True. Get Fabrizio. The kid is great. He's

faster than Trey and has better hands.'

'He wants money. He has an agent.'

'A what!'

'You heard me. Got a call last week from some slimy lawyer here who says he represents the fabulous Fabrizio and they want a contract.'

'Football agents here in Italy?'

'Afraid so.'

Rick scratched his unshaven face and pondered this disheartening news. 'Has any Italian ever received money?'

'Rumor says some of the Bergamo boys are paid, but I'm not sure.'

'How much does he want?'

'Two thousand euros a month.'

'How much will he take?'

'Don't know. We didn't get that far.'

'Let's negotiate, Sam. Without him, we're dead.'

'Bruncardo ain't spending more money, Rick, listen to me. I suggested we haul in another American player and he went through the roof.'

'Take it out of my salary.'

'Don't be stupid.'

'I'm serious. I'll chip in a thousand euros a month for four months to get Fabrizio.'

Sam sipped his coffee with a frown and studied the floor. 'He walked off the field in Milan.'

'Sure he did. He's a brat, okay, we all know that. But you and I are about to walk off the field five more times with our tails tucked if we don't find someone who can catch a football. And, Sam, he can't walk off if he's under contract.'

'Don't bet on it.'

'Pay him, and I'll bet he acts like a pro. I'll spend hours with him and we'll be so finely tuned no one can stop us. You get Fabrizio, and we won't lose again. I guarantee it.'

A nurse nodded in their direction, and they hurried in to see Trey. He was awake and very uncomfortable. He tried to smile and crack a joke, but he needed medication.

* * *

Arnie called late Monday afternoon. After a brief discussion of the merits of arena football, he moved on to the real reason for the call. He hated to pass along bad news, he said, but Rick should know about it. Check out the *Cleveland Post* online, Monday sports section. Pretty ugly stuff.

Rick read it, let fly the appropriate expletives, then went for a long walk through the center of old Parma, a town he suddenly appreciated like never before.

How many low points can one career have? Three months after he fled Cleveland, they were still eating his carcass.

* * *

Judge Franco handled matters for the team. The negotiations took place at a sidewalk café along the edge of Piazza Garibaldi, with Rick and Sam seated nearby having a beer and dying of curiosity. The judge and Fabrizio's agent ordered coffee.

Franco knew the agent and didn't like him at all. Two thousand euros was out of the question, Franco explained. Many of the Americans don't earn that much. And it was a dangerous precedent to start paying the Italians because, obviously, the team barely broke even anyway. More payroll and they might as well close shop.

Franco offered five hundred euros for three months – April, May, and June. If the team advanced to the Super Bowl in July, then a one-thousand-euro bonus.

The agent smiled politely while dismissing the offer as much too low. Fabrizio is a great player and so on. Sam and Rick nursed their beers but couldn't hear a word. The Italians haggled back and forth in animated conversation – each seemingly shocked at the other's position, then both snickering over some minor point. The negotiations seemed to be polite but tense, then suddenly there was a handshake and Franco snapped his fingers at the waiter. Bring two glasses of champagne.

Fabrizio would play for eight hundred euros a month.

Signor Bruncardo appreciated Rick's offer to help with the contract, but he declined it. He was a man of his word, and he would not downsize a player's salary.

★ ★ ★

By practice time Wednesday night, the team knew the details of Fabrizio's return. To quell resentment, Sam arranged for Nino, Franco, and Pietro to meet with their star receiver beforehand and explain a few matters. Nino handled most of the discussion and promised, with no small amount of detail, to break bones if Fabrizio pulled another stunt and abandoned the team. Fabrizio happily agreed to everything, including the broken bones. There would be no problems. He was very excited about playing again and would do anything for his beloved Panthers.

Franco then addressed the team in the locker room before practice and confirmed the rumors. Fabrizio was indeed getting paid. This didn't sit well with most of the Panthers, though no one voiced disapproval. A few were indifferent – if the kid can get some money, why not?

It will take time, Sam said to Rick. Winning changes everything. If we win the Super Bowl, they'll worship Fabrizio.

Sheets of paper had been quietly passed around the locker room. Rick had hoped the poison from Charley Cray might somehow remain in the United States, but he was wrong, thanks to the Internet. The story had been seen and copied and was now being read by his teammates.

At Rick's request, Sam addressed the matter and told the team to ignore it. Just the sloppy work of a sleazy American reporter looking for a headline. But it was unsettling for the players. They loved football and played the game for fun, so why should they be ridiculed?

Most, though, were more concerned about their quarterback. It was unfair to run him out of the league and out of the country, but to follow him to Parma seemed especially cruel.

'I'm sorry, Rick,' Pietro said as they filed out of the locker room.

* * *

Of the two teams in Rome, the Lazio Marines were usually the weaker. They had lost their first three games by an average of twenty points and had shown little spunk in doing so. The Panthers were hungry for a win, and so the five-hour bus ride south was not unpleasant at all. It was the last Sunday in April, overcast and cool, perfect for a football game.

The field, somewhere in the vast outskirts of the ancient city, miles and centuries away from the Colosseum and other splendid ruins, gave little evidence of being used for anything other than practice in the rain. The turf was thin and patchy, with hard sections of gray dirt. The yard lines had been striped by someone either drunk or crippled. Two sections of crooked bleachers held maybe two hundred fans.

Fabrizio earned his April salary in the first quarter. Lazio had not seen him on tape, had no idea who he was, and by the time they scrambled their secondary, he had caught three long passes and the Panthers were up 21–0. With such a lead, Sam began blitzing on every play, and the Marines' offense crumbled. Their quarterback, an Italian, felt the pressure before each snap.

Working solely from the shotgun, and with superb protection, Rick read the coverage, called Fabrizio's route by hand signals, then settled comfortably into the pocket and waited for the kid to jiggle and juke and pop wide open. It was target practice. By halftime, the Panthers were up 38–0, and life was suddenly good again. They laughed and played in the tiny locker room and completely ignored Sam when he tried to complain about something. By the fourth quarter, Alberto was running the offense, and Franco was thundering down the field. All forty players got their uniforms caked with dirt.

On the bus back home they resumed their verbal assaults on the Bergamo Lions. As the beer flowed and the drinking songs grew louder, the mighty Panthers were downright cocky in their predictions of their first Super Bowl.

* * *

Charley Cray had been in the bleachers, sitting among the Lazio faithful, watching his second game of *football americano*. His coverage of last week's game against Bologna had been so well received in Cleveland that his editor asked him to stay on for a week and do it again. Tough work, but someone had to do it. He'd spent five wonderful days in Rome at the paper's expense, and now he needed to justify his little vacation with another takedown of his favorite goat.

His story read:

MORE ROMAN RUINS

(ROME, ITALY). Behind the surprisingly accurate arm of Rick Dockery, the ferocious Panthers of Parma rallied from a two-game losing streak and stomped the living daylights out of the winless Marines of Lazio here today in another crucial matchup in Italy's version of the NFL. The final: 62–12.

Playing on what appeared to be a reclaimed gravel pit, and before 261 nonpaying fans, the Panthers and Dockery racked up almost 400 yards of passing in the first half alone. Skillfully picking apart a defensive secondary that was slow, confused, and thoroughly afraid to hit, Mr. Dockery strutted his stuff with his rifle arm and the marvelous moves of a gifted receiver, Fabrizio Bonozzi. At least twice, Mr. Bonozzi faked so deftly that the deep safety lost a shoe. Such is the level of play here in NFL Italy.

By the third quarter, Mr. Bonozzi appeared to be exhausted from scoring so many long touchdowns. Six, to be exact. And the great Dockery appeared to have a sore arm from throwing so much.

Browns fans will be astonished to learn that,

for the second week in a row, Dockery failed to throw the ball to the other team. Amazing, isn't it? But I swear. I saw it all.

With the win, the Panthers are back in the hunt for the Italian championship. Not that anyone here in Italy really cares.

Browns fans can only thank God that such leagues exist. They allow riffraff like Rick Dockery to play the game far away from where it matters.

Why, oh why, didn't Dockery discover this league a year ago? I almost weep when I ponder this painful question. Ciao.

Chapter 19

The bus rolled into the parking lot at Stadio Lanfranchi a few minutes after three on Monday morning. Most of the players were due at work in a few hours. Sam yelled to wake up everyone, then dismissed the team with a week off. Next weekend was a bye. They stumbled off the bus, unpacked their gear, and headed home. Rick gave a ride to Alberto, then drove through downtown Parma without seeing another car. He parked at a curb three blocks from his apartment.

Twelve hours later he awoke to the buzzing of his cell phone. It was Arnie, abrupt as always. 'Déjà vu, pal. Have you seen the *Cleveland Post?*'

'No. Thank God we don't get it over here.'

'Go online, check it out. That worm was in Rome yesterday.'

'No.'

'Afraid so.'

'Another story?'

'Oh yes, and just as nasty.'

Rick rubbed his hair and tried to remember the crowd at Lazio. A very small crowd, scattered throughout some old bleachers. No, he didn't take the time to study faces, and, anyway, he had no idea what Charley Cray looked like. 'Okay, I'll read it.'

'Sorry, Rick. This is really uncalled for. If I thought it would help, I'd call the paper and raise hell. But they're having way too much fun. It's best to ignore it.'

'If he shows up in Parma again, I'll break his neck. I'm in tight with a judge.'

'Atta boy. Later.'

Rick found a diet soda, took a quick cool shower, then turned on his computer. Twenty minutes later he was zipping through traffic in his Punto, shifting effortlessly, smoothly, like a real Italian. Trey's apartment was just south of the center, on the second floor of a semimodern building designed to cram a lot of people into as few square meters as possible.

Trey was on the sofa with his leg propped up on pillows. The small den resembled a landfill – dirty dishes, empty pizza cartons, a few beer and soda cans. The TV was running old *Wheel of Fortune* shows, and a stereo in the bedroom was playing old Motown.

'Brought you a sandwich,' Rick said, placing a bag on the cluttered coffee table. Trey waved the remote and the TV went mute.

'Thanks.'

'How's the leg?'

'Great,' he said with a hard frown. A nurse stopped by three times a day to tend to his needs and bring the painkillers. He had been very uncomfortable and complained about the pain. 'How'd we do?'

'Easy game, beat 'em by fifty points.'

Rick settled himself into a chair and tried to ignore the debris.

'So you didn't miss me.'

'Lazio is not very good.'

The easy smile and carefree attitude were gone, replaced by a sour mood and truckload of self-pity. That's what a compound fracture will do to a young athlete. The career, however Trey defined it, was over, and the next phase of life was beginning. Like most young athletes, Trey had given little thought to the next step. When you're twenty-six years old, you'll play forever.

'Is the nurse taking care of you?' Rick asked.

'She's good. I get a new cast Wednesday, and leave Thursday. I need to get home. I'm going crazy here.'

They watched the silent TV screen for a long time. Rick had stopped by daily since Trey left the hospital, and the tiny apartment was growing smaller. Maybe it was the trash piling up, or the unwashed laundry, or the windows closed tight and covered. Maybe it was just Trey sinking further into his gloominess. Rick was happy to hear he would be leaving so soon.

'I never got hurt on defense,' Trey said,

staring at the TV. 'I'm a defensive back, never got hurt. Then you put me on offense, and here I am.' He tapped the cast hard for dramatic effect.

'You're blaming me for your injury?'

'I never got hurt on defense.'

'That's a bunch of crap. You saying only offensive players get hurt?'

'I'm just talking about me.'

Rick was bristling and ready to bark, but he took a breath, swallowed hard, looked at the cast, then let it pass. After a few minutes, he said, 'Let's go to Polipo's for pizza tonight?'

'No.'

'Would you like for me to bring you a pizza?'

'No.'

'A sandwich, a steak, anything?'

'No.' And with that, Trey lifted the remote, punched a button, and a happy little housewife purchased a vowel.

Rick eased from the chair and quietly left the apartment.

He sat in the late-afternoon sunshine at an outdoor table and drank a Peroni from a frosty mug. He puffed on a Cuban cigar and watched the ladies walk by. He felt very alone and wondered what on earth he might do for an entire week to keep himself occupied.

Arnie called again, this time with some excitement in his voice. 'The Rat is back,' he announced triumphantly. 'Got hired yesterday by Saskatchewan, head coach. First call he made was to me. He wants you, Rick, right now.'

'Saskatchewan?'

'You got it. Eighty grand.'

'I thought Rat hung it up years ago.'

'He did, moved to a farm in Kentucky, shoveled horse shit for a few years, got bored. Saskatchewan fired everybody last week, and they've coaxed Rat out of retirement.'

Rat Mullins had been hired by more pro teams than Rick. Twenty years earlier he had created a wacky machine-gun offense that passed on every play and sent waves of receivers racing in all directions. He became notorious, for a spell, but over the years fell out of favor when his teams couldn't win. He had been the offensive co-ordinator for Toronto when Rick played there, and the two had been close. If Rat had been the head coach, Rick would've started every game and thrown fifty times.

'Saskatchewan,' Rick mumbled as he flashed back to the city of Regina and the vast wheat plains around it. 'How far is that from Cleveland?'

'A million miles. I'll buy you an atlas. Look, they draw fifty thousand a game, Rick. It's great football, and they're offering eighty grand. Right now.'

'I don't know,' Rick said.

'Don't be silly, kid. I'll have it up to a hundred by the time you get here.'

'I can't just walk away, Arnie, come on.'

'Of course you can.'

'No.'

'Yes. It's a no-brainer. This is your comeback. It starts right now.'

'I have a contract here, Arnie.'

'Listen to me, kid. Think about your career. You're twenty-eight years old, and this opportunity won't come again. Rat wants you in the pocket with that great arm of yours firing bullets all over Canada. It's beautiful.'

Rick chugged his beer and wiped his mouth.

Arnie was on a roll. 'Pack your bags, drive to the train station, park the car, leave the keys on the seat, and say adios. What're they gonna do, sue you?'

'It's not right.'

'Think about yourself, Rick.'

'I am.'

'I'll call you in two hours.'

Rick was watching television when Arnie called again. 'They're at ninety grand, kid, and they need an answer.'

'Has it stopped snowing in Saskatchewan?'

'Sure, it's beautiful. First game's in six weeks. The mighty Roughriders, played for the Grey Cup last year, remember? Great organization and they're ready to roll, pal. Rat's standing on his head to get you there.'

'Let me sleep on it.'

'You're thinking too much, kid. This ain't complicated.'

'Let me sleep on it.'

208

Chapter 20

Sleep, though, was impossible. He rambled through the night, watched television, tried to read, and tried to shake the numbing guilt that consumed any thought of running away. It would be so easy, and could be done in such a way that he would never be forced to face Sam and Franco and Nino and all the rest. He could flee at dawn and never look back. At least that's what he told himself.

At 8:00 a.m. he drove to the train station, parked the Fiat, and walked inside. He waited an hour for his train.

*　*　*

Three hours later he arrived in Florence. A cab took him to the Hotel Savoy, overlooking the Piazza della Repubblica. He checked in, left his bag in the room, and found a table outside at one of the many cafés around the bustling piazza. He punched the number for Gabriella's cell, got a recording in Italian, but decided not to leave a message.

Halfway through lunch, he called her again. She seemed reasonably pleased to hear his voice, a little surprised maybe. A few stutters here and there but she warmed up considerably as they chatted. She was at work, though she didn't explain what she was doing. He suggested they meet for a drink at Gilli's, a popular café across from his hotel and, according to his guidebook, a great place for a late-afternoon drink. Sure, she eventually said, at 5:00 p.m.

He drifted along the streets around the piazza, flowing with the crowd, admiring the ancient buildings. At the duomo, he was almost crushed by a mob of Japanese tourists. He heard English, and lots of it, all coming from packs of what appeared to be American college students, almost all of whom were female. He browsed the shops on the Ponte Vecchio, the ancient bridge over the Arno River. More English. More college girls.

When Arnie called, he was having an espresso and studying his guidebook at a café at the Piazza della Signoria, near the Uffizi, where mobs of tourists waited to see the world's greatest collection of paintings. He had decided he would not tell Arnie where he was.

'Sleep well?' Arnie began.

'Like a baby. It's not going to work, Arnie. I'm not walking out in the middle of the season. Maybe next year.'

'There won't be a next year, kid. It's now or never.'

'There's always next year.'

'Not for you. Rat'll find another quarterback, don't you understand?'

'I understand better than you, Arnie. I've made the circuit.'

'Don't be stupid, Rick. Trust me on this.'

'What about loyalty?'

'Loyalty? When was the last time a team was loyal to you, kid? You've been cut so many times . . .'

'Careful, Arnie.'

A pause, then, 'Rick, if you don't take this deal, then you can find another agent.'

'I was expecting that.'

'Come on, kid. Listen to me.'

Rick was napping in his room when his agent called again. An answer of no was only a temporary setback for Arnie. 'Got 'em up to a hundred grand, okay? I'm working my ass off here, Rick, and I'm getting nothing from your end. Nothing.'

'Thanks.'

'Don't mention it. Here's the deal. The team will buy you a ticket to fly over and meet with Rat. Today, tomorrow, soon, okay? Real soon. Will you please do this just for me?'

'I don't know . . .'

'You got a week off. Please, Rick, as a favor for me. God knows I deserve it.'

'Let me think about it.'

He slowly closed the phone while Arnie was still talking.

* * *

A few minutes before five he found a table outside of Gilli's, ordered Campari on the rocks, and tried not to look at every female who crossed the piazza. Yes, he admitted to himself, he was quite nervous but also excited. He had not seen Gabriella in two weeks, nor had he spoken with her on the phone. No e-mails. No contact whatsoever. This little rendezvous would determine the future of the relationship, if indeed there was a future. It could be a warm reunion with one drink leading to another, or it could be stiff and awkward and the final dose of reality.

A small pack of college girls descended on a table close by. They all talked at once – half on cell phones, the others rattling on at full volume. Americans. Accents from the South. Eight of them, six blondes. Jeans mainly, but a couple of very short skirts. Tanned legs. Not a single textbook or notebook among them. They slid two tables together, pulled chairs, arranged bags, hung jackets, and in the flurry of properly settling in, all eight managed to keep talking.

Rick thought about moving, but then changed his mind. Most of the girls were cute, and the English was comforting, even if it came in torrents. From somewhere inside Gilli's, a waiter pulled the short straw and ventured forth to take their orders, primarily wine, with none of the requests in Italian.

One spotted Rick, then three more glanced over. Two lit cigarettes. For the moment, no cell phones were in use. It was now ten minutes after five.

Ten minutes later, he called Gabriella's cell and listened to the recording. The southern belles were discussing, among other things, Rick and whether he was Italian or American. Could he even understand them? They really didn't care.

He ordered another Campari, and this, according to one of the brunettes, was clear evidence that he was not an American. They suddenly dropped him when someone mentioned a shoe sale at Ferragamo.

Five thirty came and went, and Rick was beginning to worry. Surely she would call if there was a delay, but maybe she wouldn't if she decided not to meet him.

One of the brunettes in one of the miniskirts appeared at his table and quickly fell into the chair across from him. 'Hello,' she said with a dimpled smile. 'Can you settle a bet?' She glanced at her friends, and so did Rick. They were watching with curiosity. Before he could say anything, she continued: 'Are you waiting on a man or a woman? It's half-and-half at our table. The losers buy the drinks.'

'And your name is?'

'Livvy. Yours?'

'Rick.' And for a millisecond he was terrified of using his last name. These were Americans here. Would they recognize the name of the Greatest Goat in the history of the NFL?

'What makes you think I'm waiting on anyone?' Rick asked.

'It's pretty obvious. You glance at your watch, dial a number, don't say anything, watch the crowd, check the time again. You're definitely waiting on someone. It's just a silly bet. Pick one – male or female.'

'Texas?'

'Close, Georgia.'

She was really cute – soft blue eyes, high cheekbones, silky dark hair that fell almost to her shoulders. He wanted to talk. 'A tourist?'

'Exchange student. And you?'

Interesting question with a complicated answer. 'Just business,' he said.

Quickly bored, most of her friends were talking again, something about a new disco where the French boys hung out.

'What do you think, man or woman?' he asked.

'Maybe your wife?' Her elbows were on the table and she was leaning closer, thoroughly enjoying the conversation.

'Never had one.'

'Didn't think so. I'd say you're waiting on a woman. It's after business hours. You don't look like the corporate type. You're definitely not gay.'

'That obvious, huh?'

'Oh, definitely.'

If he admitted he was waiting on a woman, then he might look like a loser who was being stiffed. If he said he was waiting on a man, then he would look stupid when (and if) Gabriella arrived. 'I'm not waiting on anyone,' he said.

She smiled because she knew the truth. 'I doubt that.'

'So where do the American college girls hang out in Florence?'

'We have our places.'

'I might be bored later.'

'Care to join us?'

'Certainly.'

'There's a club called . . .' She paused and looked at her friends, who had moved on to the urgent matter of another round of drinks. Instinctively, Livvy decided not to share. 'Give me your cell number and I'll call you later, after we make some plans.'

They swapped numbers. She said, 'Ciao,' and returned to her table, where she announced to the pack that there were no winners, no losers. Rick over there was waiting on no one.

After waiting for forty-five minutes, he paid for his drinks, winked at Livvy, and got lost in the crowd. One more phone call to Gabriella, one final effort, and when he heard the recording, he cursed and slapped the phone shut.

An hour later he was watching TV in his room when his phone rang. It wasn't Arnie. It wasn't

Gabriella. 'The girl didn't show, did she?' Livvy began cheerily.

'No, she didn't.'

'So you're all alone.'

'Very much.'

'Such a waste. I'm thinking about dinner. You need a date?'

'Indeed I do.'

They met at Paoli's, a short walk from his hotel. It's an ancient place, with one long dining hall under a vaulted ceiling covered with medieval frescoes. It was packed, and Livvy happily confessed that she had pulled strings to get a table. It was a small one, and they sat very close together.

They sipped white wine and worked through the preliminaries. She was a junior at the University of Georgia, finishing her last semester abroad, majoring in art history, not studying too hard, and not missing home.

There was a boy at Georgia, but he was a temp. Disposable.

Rick swore he had no wife, no fiancée, no steady relationship. The girl who didn't show was an opera singer, which of course changed the direction of the conversation considerably. They ordered salads, *pappardelle* with rabbit, and a bottle of Chianti.

After a hearty pull of wine, he gritted his teeth and addressed the issue of football head-on. The good (college), the bad (the nomadic pro career), and the ugly (his brief appearance last

January for the Cleveland Browns).

'I haven't missed football,' she said, and Rick wanted to hug her. She explained that she had been in Florence since September. She did not know who won the SEC or national title, and really didn't care. Nor did she have any interest in pro football. She had been a cheerleader in high school and had endured enough football to last a lifetime.

Finally, a cheerleader in Italy.

He briefly described Parma, its Panthers, the Italian league, then moved the topics back to her side of the table. 'There seem to be a lot of Americans here in Florence,' he said.

She rolled her eyes as if she was fed up with Americans. 'I couldn't wait to study abroad, dreamed about it for years, and now I'm living with three of my sorority sisters from Georgia, none of whom has any interest in learning the language or absorbing the culture. It's all shopping and discos. There are thousands of Americans here, and they stick together like geese.' She might as well be in Atlanta. She often traveled alone to see the countryside and to get away from her friends.

Her father was a noted surgeon who was having an affair that was causing a protracted divorce. Things were messy back home, and she was not excited about leaving Florence when the semester ended in three weeks. 'Sorry,' she said, when she wrapped up the family summary.

'No problem.'

'I'd like to spend the summer traveling in Italy, away, finally, from my sorority, away from the frat boys who get drunk every night, and very far away from my family.'

'Why not?'

'Daddy's paying the bills and Daddy says to come home.'

He had no plans beyond the season, which might stretch into July. For some reason, he mentioned Canada, maybe to impress her. If he played there, the season would go into November. This did not make an impression.

The waiter delivered heaping plates of *pappardelle* and rabbit, a rich meat sauce that looked and smelled divine. They talked about Italian food and wine, about Italians in general, about the places she had already visited and the ones on her wish list.

They ate slowly, like everyone else at Paoli's, and when they finished with the cheese and port, it was after eleven.

'I don't really want to go to a club,' she admitted. 'I'll be happy to show you a couple, but I'm not in the mood. We go out so often.'

'What's on your mind?'

'Gelato.'

They walked across the Ponte Vecchio and found an ice cream shop that offered fifty flavors. Then he walked her to her apartment and kissed her good night.

Chapter 21

'It's five o'clock in the morning here,' Rat began pleasantly. 'Why the hell am I wide awake and calling you at five in the morning? Why? Answer me that, blockhead.'

'Hello, Rat,' Rick said as he visually choked Arnie for giving away his phone number.

'You're a moron, you know that. A first-class idiot, but then we knew that five years ago, didn't we? How are you, Ricky?'

'I'm fine, Rat, and you?'

'Super, off the charts, kicking ass already and the season hasn't started.' Rat Mullins talked in a high pitch at full throttle and seldom waited for a response before he launched into his next verbal assault. Rick had to smile. He had not heard the voice in years, and it brought back fond memories of one of the few coaches who had believed in him. 'We're gonna win, baby, we're gonna score fifty points a game, other team scores forty I don't care, because they'll never

219

catch us. Told the boss yesterday that we need a new scoreboard, old one can't count fast enough for me and my offense and my great quarterback, Blockhead Dockery. Are you there, boy?'

'I'm listening, Rat, as always.'

'So here's the deal. The boss has already bought a round-trip ticket, first-class, you ass, didn't spring one for me, rode back in coach, leaving Rome in the morning at eight, nonstop to Toronto, then to Regina, first-class again, Air Canada, a great airline, by the way. We'll have a car at the airport when you touch down and tomorrow night we'll be having dinner and creating brand-new, never-before-heard-of pass routes.'

'Not so fast, Rat.'

'I know, I know. You can be very slow. How well I remember, but—'

'Look, Rat, I can't walk away from my team right now.'

'Team? Did you say team? I've been reading about your team. The guy in Cleveland, what's his name, Cray, he's all over your ass. A thousand fans for a home game. What is it, touch football?'

'I signed a contract, Rat.'

'And I got another one for you to sign. A much bigger one, with a real team in a real league with real stadiums that hold real fans. Television. Endorsements. Shoe contracts. Marching bands and cheerleaders.'

'I'm happy here, Rat.'

There was a pause as Rat caught his breath.

Rick could see him in the locker room, at halftime, pacing frantically and talking wildly as both hands thrashed the air, then a sudden stop for air as he sucked in mightily before launching into the next tirade.

An octave lower and trying to sound wounded, he began, 'Look, Ricky, don't do this to me. I'm sticking my neck out. After what happened in Cleveland, well—'

'Drop it, Rat.'

'Okay, okay. Sorry. But will you just come see me? Come visit and let me talk to you face-to-face? Can't you do that for your old coach? No strings attached. The ticket's bought, no refund, please, Ricky.'

Rick closed his eyes, massaged his forehead, and reluctantly said, 'Okay, Coach. Just a visit. No strings.'

'You're not as dumb as I thought. I love you, Ricky. You won't be sorry.'

'Who picked the airport at Rome?'

'You're in Italy, right?'

'Yes, but—'

'That's where Rome is, last I checked. Now find the damned airport and come see me.'

★ ★ ★

He knocked back two quick Bloody Marys before takeoff and managed to sleep for most of the eight-hour flight to Toronto. Landing anywhere in North America made him anxious,

221

regardless of how ridiculous such thoughts were. Killing time as he waited for the flight to Regina, he called Arnie and reported his whereabouts. Arnie was very proud. Rick e-mailed his mother, but did not say where he was. He e-mailed Livvy with a quick hello. He checked the *Cleveland Post* just to make sure Charley Cray had moved on to other targets. There was a note from Gabriella: 'Rick, I am so sorry, but it would not be wise to see you. Please forgive me.'

He stared at the floor and decided not to reply to it. He called Trey's cell, but there was no answer.

His two years in Toronto had not been unpleasant. It seemed so long ago, and he seemed so much younger back then. Fresh from college with big dreams and a long career ahead of him, he thought he was invincible. He was a work in progress, a greenhorn with all the tools, he just needed a little polish here and there, and before long he would start in the NFL.

Rick wasn't sure if he still dreamed of playing in the big league.

An announcement mentioned Regina. He walked to a monitor and realized his flight had been delayed. He inquired at the gate and was told the delay was weather related. 'It's snowing in Regina,' the clerk said.

He found a coffee bar and ordered a diet soda. He checked out Regina and, yes, there was snow, and lots of it. 'A rare Spring blizzard' was one description.

Killing time, he browsed through the Regina daily, the *Leader-Post*. There was football news. Rat was making noise, hiring a defensive coordinator, evidently one with very little experience. He'd cut a tailback, leading to speculation that a running game would not be necessary. Season tickets sales had topped thirty-five thousand, a record. A columnist, the type who drags himself to the typewriter and manages to write six hundred words four times a week, for thirty years now, regardless of how absolutely dead the sports world happens to be in Saskatchewan or wherever, mailed in a gossipy potpourri of things 'heard on the street.' A hockey player had said no to surgery until the season was over. Another had separated from his wife, who had a suspicious broken nose.

Last paragraph: Rat Mullins confirmed that the Roughriders were talking to Marcus Moon, a scrambling-style quarterback with a quick arm. Moon spent the past two seasons with the Packers and was 'anxious to play every day.' And Rat Mullins refused to confirm or deny that the team was talking to Rick Dockery, who 'when last seen was throwing gorgeous interceptions for the Cleveland Browns.'

Rat was quoted as offering a gruff 'No comment' to the Dockery rumor.

Then, with a wink, the sportswriter passed along a little tidbit too rich to ignore. The use of parentheses gave him some distance from his own gossip:

(For more on Dockery go to charleycray@clevelandpost.com.)

No comment? Rat is too afraid or too ashamed to comment? Rick asked this question out loud and got a stare or two. He slowly closed his laptop and went for a long hike through the concourse.

* * *

When he boarded an Air Canada commuter flight two hours later, he was headed not to Regina but to Cleveland. There he took a cab downtown. The *Cleveland Post* building was a bland modern structure on Slate Avenue. Oddly, it was four blocks north of the community of Parma.

Rick paid the cabdriver and told him to wait around the corner, a block away. On the sidewalk he paused only for a second to absorb the fact that he was really once again in Cleveland, Ohio. He could have made peace with the city, but the city was determined to torment him.

If there was any hesitation about doing what he was about to do, he did not remember it later.

In the front lobby there was a bronze statue of some unrecognizable person with a pretentious quotation about truth and freedom. A guard station was just beyond it. All guests were required to sign in. Rick was wearing a Cleveland

224

Indians baseball cap, purchased moments earlier at the airport for thirty-two dollars, and when the guard said, 'Yes, sir,' Rick was quick to respond, 'Charley Cray.'

'And your name?'

'Roy Grady. I play for the Indians.'

This pleased the guard greatly, and he slid the clipboard over for a signature. Roy Grady, according to the Indians' Web site, was the newest member of the team's pitching staff, a youngster just called up from AAA who so far had pitched in three innings with very mixed results. Cray would probably recognize the name, but maybe not the face.

'Second floor,' the guard said with a big smile.

Rick took the stairs because he planned to leave by them. The second-floor newsroom was what he expected – a vast open area crammed with cubicles and workstations and papers stacked everywhere. Around the edges were small offices, and Rick began to walk while looking for names by the doors. His heart was pounding and he found it hard to appear nonchalant.

'Roy,' someone called from the side, and Rick stepped in his direction. He was about forty-five, balding, with a few long strands of oily gray hair sprouting from just over his ears, unshaven, cheap reading glasses halfway down his nose, overweight, and with the body type that never earned a letter in high school, never got a uniform, never got the cheerleader. A disheveled sports geek who couldn't play the games and now made a living criticizing those who did. He was standing in the door of his small, cluttered office, frowning at Roy Grady, suspicious of something.

'Mr. Cray?' Rick said, five feet away and closing fast.

'Yes,' he answered with a sneer, then a look of shock.

Rick shoved him quickly back into the office and slammed the door. He yanked off his cap with his left hand as he took Cray's throat with his right. 'It's me, asshole, Rick Dockery, your favorite goat.' Cray's eyes were wide, his glasses fell to the floor.

There would be only one punch, Rick had decided after much thought. A hard right to the head, one that Cray could clearly see coming. No cheap shots, kicks in the crotch, nothing like that. Face-to-face, man-to-man, flesh to flesh, without the aid of any weapon. And, hopefully, no broken bones and no blood.

It wasn't a jab and it wasn't a hook, just a hard right cross that began months ago and was now being delivered from across the ocean. With no resistance because Cray was too soft and too scared and spent too much time hiding behind his keyboard, the punch landed perfectly on the left chinbone, with a nice crunch that Rick would pleasantly remember many times in the weeks afterward. He dropped like a bag of old potatoes, and for a second Rick was tempted to kick him in the ribs.

He had thought about what he might say, but nothing seemed to work. Threats wouldn't be taken seriously – Rick was stupid enough to show up in Cleveland, surely he wouldn't do it again. Cursing Cray would only make him happier, and whatever Rick said would soon be in print. So he left him there, crumpled on the floor, gasping in horror, semiconscious from the blow, and never, not for the slightest moment, did Rick feel sorry for the creep.

He eased out of the office, nodded to a couple of reporters who looked remarkably similar to Mr. Cray, then found the stairs. He raced down to the basement, and after a few minutes of drifting found a door to a loading dock. Five minutes after the knockout, he was back in the cab.

The return flight to Toronto was also on Air Canada, and when Rick landed on Canadian soil, he began to relax. Some three hours later he was bound for Rome.

Chapter 22

A heavy rainstorm settled over Parma late Sunday morning. The rain fell straight and hard, and the clouds looked as though they might be around for a week. Thunder finally woke Rick, and the first sight caught by his swollen eyes was red toenails. Not the red toenails of that last gal in Milan, nor the pink or orange or brown ones of countless, nameless others. No sir. These were the meticulously manicured (not by the owner) and painted (Chanel Midnight Red) toenails of the elegant and sensual and quite naked Miss Livvy Galloway of Savannah, Georgia, by way of the Alpha Chi Omega sorority house in Athens and, of late, a crowded apartment in Florence. Now she was in a slightly less crowded apartment in Parma, on the third floor of an old building on a quiet street, far from her suffocating roommates and very far away from her warring family.

Rick closed his eyes and pulled her close, under the sheets.

She arrived late Thursday night on a train from Florence, and after a lovely dinner they retired to his room for a long session in bed, their first. And though Rick had certainly been ready for it, Livvy was just as eager. Originally, his plans for Friday had been to spend the day in bed or somewhere close to it. She, however, had radically different ideas. On the train she had read a book on Parma. It was time to study the city's history.

With a camera and her notes, they launched a tour of the city center, studiously inspecting the interiors of buildings Rick had hardly noticed in passing. The first was the duomo – Rick had peeked inside once out of curiosity – where Livvy took on a Zen-like meditative state as she dragged him from corner to corner. He wasn't sure what she was thinking, but occasionally she offered helpful sentences such as 'It's one of the finest examples of Romanesque architecture in the Po valley.'

'When was it built?' he always asked.

'It was consecrated in 1106 by Pope Pasquale, then destroyed by an earthquake in 1117. They started again in 1130 and, typically, worked on it for three hundred years or so. Magnificent, isn't it?'

'Truly.' He tried hard to sound engaged, but Rick had already learned that it didn't take long for him to examine a cathedral. Livvy, however, was in another world. He tagged along, followed close, still thinking about their first night together, glancing occasionally at her fine rear end, and already planning an afternoon assault.

In the center aisle, staring straight up, she said, 'The dome was frescoed by Correggio in the 1520s. It depicts the Assumption of the Virgin. Breathtaking.' Far above them, in the vaulted ceiling, old Correggio had somehow managed to paint an extravagant scene of Mary surrounded by angels. Livvy looked at it as if she might be overcome with emotion. Rick looked at it with an aching neck.

They shuffled through the main nave, the crypt, the numerous bays, and they studied the tombs of ancient saints. After an hour, Rick was desperate for sunshine.

Next was the baptistery, a handsome octagonal building near the duomo, and they stood motionless for a long time before the north portal, the Portal of the Virgin. Elaborate sculptures above the door portrayed events from the life of Mary. Livvy checked her notes but seemed to know the details.

'Have you stopped here?' she asked.

If he told the truth and answered no, then she would consider him a rube. If he lied and said yes, it wouldn't matter anyway because Livvy was about to inspect another building. In truth, he had passed it a hundred times and knew that it was indeed a baptistery. He wasn't certain exactly what a baptistery was used for nowadays, but nonetheless he pretended to.

She was talking softly, almost to herself, as

well she might have been. 'Four tiers in red Verona marble. Started in 1196, a transition between Romanesque and Gothic.' She took some photos of the exterior, then led him inside, where they gawked at another dome. 'Byzantine, thirteenth century,' she was saying. 'King David, the flight from Egypt, the Ten Commandments.' He nodded along, his neck beginning to ache.

'Are you Catholic, Rick?' she asked.

'Lutheran. You?'

'Nothing really. Family's some strain of Protestant. I dig this stuff, though, the history of Christianity and the origins of the early Church. I love the art.'

'There are plenty of old churches here,' he said. 'All Catholic.'

'I know.' And she did. Before lunch they toured the Renaissance church of San Giovanni Evangelista, still in the religious center of the city, as well as the church of San Francesco del Prato. According to Livvy, it was one of the 'most remarkable examples of Franciscan Gothic architecture in Emilia.' To Rick, the only interesting detail was the fact that the beautiful church had once been used as a jail.

At one, he insisted on lunch. They found a table at Sorelle Picchi on Strada Farini, and as he studied the menu, Livvy made more notes. Over *anolini*, the best in town in Rick's opinion, and a bottle of wine, they talked about Italy and the places she'd been. Eight months in Florence, she had visited eleven of the country's twenty

231

regions, often traveling alone on weekends because her roommates were too lazy or apathetic or hungover. Her goal had been to see every region, but she was out of time. Exams were in two weeks, then her long holiday was over.

Instead of a nap, they attacked the churches of San Pietro Apostolo and San Rocco, then wandered through the Parco Ducale. She took photos and notes and absorbed the history and art, while Rick gamely trudged on in a sleepwalk. He collapsed in the sunshine and warm grass of the park, with his head in her lap, while she studied a map of the city. When he awoke, he finally coaxed her back to his apartment for a proper nap.

At Polipo's Friday night after practice, Livvy was the star attraction. Their quarterback had found a lovely American girl, a former cheer-leader at that, and the Italian boys were anxious to impress her. They sang bawdy songs and drained pitchers of beer.

The story of Rick's mad dash to Cleveland to punch out Charley Cray had taken on legendary status. The spin, started by Sam and inadver-tently aided by Rick and his refusal to talk about the episode, had stayed fairly close to the facts. The glaring omission was that Rick left Parma to explore another contract, one that would require him to abandon the Panthers in mid-season, but no one in Italy knew this, nor would they ever.

The evil Charley Cray had traveled to their

Italy to write nasty things about their team and their quarterback. He had insulted them, and Rick tracked him down, at what appeared to be considerable expense, decked him, then hustled back to Parma, where he was safe. Damned right he was safe. Anybody coming after Reek on their turf would get hurt.

The fact that Rick was now a fugitive added a level of daring and romance that the Italians found irresistible. In a country where laws are flaunted and those who flaunt them are often glamorized, the pursuit by the police was the dominant topic whenever two or more Panthers got together. In a crowded room they buzzed with the story, often adding their own details.

In truth, Rick was not being pursued. There was a warrant for his arrest for simple assault, a misdemeanor, and, according to his new lawyer in Cleveland, no one was chasing him with handcuffs. The authorities knew where he was, and if he ever came to Cleveland again, he'd be prosecuted.

Still, Rick was on the run, and the Panthers had to protect him, both on the field and off.

* * *

Saturday proved to be as educational as Friday. Livvy led him through the Teatro Regio, a place he was extremely proud to have already seen, then the Diocesan Museum, the church of San Marcellino, the chapel of San Tommaso

Apostolo. For lunch they ate a pizza on the grounds of the Palazzo della Pilotta.

'I will not set foot in another church,' Rick announced in defeat. He was stretched out on the grass, soaking in the sunshine.

'I'd like to see the National Gallery,' she said as she curled next to him, tanned legs everywhere.

'What's in it?'

'Lots of paintings, from all over Italy.'

'No.'

'Yes, then the archaeological museum.'

'Then what?'

'I'll be tired then. We go to bed, take a nap, think about dinner.'

'I have a game tomorrow. Are you trying to kill me?'

'Yes.'

* * *

After two days of diligent tourism, Rick was ready for football, rain or not. He couldn't wait to drive past the old churches, go to the field, put on a uniform, then get it muddy and maybe even hit someone.

'But it's raining,' Livvy cooed from under the sheets.

'Too bad, cheerleader. The show must go on.'

She rolled over and flung a leg across his stomach. 'No,' he said with conviction. 'Not before a game. My knees are weak anyway.'

'I thought you were the stud quarterback.'

'Just the quarterback for now.'

She removed the leg and swung it off the bed. 'So who are the Panthers playing today?' she asked, standing, turning, enticing.

'The Gladiators of Rome.'

'What a name. Can they play?'

'They're pretty good. We need to go.'

He parked her under the canopy on the home side, one of fewer than ten fans there an hour before the game. She was covered in a poncho and huddled under an umbrella, more or less waterproof in the driving rain. He almost felt sorry for her. Twenty minutes later he was on the field in full uniform, stretching, bantering with his teammates, and keeping an eye on Livvy. He was in college again, or maybe in high school, anxious to play for the love of the game, for the glory of winning, but also for a very cute girl up in the stands.

The game was a mudbowl; the rain never stopped. Franco fumbled twice in the first quarter, and Fabrizio dropped two slippery passes. The Gladiators got bogged down as well. With a minute to go before the half, Rick scrambled out of the pocket and sprinted thirty yards for the first score of the game. Fabrizio bobbled the snap and the score was 6–0 at the half. Sam, who had not had the chance to bitch and yell at them for two weeks, unloaded in the locker room and everyone felt better.

By the fourth quarter, water was standing in

235

large puddles across the field, and the game became a slugfest at the line of scrimmage. On a second and two, Rick faked to Franco, faked to Giancarlo, the third-string tailback, and lofted a long soft pass to Fabrizio, flying downfield on a post. He bobbled it, then snatched it and ran twenty yards untouched. With a two-touchdown lead, Sam began blitzing on every play, and the Gladiators couldn't get a first down. They racked up five for the entire game.

* * *

Rick said good-bye to Livvy at the train station Sunday night, then watched the Eurostar pull away with both sadness and relief. He had not realized the extent of his loneliness. He had been reasonably certain that he greatly missed the companionship of a woman, but Livvy made him feel like a college boy again. At the same time, she was not exactly low maintenance. She demanded his attention and had a strong streak of hyperactivity. He needed some rest.

Late Sunday e-mail from his mother:

Dear Ricky: Your father has decided that he will not make the trip to Italy after all. He is quite angry with you and that stunt in Cleveland – the game was bad enough but now reporters are calling all the time asking about the assault and battery. I despise these people. I'm beginning to understand

236

why you slugged that poor man in Cleveland. But you could've stopped by and said hello while you were here. We haven't seen you since Christmas. I would try to come alone but my diverticulosis might be flaring up. Best if I stay close. Please tell me you'll be home in a month or so. Are they really going to arrest you? Love, Mom

She treated her diverticulosis like an active volcano – always down there in the colon awaiting an eruption in the event she was expected to do something she really didn't want to do. She and Randall had made the mistake five years earlier of traveling to Spain with a group of retirees, and they were still bitching about the cost, the air travel, the rudeness of all Europeans, the shocking ignorance of people who cannot speak English.

Rick really didn't want them in Italy.

E-mail back to his mother:

Dear Mom: I'm so sorry you guys can't make it over, but the weather has been awful. I am not going to be arrested. I have lawyers working on things – it was just a misunderstanding. Tell Dad to relax – everything will be fine. Life is good here but I sure am homesick. Love, Rick

Late Sunday e-mail from Arnie:

Dear Turd:

The lawyer in Cleveland has worked out a deal whereby you plead guilty, pay a fine, slap on the wrist. But, if you plead guilty, then Cray can use that against you in a civil suit. He's claiming he has a broken jaw and is making noise about a suit. I'm sure all of Cleveland is egging him on. How would you like to face a jury in Cleveland? They'd give you the death penalty just for the assault. And they'll give Cray a billion bucks in punitive in a civil suit. I'm working on it, not sure why.

Rat cursed me yesterday for the last time, I hope. Tiffany gave birth early and the child appears to be of mixed race; guess you're off the hook.

I am now officially losing money as your agent, just thought you'd like to know that.

E-mail back to Arnie:

I love you, man. You're the greatest, Arn. Keep on keeping the vultures at bay. Mighty Panthers rolled today, shut out the Rome Gladiators in a flood. Yours truly was magnificent.

If Cray has a broken jaw, then he needs two. Tell him to sue me and I'll file for bankruptcy – in Italy! Let his lawyers chew on that.

The food and women continue to

astound. Thanks so much for skillfully guiding me to Parma. RD

E-mail to Gabriella:

Thanks for your kind note a few days ago. Don't worry about the episode in Florence. I've been stiffed by better women. No need to worry about future contact.

Chapter 23

The pretty town of Bolzano is in the mountainous northeastern part of the country, in the Trentino-Alto Adige region, a recent addition to Italy that was chipped away from Austria in 1919 by the Allies as a reward to the Italians for fighting the Germans. Its history is complicated. Its boundaries have been rigged and gerrymandered by whoever happened to have the larger army. Many of its residents consider themselves to be of Germanic stock and certainly look like it. Most speak German first and Italian second, often reluctantly. Other Italians are known to whisper, 'Those people aren't real Italians.' Efforts to Italianize, Germanize, and homogenize the population all failed miserably, but over time a pleasant truce evolved, and life is good. The culture is pure Alpine. The people are conservative, hospitable, and prosperous, and they love their land.

The scenery is stunning – ragged mountain

peaks, lakeside vineyards and olive groves, valleys carpeted with apple orchards, and thousands of square miles of protected forests.

Rick got all this from his guidebook. Livvy, however, piled on the details. Since she had not been to the region, she had initially planned to make the trip. Exams, though, intervened, plus Bolzano was at least a six-hour train ride from Florence. So she passed along her research in a series of windy e-mails. Rick scanned them as they arrived during the week, then left them on his kitchen table. He was much more concerned with football than with how Mussolini screwed up the region between the wars.

And football was plenty to worry about. The Bolzano Giants had lost only once, to Bergamo, and by only two points. He and Sam had watched the film of the game twice and agreed that Bolzano should have won. A bad snap on an easy field goal made the difference.

Bergamo. Bergamo. Still undefeated, the winning streak now at sixty-six. Everything the Panthers did had something to do with Bergamo. Their game plan against Bolzano was impacted by their next game against Bergamo.

The bus ride lasted three hours, and halfway through it the landscape began to change. The Alps appeared to the north. Rick sat near the front with Sam, and when they weren't napping, they talked about the outdoors – hiking the Dolomites, skiing, and camping in the lake region. With no children, Sam and Anna spent weeks each autumn exploring northern Italy and southern Austria.

★ ★ ★

Playing against the Giants.

If Rick Dockery had one game to remember in his sad little tour of the NFL, it was against the Giants, on a foggy Sunday night at the Meadowlands, on national television, in front of eighty thousand raucous fans. He was with Seattle, in his customary role as the number-three quarterback. Number one got knocked out in the first half, and number two was throwing interceptions when he wasn't fumbling. Down twenty points late in the third, the Seahawks threw in the towel and called on Dockery. He completed seven passes, all to his teammates, for ninety-five yards. Two weeks later he was on waivers.

He could still hear the deafening roar of Giants Stadium.

The stadium in Bolzano was much smaller and a lot quieter, but much prettier. With the Alps looming in the background, the teams lined up for the kickoff in front of two thousand fans. There were banners, a mascot, chants, and flares.

On the second play from scrimmage, the nightmare began. His name was Quincy Shoal, a thick tailback who once played at Indiana State. After the usual stints in Canada and arena ball, Quincy arrived in Italy ten years earlier and found a home. He had an Italian wife and Italian kids and held almost all Italian records for running the football.

Quincy rambled seventy-eight yards for a touchdown. If anyone touched him, it would not be evident on the game film. The crowd went berserk; more flares and even a smoke bomb. Rick tried to imagine smoke bombs at the Meadowlands.

Because Bergamo was next on the schedule, and because Sam knew they were there scouting the game, he and Rick had decided to run the ball and downplay Fabrizio. It was a risky strategy, the kind of gamble Sam enjoyed. Both felt confident that the offense could pass at will, but they preferred to save something for Bergamo.

Since Franco usually fumbled his first handoff each game, Rick called a pitchout to Giancarlo, a young tailback who had started the season as a third-stringer but was improving each week. Rick liked him primarily because he had a soft spot for third-stringers. Giancarlo had a unique running style. He was small, 175 pounds or so, and not muscular at all, and he really didn't like to get hit. He had been a swimmer and diver as a young teenager, and possessed quick and light feet. When faced with imminent contact, Giancarlo often hurled himself upward and forward, picking up additional yardage with each vault. His runs were becoming spectacular, especially the sweeps and pitchouts that allowed him to build momentum before hurdling over tacklers.

Sam had given him the advice every young runner gets in the seventh grade: Do not leave your feet! Lower your head, protect the ball, and by all means protect your knees, but do not leave your feet! Thousands of college careers had been ended suddenly by showy leaps over the pile. Hundreds of professional running backs had been maimed for life.

Giancarlo had no use for such wisdom. He loved sailing through the air and was unafraid of a hard landing. He ran eight yards to the right, then flew for three more. Twelve to the left, including four from a half gainer. Rick boot-legged for fifteen, then called a dive to Franco.

'Don't fumble!' he growled as he grabbed Franco's face mask when they broke huddle. Franco, wild-eyed and psychotic, grabbed Rick's and said something nasty in Italian. Who grabs the quarterback's face mask?

He didn't fumble, but instead lumbered for ten yards until half the defense buried him at the Giants' 40. Six plays later, Giancarlo soared into the end zone and the game was tied.

It took Quincy all of four plays to score again. 'Let him run,' Rick said to Sam on the sideline. 'He's thirty-four years old.'

'I know how old he is,' Sam snapped. 'But I'd like to keep him under five hundred yards in the first half.'

Bolzano's defense had prepared for the pass

and was confused by the run. Fabrizio did not touch the ball until almost halftime. On a second and goal from the 6, Rick faked to Franco, bootlegged, and flipped it to his receiver for an easy score. A neat, tidy game – each team had two touchdowns in each quarter. The noisy crowd had been thoroughly entertained.

★ ★ ★

During halftime, the first five minutes inside a locker room are dangerous. The players are hot, sweating, some bleeding. They throw helmets, curse, criticize, scream, exhort one another to step it up and do whatever is not getting done. As the adrenaline slowly settles, they relax a bit. Drink some water. Maybe take off the shoulder pads. Rub a wound or two.

It was the same in Italy as it was in Iowa. Rick had never been an emotional player, and he preferred to hunker in the background and let the hotheads rally the team. Tied with Bolzano, he was not at all worried. Quincy Shoal's tongue was hanging, and Rick and Fabrizio had yet to play pitch and catch.

Sam knew when to enter, and after five minutes he stepped into the room and took over the yelling. Quincy was eating their lunch – 160 yards, four touchdowns. 'What a great strategy!' Sam ranted. 'Let him run until he collapses!' 'I've never heard of that before!' 'You guys are brilliant!' And so on.

As the season progressed, Rick was impressed more and more by Sam's tongue-lashings. He, Rick, had been chewed out by many experts, and though Sam usually left him alone, he showed real talent when going after the others. And the fact that he could do it in two languages was awesome.

*　*　*

But the locker room rave had little effect. Quincy, with a twenty-minute rest and quick rubdown, picked up where he left off. Touchdown number five came on the Giants' first drive of the second half, and number six was a fifty-yard gallop a few minutes later.

A heroic effort, but not quite enough. Whether it was old age (thirty-four), or too much pasta, or simply overuse, Quincy was finished. He stayed in the game until the end, but was too tired to save his team. In the fourth quarter, the Panthers' defense sensed his demise and came to life. When Pietro stuffed him on a third and two and flung him to the ground, the game was over.

With Franco pounding the middle and Giancarlo bunny-hopping around the ends, the Panthers tied it with ten minutes to go. A minute later they scored again when Karl the Dane scooped up a fumble and wobbled thirty yards for perhaps the ugliest touchdown in Italian history. Two tiny Giants rode his back like insects for the last ten yards.

For good measure, and to keep sharp, Rick and Fabrizio hooked up on a long post with three minutes on the clock. The final was 56–41.

* * *

The locker room was far different after the game. They hugged and celebrated, and a few seemed on the verge of tears. For a team that only weeks earlier seemed listless and dead, they were suddenly close to a great season. Mighty Bergamo was next, but the Lions had to travel to Parma.

Sam congratulated his players and gave them exactly one more hour to revel in the win. 'Then shut if off and start thinking about Bergamo,' he said. 'Sixty-seven consecutive wins, eight straight Super Bowl titles. A team we have not beaten in ten years.'

Rick sat on the floor in a corner, his back to the wall, fiddling with his shoelaces and listening to Sam speak in Italian. Though he couldn't understand his coach, he knew exactly what he was saying. Bergamo this and Bergamo that. His teammates hung on every word, their anticipation already building. A slight wave of nervous energy swept over Rick, and he had to smile.

He was no longer a hired gun, a ringer brought in from the Wild West to run the offense and win games. He no longer dreamed of NFL glory and riches. Those dreams were behind him

now, and fading fast. He was who he was, a
Panther, and as he looked around the cramped
and sweaty locker room, he was perfectly happy
with himself.

Chapter 24

Much less beer was consumed Monday night during the film session. There were fewer wise-cracks, insults, laughter. The mood wasn't somber, they were still quite proud of their road win the day before, but it was not the typical Monday night at the movies. Sam raced through the Bolzano highlights, then switched to a collage of Bergamo clips he and Rick had worked on all day.

They agreed on the obvious – Bergamo was well coached, well financed, and well organized and had talent that was slightly above the rest of the league, at some positions, but certainly not across the board. Their Americans were: a slow quarterback from San Diego State, a strong safety who hit hard and would try to kill Fabrizio early in the game, and a cornerback who could shut down the outside running game but was rumored to have a pulled hamstring. Bergamo was the only team in the league with two of their three Americans on defense. Their key player, though, was not an American. The middle linebacker was an Italian named Maschi, a flamboyant showman with long hair and white shoes and a me-first attitude he'd copied from the NFL, where he happened to think he belonged. Quick and strong, Maschi had great instincts, loved to hit, the later the better, and was usually at the bottom of every pile. At 220 pounds, he was big enough to wreak havoc in Italy and could have played for most Division I schools in the United States. He wore number 56 and insisted on being called L.T. to mimic his idol, Lawrence Taylor.

Bergamo was strong defensively but not overly impressive with the ball. Against Bologna and Bolzano – all those killer bees – they trailed until the fourth quarter and could've easily lost both. Rick was convinced the Panthers were a better team, but Sam had been beaten by Bergamo so many times he refused to be confident, at least in private. After eight straight Super Bowl titles, the Bergamo Lions had achieved an aura of invincibility that was worth at least ten points a game.

Sam replayed the tape and hammered away at Bergamo's weaknesses on offense. Their tailback was quick to the line but reluctant to lower his head and take a shot. They rarely passed until they had to, always on third down, primarily because they lacked a dependable receiver. The offensive line was big and fundamentally sound, but often too slow to pick up the blitz.

When Sam finished, Franco addressed the team, and in superb lawyerly fashion gave a rousing, emotional appeal for a hard, dedicated week, one that would lead to a mighty victory. In closing, he suggested that they practice every night until Saturday. The idea was unanimously approved. Then Nino, not to be outdone, took the floor and began by announcing that to show the gravity of the moment, he had decided to stop smoking until after the game, after they had thrashed Bergamo. This was greeted warmly because, evidently, Nino had made such a commitment before and Nino, deprived of nicotine, was a frightening force on the field. Then he announced there would be a team dinner at Café Montana Saturday night, on the house. Carlo was already working on the menu.

The Panthers were edgy with anticipation. Rick flashed back to the Davenport Central game, the biggest of the year for Davenport South. Starting on Monday, the school planned the entire week and the town talked of little else. By Friday afternoon, the players were so anxious some were nauseous and threw up hours before the game.

Rick doubted if any Panther would be so overcome with nerves, but it was certainly possible.

They left the locker room with a solemn determination. This was their week. This was their year.

Thursday afternoon, Livvy arrived in all her splendor, and with a surprising amount of luggage. Rick had been at the field with Fabrizio and Claudio, working relentlessly on precision routes and quick audibles, when he took a break and checked his cell phone. She was already on the train.

As they drove from the station to his apartment, he learned that she was (1) finished with exams, (2) sick of her roommates, (3) thinking seriously of not returning to Florence for the final ten days of her semester abroad, (4) disgusted with her family, (5) not speaking to anyone in her family, not even her sister, a person she had feuded with since kindergarten and who was now way too involved in their parents' divorce, (6) in need of a place to crash for a few days, thus the luggage, (7) worried about her visa because she wanted to stay in Italy for some vague period of time, and (8) really ready to hop in the sack. She wasn't whining and she wasn't looking for sympathy; in fact, she covered her plethora of problems with a cool detachment that Rick found admirable. She needed someone, and she had fled to him.

He hauled the remarkably heavy bags up the three flights, and did so with ease and energy. Happy to do so. The apartment was too quiet, almost lifeless, and Rick had found himself spending more time away from it, walking the streets of Parma, drinking coffee and beer at the sidewalk cafés, browsing the meat markets and wine shops, even taking quick detours through ancient churches, anything to keep away from the numbing tedium of his empty apartment. And he was always alone. Sly and Trey had left him, and his e-mails to them were rarely returned. It was hardly worth the trouble. Sam kept busy most days, plus he was married and had a different life. Franco, his favorite team-mate, was good for lunch occasionally but had a demanding job. All the Panthers worked; they had to. They could not afford to sleep until noon, spend a couple of hours in the gym, and roam around Parma, killing time and earning nothing.

Rick was not, however, in the market for a full-time live-in. That entailed complications and required a commitment that he had trouble even addressing. He had never lived with a woman, had not in fact lived with anyone since his days in Toronto, and he was not contem-plating a full-time companion.

As she unpacked, he wondered, for the first time, exactly how long she planned to stay.

They postponed the lovemaking until after practice. It was to be a light workout, no pads, but still he preferred to have the full use of his legs and feet.

Livvy sat in the stands and read a paperback while the boys went through their drills and plans. There were a handful of other wives and girlfriends scattered about, even a few small children bouncing up and down the grandstand.

At 10:30 Thursday night, a city employee arrived and made his presence known to Sam. His job was to turn off the lights.

* * *

There were castles waiting. Rick first heard this news around 8:00 a.m., but managed to roll over and go back to sleep. Livvy threw on her jeans and went to find coffee. When she returned in thirty minutes, with two large cups of takeaway, she announced again that castles were waiting and she wanted to begin with one in the town of Fontanellato.

'It's very early,' Rick said, taking a sip, sitting up in bed, trying to orient himself to such an odd hour.

'Have you been to Fontanellato?' she asked as she removed the jeans, picked up a guidebook with her notes, and returned to her side of the bed.

'I've never heard of it.'

'Have you left Parma since you got here?'

'Sure. We had a game in Milan, one in Rome, one in Bolzano.'

'No, Ricky, I'm talking about hopping in your little copper Fiat and sightseeing through the countryside.'

'No, why—'

'Aren't you the least bit curious about your new home?'

'I've learned not to get attached to new homes. They're all temporary.'

'That's nice. Look, I'm not lounging around this apartment all day, having sex every hour, and thinking about nothing but lunch and dinner.'

'Why not?'

'I'm doing a road trip. Either you're driving or I'll catch a bus. There's too much to see. We're not even finished with Parma yet.'

They left half an hour later and drove northwest in search of Fontanellato, a fifteenth-century castle Livvy was desperate to inspect. The day was warm and sunny. The windows were down. She wore a short denim skirt and a cotton blouse, and the wind rushed across everything nicely and kept him engaged. He groped her legs, and she pushed him away with one hand as she read a guidebook with the other.

'They make 120,000 tons of Parmesan cheese here every year,' she was saying as she looked at the countryside. 'Right here, on these farms.'

'At least that much. These folks put it in their coffee.'

'Five hundred dairies, all in a tightly defined area around Parma. It's regulated by law.'

'They make ice cream out of it.'

'And ten million Parma hams each year. That's hard to believe.'

'Not if you live here. They put it on your table before you sit down. Why are we talking about food? You were in such a hurry we got no breakfast.'

She put her book down and announced, 'I'm starving.'

'How about some cheese and ham?'

They were on a narrow road with little traffic and soon came to the village of Baganzola, where they found a bar with coffee and croissants. She was anxious to practice her Italian, and while it sounded proficient to Rick, the signora at the counter struggled. 'A dialect,' Livvy said as they headed for the car.

The Rocca, or fortress, at Fontanellato had been built some five hundred years earlier, and it certainly looked impregnable. It was surrounded by a moat and anchored by four massive towers with wide openings for observation and weaponry. Inside, however, there was a marvelous palace with walls covered in art and remarkably decorated rooms. After fifteen minutes, Rick had seen enough, but his lady friend was just getting started.

When he finally got her back into the car, they continued north, at her direction, to the town of Soragna. It was situated on fertile plains on the left bank of the river Stirone and had been the site of many ancient battles, according to their car's historian, who could not digest the details fast enough. As she rattled them off, Rick drifted away to the Bergamo Lions and especially Signor Maschi, the very agile middle linebacker who, in Rick's opinion, was the key to the game. He thought of all the plays and schemes devised by brilliant coaches to neutralize a great middle linebacker. They rarely worked.

The castle at Soragna (still home to a real prince!) dated back only to the seventeenth century, and after a quick tour they found lunch at a small deli. Then onward, to San Secondo, famous nowadays for *spalla*, a boiled ham. The town's castle, built in the fifteenth century as a fortress, played a role in many important battles. 'Why did these people fight so much?' Rick asked at one point.

Livvy shot him a quick answer but had little interest in the wars. She was more attracted to the art, the furniture, the marble fireplaces, and so on. Rick sneaked away and took a nap under a tree.

They finished at Colorno, nicknamed the 'little Versailles of the Po.' It was a majestic fortress that had been remodeled into a splendid home, complete with vast gardens and court-yards. When they arrived, Livvy was just as excited as she'd been seven hours earlier when they got to the first castle, one that Rick could barely remember. He gamely plodded on through the exhaustive tour, then finally quit.

'Meet me at the bar,' he said, and left her alone in a massive hallway, gawking at frescoes high above and lost in another world.

* * *

Rick balked on Saturday, and they argued briefly. It was their first dustup, and both found it amusing. It was over quickly, and neither seemed to hold a grudge, a promising sign.

She had in mind a road trip to the south, to Langhirano, through the wine country, with only a couple of important castles to examine. He had in mind a quiet day, off his feet, as he tried to focus more on Bergamo and less on her legs. They compromised on a plan to stay in town and finish off a couple of churches.

He was clear-eyed and rested, primarily because the team had decided to skip the Friday ritual of pizza and buckets of beer at Polipo's. They had hustled through a quick workout in shorts, listened to more game planning from Sam, listened to yet another emotional speech, this one from Pietro, and finally quit at ten Friday night. They had practiced enough.

Saturday night they gathered at Café Montana for the pregame meal, a three-hour gastronomic fiesta with Nino on center stage and Carlo roaring in the kitchen. Signor Bruncardo was present and addressed his team. He thanked them for a thrilling season, one that would not, however, be complete unless they thrashed Bergamo tomorrow.

There were no women present – the little restaurant was packed with just the players – and this fact led to two raunchy poems and a final farewell, a profanity-laced ode composed by the lyrical Franco and delivered in a hysterical style.

Sam sent them home before eleven.

Chapter 25

Bergamo traveled well. They brought an impressive number of fans who arrived early and loud, unfurled banners, practiced horn blowing and chants, and in general made themselves quite at home at Stadio Lanfranchi. Eight straight Super Bowls bestowed upon them the right to go anywhere in NFL Italy and take over the stadium. Their cheerleaders were dressed appropriately in skimpy gold skirts and knee-high black boots, and this proved to be a distraction for the Panthers during the lengthy pregame warm-up. Focus was lost, or at least temporarily detoured, as the girls stretched and jiggled and limbered up for the big game.

'Why can't we have cheerleaders?' Rick asked Sam when he walked by.

'Shut up.'

Sam stalked around the field, growling at his players, as nervous as any NFL coach before a big game. He chatted briefly with a reporter from the *Gazzetta di Parma*. A television crew shot some footage, as much of the cheerleaders as of the players.

The Panthers' fans were not to be outdone. Alex Olivetto had spent the week rounding up the younger players from the flag football leagues, and they packed together at one end of the home stands and were soon yelling at the Bergamo supporters. Many ex-Panthers were there, along with families and friends. Anyone with a passing interest in *football americano* had a seat long before kickoff.

The locker room was intense, and Sam made no effort to calm his players. Football is a game of emotion, most of it grounded on fear, and every coach wants his team clamoring for violence. He issued the standard warnings against penalties and turnovers and stupid mistakes, then turned them loose.

When the teams lined up for the opening kickoff, the stadium was full and noisy. Parma received, and Giancarlo zipped along the far sideline with the return until he was pushed into the Bergamo bench at the 31. Rick trotted out with his offense, outwardly cool but with a hard knot deep in his stomach.

The first three plays were scripted, and none was designed to score. Rick called a quarterback sneak, and no translation was needed. Nino was shaking with rage and nicotine deprivation. His glutes were in full arrest, but the snap was quick and he lunged like a rocket at Maschi, who fought him off and stopped the play after a one-yard gain.

'Nice run, Goat,' Maschi yelled in a thick accent. The nickname would be thrown at Rick many times in the first half.

The second play was another quarterback sneak. It went nowhere, which was the plan. Maschi blitzed hard on every third and long without exception, and some of his sacks were acts of brutality. His tendency, though, perhaps through lack of experience and perhaps because he loved to be seen, was to 'blitz tall,' to come in high. In the huddle, Rick called their special play: 'Kill Maschi.' The offense had been running the play for a week now. In the shotgun, with no tailback and three wideouts, Franco lined up close behind Karl the Dane at left tackle. He squatted low to hide himself. On the snap, the offensive line double-teamed the tackles, leaving a gaping hole for Signor 'L.T.' Maschi to come crashing through, a straight shot at Rick. He took the bait, and his quickness almost killed him. Rick dropped deep to pass, hoping the play would work before the linebacker assaulted him. As Maschi exploded through the middle, tall and confident and thrilled for a chance at Rick so soon, Judge Franco suddenly shot up from nowhere and caused a mighty collision between two players who each weighed 220 pounds. Franco's helmet landed perfectly, just under Maschi's face mask, ripping off the chin strap and causing the gold Bergamo helmet to shoot high into the air. Maschi flipped, his feet soon chasing his helmet, and when he landed on his head, Sam thought they might have killed him. It was a classic beheading, a super highlight, the type of play that would be repeated a million times on the sports channels in the United States. Perfectly legal, perfectly brutal.

Rick missed it because he had the ball with his back to the play. He heard it, though, the crack and crunch of the extremely nasty hit, every bit as violent as something from the real NFL.

As the play developed, things became complicated, and when it was over, the referees needed five minutes to sort it all out. At least four flags were on the field, along with what appeared to be three dead bodies.

Maschi wasn't moving, and not far away Franco wasn't either. But there was no penalty on that part of the play. The first flag went down in the secondary. The safety was a little thug named McGregor, a Yank from Gettysburg College who fancied himself to be from the assassin school of roving safeties. In an attempt to establish turf, intimidate, bully, and simply start the game with the right tone, he delivered a vicious clothesline to Fabrizio as he ran benignly across the field, far away from the action. Fortunately, a referee saw it. Unfortunately, Nino did, too, and by the time Nino sprinted to McGregor and knocked him down, there were more flags. Coaches ran onto the field and barely prevented a brawl.

The final flags floated down in the area where Rick had been tackled, after a five-yard gain. The cornerback, nicknamed The Professor, had played sparingly at Wake Forest as a youth, and now, in his mid-thirties, he was pursuing yet another degree in Italian literature. When he wasn't studying or teaching, he was playing and coaching for the Bergamo Lions. Far from a soft academic, The Professor went for the head and was fond of the cheap shot. If his hamstring was bothering him, it wasn't apparent. After a hard hit on Rick, he yelled, like a crazy man, 'Great run, Goat! Now throw me a pass!' Rick gave him a shove, The Professor shoved back, and there were flags.

While the officials huddled frantically and seemed completely clueless about what to do, the trainers tended to the wounded. Franco was the first up. He jogged to the sideline, where he was mobbed by his teammates. Kill Maschi had worked to perfection. On the ground, Maschi's legs were moving, so there was some relief around the stadium. Then his knees bent, the trainers stood, and Maschi bounded to his feet. He walked to the sideline, found a seat on the bench, and began taking oxygen. He would be back, and soon, though his enthusiasm for the blitz would not return that day.

Sam was screaming at the referees to eject McGregor, and it was deserved. But they would have to eject Nino as well for throwing a punch. The compromise was a fifteen-yard penalty against the Lions – first down Panthers. When Fabrizio saw the penalty being marked off, he slowly got to his feet and went to the bench.

No permanent injuries. Everybody would be back. Both sidelines were furious, and all the coaches were yelling at the officials in a heated mixture of languages.

Rick was fuming from the encounter with The Professor, so he called his number again. He swept to the right, cut around the end, and went straight for him. The collision was impressive, especially for Rick, the non-hitter, and when he rammed The Professor in front of the Panther bench, his teammates yelled with delight. Gain of seven. The testosterone was pumping now. His entire body throbbed from two straight collisions. But his head was clear, and there was no residue from the old concussions. Same play, quarterback sweep right. Claudio got a block on The Professor, and when he spun around, Rick was charging at full speed, head low, helmet aimed at his chest. Another impressive collision. Rick Dockery, a headhunter.

'What the hell are you doing?' Sam barked when Rick jogged by.

'Moving the ball.'

If unpaid, Fabrizio would have gone to the locker room and called it a day. But the salary had brought a responsibility that the kid had maturely accepted. And, he still wanted to play college ball in the United States. Quitting wouldn't help that dream. He jogged back on the

264

field, along with Franco, and the offense was intact.

And Rick was tired of running. With Maschi on the bench, Rick worked the middle with Franco, who had vowed on his mother's grave not to fumble, and pitched to Giancarlo around the ends. He bootlegged twice, running for nice gains. On a second and two from the 19, he faked to Franco, faked to Giancarlo, sprinted right on another bootleg, then pulled up at the line and hit Fabrizio in the end zone. McGregor was close, but not close enough.

'Whatta you think?' Sam asked Rick as they watched the teams line up for the kickoff.

'Watch McGregor. He'll try to break Fabrizio's leg, I guarantee it.'

'You hearing all that "Goat" shit?'

'No, Sam, I'm deaf.'

The Bergamo tailback, the one the scouting report said didn't like to hit, grabbed the ball on the third play and managed to hit (hard) every member of the Panther defense on his way to a beautiful seventy-four-yard gallop that electrified the fans and sent Sam into hysterics.

After the kickoff, Mr. Maschi strutted onto the field, but with a bit less spring in his gait. He hadn't been killed after all. 'I'll get him,' Franco said. Why not? thought Rick. He called a dive play, handed it to Franco, and watched in horror as the ball was dropped. It somehow got kicked by a churning knee that propelled it high over the line of scrimmage. In the melee that followed,

265

half the players on the field touched the loose ball as it rolled and hopped from pile to pile and finally careened, unpossessed, out of bounds. Still Panthers' ball. Gain of sixteen.

'This might be our day,' Sam mumbled to no one.

Rick reshifted the offense, spread Fabrizio to the left, and hit him for eight yards on a down and out. McGregor shoved him out of bounds, but there was no foul. Back to the right, same play, for eight more. The short pass game worked for two reasons: Fabrizio was too fast to play tight, so McGregor had to yield space underneath; and Rick's arm was too strong to be stopped in the short game. He and Fabrizio had spent hours on the timing patterns – the quick-outs, slants, hooks, curls.

The key would be how long Fabrizio was willing to take shots from McGregor after he caught Rick's passes.

The Panthers scored late in the first quarter when Giancarlo leaped over a wave of tacklers, landed on his feet, then sprinted ten yards to the end zone. It was an amazing, fearless, acrobatic maneuver, and the Parma faithful went berserk. Sam and Rick shook their heads. Only in Italy.

The Panthers led 14–7.

The punting game took over in the second quarter as both offenses sputtered. Maschi was slowly shaking off the cobwebs and returning to form. Some of his plays were impressive, at least from the safety of the deep pocket where Rick had a good view. Maschi did not, however, seem inclined to return to his kamikaze blitzing. Franco was always lurking nearby, near his quarterback.

With a minute to go before the half, and the Panthers up by a touchdown, the game turned on its most crucial play. Rick, who hadn't thrown an interception in five games, finally did so. It was a curl to Fabrizio, who was open, but the ball sailed high. McGregor caught it at midfield and had a good shot at the end zone. Rick bolted toward the sideline, as did Giancarlo. Fabrizio caught McGregor enough to spin him and slow him, but he stayed on his feet and kept running. Giancarlo was next, and when McGregor juked him, he was suddenly on a collision course with the quarterback.

A quarterback's dream is to murder the safety who just picked off his pass, a dream that never comes true because most quarterbacks really don't want to get near a safety who has the ball and really wants to score. It's just a dream.

But Rick had been smashing helmets all day, and for the first time since high school he was looking for contact. Suddenly he was a roving hit man, someone to be feared. With McGregor in the crosshairs, Rick left his feet, launched himself, abandoned any and all concern for his own body and safety, and aimed at his target. The impact was loud and violent. McGregor fell back as if he'd been shot in the head. Rick was dazed for a second but jumped to his feet as if it were just another kill. The crowd was stunned but also thrilled by such mayhem.

Giancarlo fell on the ball and Rick chose to run out the clock. As they left the field for half-time, Rick glanced at the Bergamo bench and saw McGregor walking gingerly with a trainer, much like a boxer who'd been flattened.

'Did you try to kill him?' Livvy would ask later, not in disgust but certainly not in admiration.

'Yes,' Rick answered.

★　★　★

McGregor did not answer the bell, and the second half quickly became the Fabrizio show. The Professor stepped over and immediately got burned on a post. If he played tight, Fabrizio ran by him. If he played loose, which he preferred to do, Rick tossed the ten-yarders that quickly added up. The Panthers scored twice in the third quarter. In the fourth, the Lions engaged the strategy of a double-team, half of it being The Professor, who was by then quite winded and by any means overmatched, and the other half being an Italian who was not only too small but too slow. When Fabrizio outran them on a fly and hauled in a long, beautiful pass that Rick had launched from midfield, the score was 35–14, and the celebrating began.

The Parma fans lit fireworks, chanted non-stop, waved huge soccer-style banners, and someone tossed the obligatory smoke bomb. Across the field, the Bergamo fans were still and bewildered. If you win sixty-seven in a row, you're never supposed to lose. Winning becomes automatic.

A loss in a tight game would be heartbreaking enough, but this was a romp. They rolled up their banners, packed their stuff. Their cute little cheerleaders were silent and very sad.

Many of the Lions had never lost, and as a whole they did so gracefully. Maschi, surprisingly, was a good-natured soul who sat on the grass with his shoulder pads off and chatted with several of the Panthers long after the game was over. He admired Franco for the brutal hit, and when he heard about the 'Kill Maschi' play, he took it as a compliment. And he admitted that the long winning streak had created too much pressure, too many expectations. In a way, there was relief in getting it out of the way. They would meet again soon, Parma and Bergamo, probably in the Super Bowl, and the Lions would return to form. That was his promise.

Normally, the Americans from both teams met after the game for a quick hello. It was nice to hear from home and compare notes on players each had met along the way. But not today. Rick resented the 'Goat' calling and hustled off the field. He showered and changed quickly, celebrated just long enough, then hurried away with Livvy in tow.

He'd been dizzy in the fourth quarter, and a

headache was settling in at the base of his skull. Too many blows to the head. Too much football.

Chapter 26

They slept till noon in their tiny room in a small *albergo* near the beach, then gathered their towels, sunscreen, water bottles, and paperbacks and stumbled, still groggy, to the edge of the Adriatic Sea, where they set up camp for the afternoon. It was early June and hot, the tourist season fast approaching, but the beach was not yet crowded.

'You need sun,' Livvy said as she covered herself with oil. Her top came off, leaving nothing but a few strings where they were absolutely necessary.

'I guess that's why we're here at the beach,' he said. 'And I haven't seen a single tanning salon in Parma.'

'Not enough Americans.'

They'd left Parma after the Friday practice and the Friday pizza at Polipo's. The drive to Ancona took three hours, then another half hour south along the coast to the Conero Peninsula,

271

and finally to the small resort town of Sirolo. It was after 3:00 a.m. when they checked in. Livvy had booked the room, found the directions, and knew where the restaurants were. She loved the details of travel.

A waiter finally noticed them and trudged over for a tip. They ordered sandwiches and beer and waited a good hour for both. Livvy kept her nose stuck in a paperback while Rick managed to drift in and out of consciousness, or if fully awake he would shift to his right side and admire her, topless and sizzling in the sun.

Her cell phone buzzed from somewhere deep in the beach bag. She grabbed it, stared at the caller ID, and decided not to answer. 'My father,' she said with distaste, then returned to her mystery.

Her father had been calling, as had her mother and sister. Livvy was ten days past due from her year of study abroad and had dropped more than one hint that she might not come home. Why should she? Things were much safer in Italy.

Though she was still guarded with some of the details, Rick had learned the basics. Her mother's family was a strain of Savannah blue bloods, miserable people, according to Livvy's succinct descriptions, and they had never accepted her father, because he was from New England. Her parents had met at the University of Georgia, the family school. Their wedding had been hotly opposed in private by her family, and this had only inspired her mother to go on with it. There was infighting at many levels, and the marriage was doomed from the beginning.

The fact that he was a prominent brain surgeon who earned lots of money meant little to his in-laws, who actually had very little cash but had been forever blessed with the status of 'family money.'

Her father worked brutal hours and was thoroughly consumed by his career. He ate at the office, slept at the office, and evidently was soon enjoying the companionship of nurses at the office. This went on for years, and in retribution her mother began seeing younger men. Much younger. Her sister, and only sibling, was in therapy by the age of ten. 'A totally dysfunctional family' was Livvy's assessment.

She couldn't wait to leave for boarding school at fourteen. She picked one in Vermont, as far away as possible, and for four years dreaded the holidays. Summers were spent in Montana, where she worked as a camp counselor.

For this summer, upon her return from Florence, her father had arranged an internship with a hospital in Atlanta where she would work with brain-damaged accident victims. He planned for her to be a doctor, no doubt a great one like himself. She had no plans, except those that would take her far from the routes chosen by her parents.

The divorce trial was scheduled for late September, with a lot of money at stake. Her mother was demanding that she testify on her behalf, specifically about an incident three years earlier when Livvy surprised her father at the hospital and caught him groping a young female doctor. Her father was playing the money card. The divorce had been raging for almost two years, and Savannah couldn't wait for the public showdown between the great doctor and the prominent socialite.

Livvy was desperate to avoid it. She did not want her senior year of college wrecked by a sleazy brawl between her parents.

Rick was given this background in brief narratives, almost reluctantly, usually whenever her phone rang and she was forced to deal with her family. He listened patiently and she was grateful to have a sounding board. Back in Florence, her roommates were too absorbed with their own lives.

He was thankful for his rather dull parents and their simple lives in Davenport.

Her phone rang again. She grabbed it, grunted, then took off down the beach with the phone stuck to her head. Rick watched and admired every step. Other men adjusted themselves in beach chairs to have a look.

He guessed it was her sister because she took the call and quickly walked away, as if to spare him the details. He wouldn't know, though. When she returned, she said, 'Sorry,' then re-arranged herself in the sun and began reading.

* * *

Fortunately for Rick, the Allies leveled Ancona at the end of the war, and thus it was light on castles and palazzi. According to Livvy's collection of guidebooks, there was only an old cathedral worth looking at, and she was not keen to see it. Sunday, they slept late again, skipped the sightseeing, and finally found the football field.

The Panthers arrived by bus at 1:30. Rick was alone in the locker room waiting for them. Livvy was alone in the bleachers reading an Italian Sunday newspaper.

'Glad you could make it,' Sam growled at his quarterback.

'So you're in your usual happy mood, Coach.'

'Oh yes. A four-hour bus ride always makes me happy.'

The great victory over Bergamo had yet to wear off, and Sam, as usual, was expecting a disaster against the Dolphins of Ancona. An upset, and the Panthers would miss the play-offs. He had pushed them hard Wednesday and Friday, but they were still reveling in their stunning disruption of the Great Streak. The *Gazzetta di Parma* ran a front-page story, complete with a large action shot of Fabrizio racing down the field. There was another story on Tuesday, one that featured Franco, Nino, Pietro, and Giancarlo. The Panthers were the hottest team in the league, and they were winning big with real Italian footballers. Only their quarterback was American. And so on.

But Ancona had won only a single game, and lost six, most by wide margins. The Panthers were flat, as expected, but they had also slaughtered Bergamo, and that in itself was intimidating. Rick and Fabrizio hooked up twice in the first quarter, and Giancarlo cartwheeled and belly flopped for two more touchdowns in the second. Early in the fourth, Sam cleared the bench and Alberto took over on offense.

The regular season came to an end with the ball at midfield, both teams huddled over it like a rugby scrum, as the clock ticked down to the final seconds. The players ripped off their dirty jerseys and pads, and spent half an hour shaking hands and making promises about next year. The Ancona tailback was from Council Bluffs, Iowa, and had played at a small college in Minnesota. He had seen Rick play seven years earlier in a big Iowa-Wisconsin game, and they had a delightful time replaying it. One of Rick's better college efforts. It was nice to talk to someone with the same accent.

They chatted about players and coaches they had known. The tailback had a flight the next day and couldn't wait to get home. Rick, of course, would stay through the play-offs, and beyond that had no plans. They wished each other well and promised to catch up later.

Bergamo, evidently anxious to start a new streak, beat Rome by six touchdowns and finished the season at 7–1. Parma and Bologna tied for second at 6–2 and would play each other in the semifinals. The big news of the day was the upset at Bolzano. The Rhinos from Milan scored on the final play and sneaked into the play-offs.

* * *

They worked on their tans for another day, then grew tired of Sirolo. They drifted north, stopping for a day and a night at the medieval village of Urbino. Livvy had now seen thirteen of the twenty regions, and was hinting strongly at a prolonged tour that would include the other seven. But with an expired visa, how far could she go?

She preferred not to talk about it. And she did a remarkable job ignoring her family, as long as they ignored her. As they drove along the back roads of Umbria and Tuscany, she studied the maps and had a knack for finding tiny villages and wineries and ancient palazzi. She knew the history of the regions – the wars and conflicts, the rulers and their city-states, the influence of Rome and its decline. She could glance at a small village cathedral and say, 'Baroque, late seventeenth century,' or, 'Romanesque, early twelfth century,' and for good measure she might add, 'But the dome was added a hundred years later by a classical architect.' She knew the great artists, and not just their work but also their hometowns and training and eccentricities and all the important details of their careers. She knew Italian wine and made sense of the endless variety of grapes from the regions. If they were really thirsty, she would find a hidden winery. They would do a quick tour, then settle in for a free sample.

They finally made it back to Parma, late Wednesday afternoon, in time for a very long practice. Livvy stayed at the apartment ('home') while Rick dragged himself to Stadio Lanfranchi to prepare once again for the Bologna Warriors.

Chapter 27

The oldest Panther was Tommaso, or simply Tommy. He was forty-two and had been playing for twenty years. It was his intention, shared much too often in the locker room, to retire only after Parma won its first Super Bowl. A few of his teammates thought he was long past retirement age, and his desire to hang on was just another good reason for the Panthers to hurry and win the big one.

Tommy played defensive end and was effective for about a third of any game. He was tall and weighed around two hundred pounds, but sort of quick off the ball and a decent pass rusher. On running plays, though, he was no match for a charging lineman or fullback, and Sam was careful how he used Tommy. There were several Panthers, the older guys, who needed only a few snaps per game.

Tommy was a career civil servant of some variety, with a nice secure job and thoroughly hip apartment in the center of town. Nothing was old but the building. Inside the apartment, Tommy had carefully removed any concession to age and history. The furniture was glass, chrome, and leather, the floors were unpolished blond oak, the walls were covered with baffling contemporary art, and arranged nicely throughout was every conceivable high-tech entertainment apparatus.

His lady for the evening, certainly not a wife, fit in superbly with the decor. Her name was Maddalena, as tall as Tommy but a hundred pounds lighter and at least fifteen years younger. As Rick said hello to her, Tommy hugged and pecked Livvy and acted as though he might just lead her away to the bedroom.

Livvy had caught the attention of the Panthers, and why not? A beautiful, young American girl living with their quarterback, right there in Parma. Being red-blooded Italians, they could not help but wiggle their way closer. There had always been invitations to dinner, but since her arrival Rick was really in demand.

Rick managed to pry Livvy away and began admiring Tommy's collection of trophies and football memorabilia. There was a photo of Tommy with a young football team. 'In Texas,' Tommy said. 'Near Waco. I go every year in August to practice with the team.'

'High school?'

'Sì. I take my vacation, and do what you call two-a-days. No?'

'Oh yes. Two-a-days, always in August.' Rick was stunned. He had never met anyone who voluntarily submitted himself to the horrors of August two-a-days. And by August the Italian season was over, so why bother with all that brutal conditioning?

'I know, it's crazy,' Tommy was saying.

'Yes, it is. You still go?'

'Oh no. Three years ago I quit. My wife, the second one, did not approve.' At this, he cast his eyes warily at Maddalena for some reason, then continued: 'She left, but I was too old. Those boys are just seventeen, too young for a forty-year-old man, don't you think?'

'No doubt.'

Rick moved on, still flabbergasted at the thought of Tommy, or anyone, spending his vacation in the Texas heat running wind sprints and slamming into blocking sleds.

There was a rack of perfectly matched leather notebooks, each about an inch thick, with a year embossed in gold, one for each of Tommy's twenty seasons. 'This is the first,' Tommy said. Page one was a glossy Panther game schedule, with the scores added by hand. Four wins, four losses. Then game programs, newspaper articles, and pages of photographs. Tommy pointed to himself in a group shot and said, 'That's me, number 82 back then even, thirty pounds bigger.' He looked huge, and Rick almost said some of that bulk would be welcome now. But Tommy was a fashionista, dapper and always looking good. No doubt losing the extra weight had much to do with his love life.

They flipped through a few of the yearbooks, and the seasons began to blur. 'Never a Super Bowl,' Tommy said more than once. He pointed to an empty space in the center of a bookshelf and said, 'This is the special place, Reek. This is where I put a big picture of my Panthers just after we win the Super Bowl. You will be here, Reek, no?'

'Definitely.'

He flung an arm around Rick's shoulder and led him to the dining area, where drinks were waiting – just two pals arm in arm. 'We are worried, Reek,' he was saying, suddenly very serious.

A pause. 'Worried about what?'

'This game. We are so close.' He unwrapped himself and poured two glasses of white wine. 'You are a great football player, Reek. The best ever in Parma, maybe in all of Italy. A real NFL quarterback. Can you tell us, Reek, that we will win the Super Bowl?'

The women were on the patio looking at flowers in a window box.

'No one is that smart, Tommy. The game is too unpredictable.'

'But you, Reek, you've seen so much, so many great players in magnificent stadiums. You know the real game, Reek. Surely you know if we can win.'

'We can win, yes.'

'But do you promise?' Tommy smiled and

thumped Rick on the chest. Come on, buddy, just between the two of us. Tell me what I want to hear.

'I believe strongly that we will win the next two games, thus the Super Bowl. But, Tommy, only a fool would promise that.'

'Mr. Joe Namath guaranteed it. What, in Super Bowl III or IV?'

'Super Bowl III. And I'm not Joe Namath.'

Tommy was so thoroughly nontraditional that he did not provide parmigiano cheese and prosciutto ham to nibble on while they waited on dinner. His wine came from Spain. Maddalena served salads of spinach and tomato, then small portions of a baked cod dish that would never be found in a cookbook from Emilia-Romagna. Not a trace of pasta anywhere. Dessert was a dry, brittle biscuit, dark as in chocolate but practically tasteless.

For the first time in Parma, Rick left a table hungry. After weak coffee and prolonged good-byes, they left and stopped for a large gelato on the walk home. 'He's a creep,' Livvy said. 'His hands were all over me.'

'Can't blame him for that.'

'Shut up.'

'And besides, I was groping Maddalena.'

'You were not, because I watched every move.'

'Jealous?'

'Extremely.' She shoved a spoonful of pistachio between his lips and said, without a smile, 'Do you hear me, Reek? I am insanely jealous.'

'Yes, ma'am.'

And with that they passed another little milestone, took another step together. From flirting, to casual sex, to a more intense variety. From quick e-mails to much longer chats by phone. From a long-distance romance to playing house. From an uncertain near future to one that just might be shared. And now an agreement on exclusivity. Monogamy. All sealed with a mouthful of pistachio gelato.

* * *

Coach Russo was fed up with all the Super Bowl talk. Friday night he yelled at his team that if they didn't get serious about Bologna, a team they had lost to, by the way, they would not be playing the Super Bowl. One game at a time, you idiots.

And he yelled again on Saturday as they sped through a light workout, one that Nino and Franco demanded they have. Every player showed up, most of them an hour early.

At ten the following morning, they left for Bologna by bus. They had a light lunch of sandwiches at a cafeteria on the edge of town, and at 1:30 the Panthers got off the bus and walked across the best football field in Italy.

Bologna has half a million people and a lot of fans of American football. The Warriors have a long tradition of good teams, active youth leagues, and solid owners, and their field (likewise an old rugby pitch) has been upgraded to football specs and is carefully maintained. Before the rise of Bergamo, Bologna dominated the league.

Two charter buses filled with Parma fans arrived after the team and made a rowdy entrance into the stadium. Before long, the two sides were engaged in a rousing shouting match. Banners went up. Rick noticed one on the Bologna side that read: 'Cook the Goat.'

According to Livvy, Bologna was famous for its food and, not surprisingly, claimed to have the best cuisine in all of Italy. Perhaps goat was a regional specialty.

In their first meeting, Trey Colby caught three touchdown passes in the first quarter. By halftime he had four, then his career ended early in the third quarter. Ray Montrose, a tailback who'd played at Rutgers and had easily won the regular-season rushing title at 228 yards a game, romped around and through the Panther defense for three touchdowns and 200 yards. Bologna won 35–34.

Since then the Panthers had not lost, nor had they played in a close game. Nor did Rick expect one today. Bologna was a one-man team – all Montrose. The quarterback was the typical small-college type – tough but a step slow and erratic even in the short game. The third American was a safety from Dartmouth who had been pitifully unable to cover Trey. And Trey was neither as quick nor as fast as Fabrizio.

The game would be exciting and high scoring, and Rick wanted the ball first. But the Warriors won the toss, and when the teams lined up for the opening kick, the stands were full and rocking. The return man was a tiny Italian. Rick had noticed on tape that he often held the ball low, away from his body, a no-no that would keep him on every bench in America. 'Strip the ball!' Sam had screamed a thousand times during the week. 'If number 8 takes the kick, strip the damned ball.'

But first they had to catch him. As number 8 slashed across midfield, he could smell goal line. The ball came away from his gut as he took it in his right hand. Silvio, the pint-size linebacker with great speed, caught him from the side, and jerked his right arm almost out of its socket, and the ball began rolling on the ground. A Panther recovered it. Montrose would have to wait.

On the first play, Rick faked to Franco on a dive, then pump-faked to Fabrizio on a five and out. The corner, sniffing an early and dramatic interception, took the bait, and when Fabrizio spun upfield, he was wide open for a long second. Rick threw the ball much too hard, but Fabrizio knew what was coming. He took it with his fingers, absorbed it with his upper body, then clutched it just as the safety closed in for the kill. But the safety never caught him. Fabrizio spun again, hit the afterburners, and was soon strutting across the goal line. Seven–zip.

To further prolong the entrance of Mr. Montrose, Sam called for an onside kick. They had practiced it dozens of times in the past week. Filippo, their big-footed kicker, nicked the top of the ball perfectly, and it bounced crazily across midfield. Franco and Pietro thundered behind it, not to touch it but to annihilate the nearest two Warriors. They flattened two confused boys who'd been drifting back for the wedge then changed gears and were going timidly for the kick. Giancarlo somersaulted over the pile and landed on the ball. Three plays later, Fabrizio was back in the end zone.

Montrose finally got the ball on a first and ten from the 31. The pitch to the tailback was as predictable as a sunrise, and Sam sent everybody but the free safety, just in case. A massive gang tackle ensued, but Montrose still managed to gain three. Then five, and four, and three again. His runs were short, his yardage fought for against a swarming defense. On a third and one, Bologna finally tried something creative. Sam called another blitz, and when the quarterback yanked the ball out of Montrose's belly and looked for a receiver, he found one all alone, dancing down the far sideline, waving his arms and screaming because there wasn't a Panther within twenty yards of him. The pass was long and high, and when the receiver caught up to it at the ten-yard line, the home fans stood and cheered. Both hands grabbed the ball, then both hands let it slip away, painfully, slowly, as if in suspended motion. The receiver lunged for the prize of gold as it bobbled too far from his fingertips, then fell flat on his face at the five-yard line and slapped the grass.

You could almost hear him cry.

The punter averaged twenty-eight yards a kick and managed to lower this by shanking one at his own fans. Rick sprinted the offense onto the field, and with no huddle ran three straight plays to Fabrizio – a slant across the middle for twelve yards, a curl for eleven, and a post for thirty-four yards and the third touchdown in the first four minutes of the game.

Bologna didn't panic and abandon its game plan. Montrose got the ball on every play, and on every play Sam blitzed at least nine defenders. The result was a slugfest as the offense methodically punched the ball down the field. When Montrose scored from three yards out, the first quarter expired.

The second quarter was more of the same. Rick and his offense scored easily, while Montrose and his ground it out. At the half, the Panthers led 38–13, and Sam struggled for something to complain about. Montrose had two touchdowns on twenty-one carries and almost two hundred yards, but who cared?

Sam lectured them with the usual coach-speak about second-half collapses, but it was a lame performance. The truth was that Sam had never seen a team, at any level, coalesce so beautifully and effortlessly after such a lousy start. To be certain, his quarterback was a fish out of water, and Fabrizio was not just good but great and worth every penny of his eight hundred euros a month. But the Panthers had stepped up to another level. Franco and Giancarlo ran with authority and daring. Nino, Paolo the Aggie, and Giorgio fired off the ball and seldom missed a block. Rick was rarely sacked or even pressured. And the defense, with Pietro clogging the middle and Silvio blitzing with total abandon, had become a frenzy of gang-tacklers, swarming around the ball on every play like a pack of dogs.

From somewhere, probably from the presence of their quarterback, the Panthers had obtained a cocky self-assurance that coaches dream about. They had the swagger now. This was their season and they would not lose again.

They scored on the opening drive of the second half without throwing a pass. Giancarlo zipped wide left and wide right while Franco thundered through the pit. The drive ate six minutes, and with the score 45–13 Montrose and company jogged onto the field with a sense of defeat. He didn't quit, but after thirty carries he lost a step. After thirty-five, he had his fourth touchdown, but the mighty Warriors were too far behind. The final was 51–27.

Chapter 28

In the early hours of Monday morning, Livvy hopped out of bed, turned on a light, and announced, 'We're going to Venice.'

'No,' came the response from under the pillow.

'Yes. You've never been. Venice is my favorite city.'

'So was Rome and Florence and Siena.'

'Get up, lover boy. I'm showing you Venice.'

'No. I'm too sore.'

'What a wimp. I'm going to Venice to find me a real man, a soccer player.'

'Let's go back to sleep.'

'Nope. I'm leaving. I guess I'll take the train.'

'Send me a postcard.'

She slapped him across the rump and headed for the shower. An hour later the Fiat was loaded and Rick was hauling back coffee and croissants from his neighborhood bar. Coach Russo had canceled practice until Friday. The Super Bowl, like its American imitator, took two weeks to prepare for.

To no one's surprise, the opponent was Bergamo.

Outside the city, away from the morning traffic, Livvy began with the history of Venice, and, mercifully, hit only the high points for the first two thousand years. Rick listened with his hand on her knees as she went on about how and why the city was built on mud banks in tidal areas and floods all the time. She referred to her guidebooks occasionally, but much of it came from memory. She had been there twice in the past year, for long weekends. The first time she was with a gaggle of students, which inspired her to return a month later by herself.

'And the streets are rivers?' Rick asked, more than a little concerned about the Fiat and where it might get parked.

'Better known as canals. There are no cars, only boats.'

'Those little boats are called?'

'Gondolas.'

'Gondolas. I saw a movie once where this couple went for a ride in a gondola and the little captain—'

'Gondolier.'

'Whatever, but he kept singing real loud and they couldn't get him to shut up. Pretty funny. It was a comedy.'

'That's for the tourists.'

'Can't wait.'

'Venice is the most unique city in the world, Rick. I want you to love it.'

'Oh, I'm sure I will. Wonder if they have a football team.'

'There's no mention of one in the guidebooks.' Her phone was off and she seemed unconcerned about events back home. Rick knew her parents were furious and making threats, but there was much more to the saga than she had so far divulged. Livvy could turn it off like a switch, and when she buried herself in the history and art and culture of Italy, she was once again a student thrilled with her subject and anxious to share it.

They stopped for lunch outside the city of Padua. An hour later they found a commercial lot for tourists with cars and parked the Fiat for twenty euros a day. In Mestre, they caught a ferry, and their adventure on the water began. The ferry rocked as it was loaded, then lunged across the Venetian lagoon. Livvy clutched him along the top rail and watched with great anticipation as Venice drew closer. Soon, they were entering the Grand Canal and boats were everywhere – private water taxis, small barges laden with produce and goods, the carabiniere wagon with police insignia, a vaporetto loaded with tourists, fishing boats, other ferries, and, finally, gondolas by the dozen. The murky water lapped at the front steps of elegant palazzi built door-to-door. The campanile at Piazza San Marco loomed high in the distance.

292

Rick couldn't help but notice the domes of dozens of old churches, and he had a sinking feeling he would become familiar with most of them.

They exited at a ferry stop near the Gritti Palace. On the boardwalk, she said, 'This is the only bad part of Venice. We have to roll our luggage to the hotel.' And roll they did, down the crowded streets, over the narrow footbridges, through alleys cut off from the sun. She had warned him to pack light, though her bag was still twice as large as his.

The hotel was a quaint little guesthouse tucked away from the tourists. The owner, Signora Stella, was a spry woman in her seventies who worked the front desk and pretended to remember Livvy from four months back. She put them in a corner room, tight quarters but a nice view of the skyline – cathedrals all around – and also a full bath, which, as Livvy explained, was not always the case in these tiny hotels in Italy. The bed rattled as Rick stretched out, and this concerned him briefly. She was not in the mood, not with Venice lying before them and so much to see. He couldn't even negotiate a nap.

* * *

He did manage, however, to negotiate a truce. His limit would be two cathedrals/palaces per day. After that she was on her own. They wandered over to Piazza San Marco, the first stop for all visitors, and spent the first hour at a sidewalk café sipping drinks and watching large waves of students and tourists drift around the magnificent square. It had been built four hundred years earlier, when Venice was a rich and powerful city-state, she was saying. The Doge's Palace occupied one corner, a huge fortress that had been protecting Venice for at least seven hundred years. The church, or basilica, was vast and attracted the biggest crowds.

She left to buy tickets, and Rick called Sam. The coach was watching the tape of yesterday's game between Bergamo and Milan, the usual Monday afternoon chore for any coach prepping for the Super Bowl.

'Where are you?' Sam demanded.

'Venice.'

'With that young girl?'

'She's twenty-one, Coach. And, yes, she's close by.'

'Bergamo was impressive, no fumbles, only two penalties. Won by three touchdowns. They seem much better now that the streak is off their backs.'

'And Maschi?'

'Brilliant. He knocked out their quarterback in the third quarter.'

'I've been knocked out before. I suspect they'll put the two Americans on Fabrizio and pound him. Could be a long day for the boy. There goes the passing game. Maschi can shut down the run.'

'Thank God for the punting game,' Sam sneered. 'You got a plan?'

'I got a plan.'

'Mind sharing it with me so I can sleep tonight?'

'No, it's not finished yet. A couple more days in Venice and I'll have the kinks worked out.'

'Let's meet Thursday afternoon and work on it.'

'Sure, Coach.'

Rick and Livvy trudged through the basilica of San Marco, shoulder to shoulder with some Dutch tourists, their guide prattling on in any language requested. After an hour, Rick bolted. He drank a beer in the fading sun at a café and waited patiently for Livvy.

They strolled through central Venice and crossed the Rialto Bridge without buying anything. For the daughter of a rich doctor, she was behaving frugally. Tiny hotels, cheap meals, trains, and ferries, an apparent concern with what things cost. She insisted on paying for half of everything, or at least offering. Rick told her more than once that he was certainly not wealthy nor was he highly paid, but he refused to worry about money. And he refused to let her pay for much.

Their metal-framed bed rocked halfway across the room during a late-night session, enough noise to prompt Signora Stella to whisper something discreetly to Livvy during breakfast the next morning.

'What did she say?' Rick asked when Stella disappeared.

Livvy, suddenly blushing, leaned in and whispered, 'We made too much noise last night. There were complaints.'

'What did you tell her?'

'Too bad. We can't stop.'

'Atta girl.'

'She doesn't think we should, but she might move us to another room, one with a heavier bed.'

'I love a challenge.'

* * *

Long boulevards do not exist in Venice. The streets are narrow, and they twist and curl with the canals and cross them with a variety of bridges. Someone once counted 400 bridges in the city, and by late Wednesday Rick was certain he had used them all.

He was parked under an umbrella at a sidewalk café, puffing languidly on a Cuban cigar and sipping Campari and ice, waiting for Livvy to polish off another cathedral, this one known as the church of San Fantin. He wasn't tired of her, just the opposite. Her energy and curiosity inspired him to use his brain. She was a delightful companion, easy to please and eager to do whatever looked like fun. He was still waiting for a glimpse of the pampered rich kid, the self-absorbed sorority queen. Maybe it didn't exist.

Nor was he tired of Venice. In fact, he was enchanted by the city and its endless nooks and dead ends and hidden piazzas. The seafood was incredible, and he was thoroughly enjoying this break from pasta. He'd seen enough cathedrals and palazzi and museums, but his interest in the city's art and history had been piqued.

Rick was a football player, though, and there was one game remaining. It was a game he had to win to justify his presence, his existence, and his cost, meager as it was. Money aside, he had once been an NFL quarterback, and if he couldn't put together an offense for one more win here in Italy, then it was time to hang up the spikes.

He had already dropped the hint that he needed to leave Thursday morning. She seemed to ignore it. Over dinner at Fiore, he said, 'I need to go to Parma tomorrow. Coach Russo wants to meet in the afternoon.'

'I think I'll stay here,' she said without hesitation. It was all planned.

'For how long?'

'A few more days. I'll be fine.'

And he had no doubt she would be. Though they preferred to stick together, both needed their space and each was quick to disappear. Livvy could travel the world alone, much easier than he could. Nothing flustered or intimidated her. She adjusted on the fly like any seasoned traveler and was not above using her smile and beauty to get what she wanted.

297

'You'll be back for the Super Bowl?' he asked.

'I wouldn't dare miss it.'

'Smart-ass.'

They had eel, mullet, and cuttlefish, and when they were stuffed, they walked to Harry's Bar on the Grand Canal for a nightcap. They sat huddled in a corner, watching a crowd of loud Americans and not missing home.

'When the season is over, what will you do?' she asked. She was wrapped around his right arm, and his right hand massaged her knees. They sipped slowly, as if they might be there all night.

'Not sure. What about you?' he asked.

'I need to go home, but I don't want to.'

'I don't need to and I don't want to. But I'm not quite clear on what I'm supposed to do here.'

'You wanna stay?' she asked as she somehow managed to get even closer.

'With you?'

'Got anybody else in mind?'

'That's not what I meant. Are you staying?'

'I could be talked into it.'

The heavier bed was in a larger room and solved the problem of complaints. They slept late Thursday, then said an uncomfortable good-bye. Rick waved to her as the ferry shoved off and eased through the Grand Canal.

Chapter 29

The sound was vaguely familiar. He'd heard it before, but from the depths of his coma he could not remember where, or when. He sat up in bed, saw that it was four minutes after 3:00 a.m., and finally put things together. Someone was at his door.

'Coming!' he growled, and his intruder removed his/her thumb from the white button in the hallway. Rick pulled on gym shorts and a T-shirt. He flipped on lights and suddenly remembered Detective Romo and the non-arrest months earlier. He thought of Franco, his own personal judge, and decided he had nothing to fear.

'Who is it?' he said to the door, his mouth close to the latch.

'I'd like to talk to you.' Deep scratchy voice, American. Hint of a twang.

'Okay, we're talking.'

'I'm looking for Rick Dockery.'

'You found him. Now what?'

'Please. I need to see Livvy Galloway.'

'Are you a cop of some sort?' Rick suddenly thought of his neighbors and the commotion he was creating by yelling through a closed door.

'No.'

Rick unbolted the door and came face-to-face with a barrel-chested man in a cheap black suit. Large head, thick mustache, heavy circles around the eyes. Probably a long history with the bottle. He thrust out a hand and said, 'I'm Lee Bryson, a private investigator from Atlanta.'

'A pleasure,' Rick said without shaking hands. 'Who's he?'

Behind Bryson was a sinister-faced Italian in a dark suit that cost a few bucks more than Bryson's. 'Lorenzo. He's from Milan.'

'That really explains things. Is he a cop?'

'No.'

'So we don't have any cops here, right?'

'No, we're private investigators. Please, if I could just have ten minutes.'

Rick waved them through and locked the door. He followed them into the den, where they awkwardly sat knee to knee on the sofa. He fell into a chair across the room. 'This better be good,' he said.

'I work for some lawyers in Atlanta, Mr. Dockery. Can I call you Rick?'

'No.'

'Okay. These lawyers are involved in the

300

divorce between Dr. Galloway and Mrs. Galloway, and they sent me here to see Livvy.'

'She's not here.'

Bryson glanced around the room, and his eyes froze on a pair of red high heels on the floor near the television. Then a brown handbag on the end table. All that was missing was a bra hanging from the lamp. One with leopard print. Lorenzo stared only at Rick, as if his role was to handle the killing if it became necessary.

'I think she is,' Bryson said.

'I don't care what you think. She's been here, but not now.'

'Mind if I look around?'

'Sure, just show me a search warrant and you can inspect the laundry.'

Bryson swiveled his massive head again.

'It's a small apartment,' Rick said. 'With three rooms. You can see two from where you're sitting. I promise you Livvy is not in there in the bedroom.'

'Where is she?'

'Why do you want to know?'

'I was sent here to find her. That's my job. There are folks back home who are very concerned about her.'

'Maybe she doesn't want to go home. Maybe she wants to avoid those same folks.'

'Where is she?'

'She's fine. She likes to travel. You'll have a hard time finding her.'

Bryson picked at his mustache and seemed to

smile. 'She might find it difficult to travel,' he said. 'Her visa expired three days ago.'

Rick absorbed this, but did not relent. 'That's not exactly a felony.'

'No, but things could get sticky. She needs to come home.'

'Maybe so. You're welcome to explain all this to her, and when you do, I'm sure she'll make whatever decision she damn well pleases. She's a big girl, Mr. Bryson, very capable of running her own life. She doesn't need you, me, or anyone back home.'

His nighttime raid had failed, and Bryson began his withdrawal. He yanked some papers out of his coat pocket, tossed them on the coffee table, then said, with an effort at drama, 'Here's the deal. That's a one-way ticket from Rome to Atlanta this Sunday. She shows up, no one asks questions about the visa. That little problem has been taken care of. She doesn't show, then she's AWOL here without proper documentation.'

'Oh, that's really swell, but you're talking to the wrong person. As I just said, Ms. Galloway makes her own decisions. I just provide a room when she passes through.'

'But you will talk to her.'

'Maybe, but there's no guarantee I'll see her before Sunday, or next month for that matter. She likes to wander.'

There was nothing else for Bryson to do. He was being paid to find the girl, make some threats, scare her into coming home, and hand over the ticket. Beyond that, he had zero authority. On Italian soil or otherwise.

He climbed to his feet, with Lorenzo following every movement. Rick stayed in his chair. At the door, Bryson stopped and said, 'I'm a Falcons fan. Didn't you pass through Atlanta a few years ago?'

'Yes,' Rick said quickly and without elaboration.

Bryson glanced around the apartment. Third floor, no elevator. Ancient building on a narrow street in an ancient city. A long way from the bright lights of the NFL.

Rick held his breath and waited for the cheap shot. Maybe something like: 'I guess you've finally found your place.' Or, 'Nice career move.'

Instead, he filled the gap with 'How did you find me?'

As Bryson opened the door, he said, 'One of her roommates remembered your name.'

★ ★ ★

It was almost noon before she answered her phone. She was having lunch outdoors at Piazza San Marco and feeding the pigeons. Rick replayed the scene with Bryson.

Her initial reaction was one of anger – how dare her parents track her down and force themselves into her life. Anger at the lawyers who hired the thugs who barged into Rick's apartment at such an hour. Anger at her roommate for

303

squealing. When she settled down, curiosity took over as she debated which parent was behind it. It was impossible to think they were working together. Then she remembered that her father had lawyers in Atlanta, while her mother's were from Savannah.

When she finally asked his opinion, Rick, who'd thought of little else for hours, said that she should take the ticket and go home. Once there, she could work through the visa issue, and hopefully return as soon as possible.

'You don't understand,' she said more than once, and he truly did not. Her baffling explanation was that she could never use the ticket sent by her father because he had managed to manipulate her for twenty-one years and she was fed up. If she returned to the United States, it would be on her own terms. 'I would never use that ticket, and he knows it,' she said. Rick frowned and scratched his head and was once again thankful for a dull and simple family.

And not for the first time he asked himself, How damaged might this girl be?

What about the expired visa? Well, not surprisingly, she had a plan. Italy, being Italy, had some loopholes in the immigration laws, one of which was called the *permesso di soggiorno*, or a permit to stay. It was sometimes granted to legal aliens whose visas had expired, and typically ran for another ninety days.

She was wondering if Judge Franco perhaps knew someone in immigration. Or maybe Signor

Bruncardo? And what about Tommy, the career civil servant, the defensive end who couldn't cook? Surely someone in the Panthers organization could find a string to pull.

A wonderful idea, thought Rick. And even more likely if they won the Super Bowl.

Chapter 30

Last-minute wrangling with the cable company pushed the kickoff back to eight o'clock Saturday night. Televising the game live, even on a lesser channel, was important for the league and the sport, and a Super Bowl under the lights meant a bigger gate and a rowdier crowd. By late afternoon, parking lots around the stadium were filled as football diehards celebrated the Italian version of the tailgate. Buses of fans arrived from Parma and Bergamo. Banners were stretched along the edges of the field, soccer style. A miniature hot air balloon hovered over the field. As always, it was the biggest day of the year for *football americano*, and its small but loyal base of fans arrived in Milan for the final game.

The site was a beautifully maintained little arena used by a local soccer league. For the occasion, the nets were gone and the field was meticulously striped, even down to the sideline hash marks. One end zone was painted black and white with the word 'Parma' in the center. A hundred (exactly) yards away, the Bergamo end zone was gold and black.

There were pregame speeches by league officials and introductions of former greats, a ceremonial coin toss, won by the Lions, and a prolonged announcing of the starting lineups. When the teams finally lined up for the opening kick, both sidelines were hopping with nerves and the crowd was crazy.

Even Rick, the cool, unflustered quarterback, was stomping the sideline, slapping shoulder pads, and screaming for blood. This was football the way it was meant to be.

Bergamo ran three plays and punted. The Panthers did not have another 'Kill Maschi' play ready. Maschi wasn't that stupid. In fact, the more tape Rick watched, the more he admired and feared the middle linebacker. He could wreck an offense, just like the great L.T. On first down, Fabrizio was double-teamed by the two Americans – McGregor and The Professor – just as Rick and Sam expected. A wise move for Bergamo, and the beginning of a rough day for Rick and the offense. He called a sideline route. Fabrizio caught the ball and was shoved out by The Professor, then nailed in the back by McGregor. But there were no flags. Rick jumped an official while Nino and Karl the Dane went after McGregor. Sam charged onto the field, screaming and cursing in Italian, and promptly drew a personal foul. The refs managed to prevent a brawl, but the brouhaha went on for minutes. Fabrizio was okay and limped back to the huddle. On a second and twenty, Rick pitched wide to Giancarlo, and Maschi slapped his ankles together at the line. Between plays, Rick continued to bitch at the referee while Sam chewed on the back judge.

On third and long, Rick decided to give the ball to Franco and perhaps survive the traditional first-quarter fumble. Franco and Maschi collided hard, for old times' sake, and the play gained a couple with no change of possession.

The thirty-five points they had put up against Bergamo a month earlier suddenly looked like a miracle.

The teams swapped punts as the defenses dominated. Fabrizio was smothered and, at 175 pounds, was getting shoved around on every play. Claudio dropped two short passes that were thrown much too hard.

The first quarter ended with no score, and the crowd settled into a pretty dull game. Perhaps dull to watch, but along the line of scrimmage the hitting was ferocious. Every play was the last of the season, and no one yielded an inch. On a bobbled snap, Rick raced around the right side, hoping to make it out of bounds, when Maschi appeared from thin air and nailed him, helmet to helmet. Rick jumped to his feet, no big deal, but on the sideline he rubbed his temples and tried to shake off the dust.

'You okay?' Sam growled as he walked by.

'Great.'

'Then do something.'

'Right.'

But nothing worked. As they had feared, Fabrizio was neutralized, thus so was the passing game. And Maschi could not be controlled. He was too strong up the middle, and too quick on the sweeps. He looked much better on the field than on the film. Each offense ground out a few first downs, but neither approached the red zone. The punting teams were growing tired.

With thirty seconds to go before the half, the Bergamo kicker nailed a forty-two-yarder, and the Lions took a 3–0 lead into the locker room.

Charley Cray – twenty pounds lighter, his jaw still wired, gaunt with flesh sagging from his chin and cheeks – hid in the crowd and during the half pecked out some notes on his laptop:

- Not a bad setting for a game; handsome stadium, well decorated, enthusiastic crowd of maybe 5000;
- Dockery could well be in over his head even here in Italy; in the first half he was 3 for 8, 22 yards, and no score;
- I must say, however, that this is real football. The hitting is brutal; tremendous hustle and desire; no one slacks; these guys are not playing for money, just pride, and it is a powerful incentive;

– Dockery is the only American on the Parma team, and you wonder if they would be better off without him. We shall see.

* * *

There was no yelling in the locker room. Sam praised the defense for a superb effort. Keep it up. We'll figure out a way to score.

The coaches left and the players spoke. Nino, first as always, in passionate praise of the heroic defensive efforts, then an exhortation to the offense to get some points. This is our moment, he said. Some of us may never be here again. Dig deep. Gut check. He wiped away tears when he was finished.

Tommy stood and proclaimed his love for everyone in the room. This was his last game, he said, and he desperately wanted to retire as a champion.

Pietro walked to the center. This was not his last game, but he would be damned if his career would be determined by the boys from Bergamo. He boasted loudly that they would not score in the second half.

As Franco was about to wrap things up, Rick stood beside him and raised his hand. With Franco translating, he said, 'Win or lose, I thank you for allowing me to play on your team this season.' Halt. Translation. The room was still. His teammates hung on every word.

'Win or lose, I am proud to be a Panther,

310

one of you. Thank you for accepting me.'

Translation.

'Win or lose, I consider all of you to be not just my friends but my brothers.'

Translation. Some appeared ready to cry.

'I've had more fun here than in the other NFL. And we are not going to lose this game.' When he was finished, Franco bear-hugged him and the team cheered heartily. They clapped and slapped him on the back.

Franco, eloquent as always, dwelled on history. No Parma team had ever won the Super Bowl, and the next hour would be their finest hour. They had thrashed Bergamo four weeks earlier, broken the mighty streak, sent them home in disgrace, and they could certainly beat them again.

* * *

For Coach Russo and his quarterback, the first half had been perfect. Basic football – far removed from the complexities of the major college and pro games – can often be plotted like an ancient battle. A steady attack on one front can set the stage for a surprise on another. The same monotonous movements can lull the opponent to sleep. Early on, they had conceded the passing game. They had not been creative with the run. Bergamo had stopped everything, and was confident there was nothing left.

On the second play of the second half, Rick

faked left to Franco on a dive, faked a pitch left to Giancarlo, then sprinted right on a naked bootleg. Maschi, always quick to the ball, was far to the left and badly out of position. Rick ran hard for twenty-two yards and stepped out of bounds to avoid McGregor.

Sam met him as he jogged back to the huddle. 'That'll work. Save it for later.'

Three plays later, the Panthers punted again. Pietro and Silvio sprinted onto the field, looking for someone to maul. They stuffed the run three times. More punts filled the air as the third quarter ticked away and both teams slugged it out at midfield, much like two lumbering heavyweights in the center of the ring, taking shots, throwing leather, and never backing down.

Early in the fourth, the Lions inched the ball all the way to the 19, their deepest penetration of the game, and on a fourth and five their kicker drilled an easy field goal.

Down six points with ten minutes to go, the Panthers' sideline rose to another level of panic and frenzy. Their fans followed along, and the atmosphere was electric.

'Showtime,' Rick said to Sam as they watched the kickoff.

'Yep. Don't get hurt.'

'Are you kidding? I've been knocked out by better men.'

On first down, Rick pitched left to Giancarlo for five yards. On second, he faked the same pitch, kept the ball, and dashed wide around the right side, free and clear for twenty yards until McGregor came in low and hard. Rick lowered his head and met him in a sickening collision. Both scrambled to their feet; there was no time for cobwebs or rubbery knees.

Giancarlo swept right and was decked by Maschi. Rick bootlegged left and picked up fifteen before McGregor hit his knees. The only strategy to offset quickness is misdirection, and the offense suddenly had a different look. Backs in motion, three receivers on one side, two tight ends, new plays, and new formations. Under center, in the wishbone, Rick faked to Franco, turned upfield, then flipped to Giancarlo just as Maschi hit him low. A perfect option, and Giancarlo sprinted for eleven yards. From the shotgun, another naked bootleg and Rick ran out of bounds at the 18.

Maschi was guessing now, not simply reacting. He had more to think about. McGregor and The Professor had backed off Fabrizio a step or two, suddenly under pressure to stop the scrambling quarterback. Seven tough plays moved the ball to the 3, and on fourth and goal Filippo kicked an easy field goal. Bergamo led 6–3 with six minutes to go.

Alex Olivetto huddled with the defense before the kickoff. He cursed and slapped helmets and had a fine time firing up the troops. Perhaps a bit too much. On second down, Pietro speared the quarterback and gave up fifteen precious yards on the personal foul. The drive stalled at midfield, and a great punt stopped rolling at the 5.

Ninety-five yards to go in three minutes. Rick avoided Sam as he trotted onto the field. He saw fear in the huddle, and he told them to relax, no fumbles, no penalties, just hit hard and they would soon be in the end zone. No translation was needed.

Maschi taunted him as they came to the line. 'You can do it, Goat. Throw me a pass.' Instead, he pitched to Giancarlo, who clutched the ball tightly and hopped for five yards. On second down he rolled right, looked for Fabrizio across the middle, saw too many gold jerseys, and tucked the ball. Franco, bless his soul, broke from the pile and put a nasty block on Maschi. Rick picked up fourteen yards and got out of bounds. On first down he rolled right again, tucked the ball, and sprinted upfield. Fabrizio was loafing on a curl, useless as he had been throughout the game, and when Rick scrambled, he took off, sprinting at full throttle with McGregor and The Professor far behind. Rick stopped just inches from the line. Maschi was slashing in for the kill.

It was that moment in every game when the quarterback, unprotected and vulnerable, sees an open receiver and has a split second to make a choice. Throw the pass and risk a bruising tackle, or yank the ball down and run for safety.

Rick planted his feet and threw the ball as far

314

as he possibly could. After the launch, Maschi's helmet landed under his chin and almost broke his jaw. The pass was a tight spiral, so high and so long that the crowd gasped in disbelief. It had the hang time of a perfect punt, a few long seconds in which everyone froze.

Everyone except Fabrizio, who was flying and trying to find the ball. At first, it was impossible to gauge where it might land, but they had practiced this Hail Mary a hundred times. 'Just get to the end zone,' Rick always said. 'The ball will be there.' As it began its descent, Fabrizio realized more speed was needed. He pumped even harder, his feet barely touching the grass. At the five-yard line, he left the ground, much like an Olympic long jumper, and sailed through the air, arms fully extended, fingers grasping for the ball. He touched leather at the goal line, hit the ground hard, bounced up like an acrobat, and waved the ball for the world to see.

And everyone saw it but Rick, who was on all fours, rocking back and forth, trying to remember who he was. As a loud roar erupted, Franco picked him up and dragged him to the sideline, where his teammates mobbed him. Rick managed to stay on his feet, but not without assistance.

Sam figured he was dead, but was too stunned by the catch to react to his quarterback.

Flags flew as the celebration spilled onto the field. The officials finally restored order and marked off fifteen yards, then Filippo crushed an extra point that would have been good from midfield.

Charley Cray would write:

> The ball traveled 76 yards in the air, without the slightest hint of a wobble, but the pass itself paled in greatness to the catch at the other end. I've witnessed great touchdowns, but frankly, sports fans, this one tops the list. A skinny Italian named Fabrizio Bonozzi saved Dockery from another humiliating defeat.

Filippo stuck his supercharged foot into the kickoff, and it soared over the end zone. On a third and long, old Tommy spun around the left tackle and sacked the quarterback. His last play as a Panther was his greatest.

On fourth and even longer, the Bergamo quarterback bobbled a bad shotgun snap and finally fell on the ball at the five-yard line. The Panthers' sideline erupted again, and their fans managed to scream even louder.

With fifty seconds on the clock, and with Rick on the bench sniffing ammonia, Alberto took over the offense and simply fell on the ball twice. Time expired, and the Panthers of Parma had their first Super Bowl trophy.

Chapter 31

They gathered triumphantly at Mario's, an old pizzeria in north-central Milan, twenty minutes from the stadium. Signor Bruncardo rented out the entire place for the celebration, an expensive proposition he might have regretted had they lost. But they certainly did not, and they arrived in buses and cabs, whooping as they walked in the front door and looking for beer. The players were given three long tables in the center of the room, and were soon surrounded by their admirers – wives, girlfriends, fans from Parma.

A videotape was inserted, and on giant screens the game played on as waiters hauled in dozens of pizzas and gallons of beer.

Everyone had a camera and a thousand photos were taken. Rick was a favorite target, and he was hugged and squeezed and pawed until his shoulders were sore. Fabrizio was also the center of attention, especially with the teenage girls. The Catch had already taken on legendary status.

Rick's neck, chin, jaws, and forehead were throbbing, and his ears still rang. Matteo, the trainer, gave him pain pills that didn't mix with alcohol, so he laid off the beer. And he had no appetite.

The video skipped the huddles, time-outs, and halftime, and as the end of the game approached, the noise died considerably. The operator switched to slow motion, and as Rick rolled out of the pocket and faked the run, the pizzeria was silent. The hit by Maschi was of highlight quality, and in the United States would have sent the talking heads into a drooling frenzy. The Monday morning cable shows would trumpet it as their 'Hit of the Day' and run it every ten minutes. In Mario's, though, there was a moment of silence for the dead as their quarter-back held his ground, sacrificed his body, and launched his bomb. There were a few muted groans as Maschi knocked him senseless – all very clean and legal and astoundingly brutal.

But there was rejoicing on the other end.

The Catch was captured beautifully and permanently on film, and watching it for the second time, then the third, was almost as exhilarating as seeing it live. Fabrizio, atypically, acted as though it was no big deal, just another day at the office. Many more where that came from.

When the pizza was gone and the game was off, the crowd settled in for a few formalities. After a long speech by Signor Bruncardo and a short one by Sam, the two posed with the Super Bowl trophy in the greatest moment in Panthers history. When the drinking songs began, Rick knew it was time to leave. A long night was about to become much longer. He eased from the pizzeria, found a cab, and returned to the hotel.

★ ★ ★

Two days later, he met Sam for lunch at Sorelle Picchi, on Strada Farini, his neighborhood. They had some business to discuss, but first they rehashed the game. Since Sam wasn't working, they split a bottle of Lambrusco with their stuffed pasta.

'When are you going home?' Sam asked.

'No plans. I'm in no hurry.'

'That's unusual. Normally, the Americans book a flight the day after the last game. You're not homesick?'

'I need to see my folks, but "home" is a fuzzy concept these days.'

Sam chewed slowly on a spoonful of pasta. 'You thought about next year?'

'Not really.'

'Can we talk about it?'

'We can talk about anything. You're buying lunch.'

'Signor Bruncardo is buying lunch, and he's in a very good mood these days. He loves to win, loves the press, the pictures, the trophies. And he wants to repeat things next year.'

'I'm sure he does.'

Sam refilled both glasses. 'Your agent, what's his name?'

'Arnie.'

'Arnie. Is he still in the picture?'

'No.'

'Good, so we can talk business?'

'Sure.'

'Bruncardo is offering twenty-five hundred euros a month, for twelve months, plus the apartment and the car for a year.'

Rick took a long pull on his wine and studied the red checkered tablecloth.

Sam continued: 'He'd rather give you the money than spend it on more Americans. He asked me if we can win again next year with the same team. I said yes. You agree?'

Rick nodded his agreement with a smirk.

'So he's sweetening your deal.'

'That's not a bad contract,' Rick said, thinking less about the salary and more about the apartment that was now apparently needed by two people. He also thought about Silvio, who worked on the family farm, and Filippo, who drove a cement truck. They would kill for such a deal, and they practiced and played as hard as Rick.

But they were not quarterbacks, were they?

Another sip of wine, and he thought about the $400,000 Buffalo paid him when he signed six years earlier, and he thought about Randall Framer, a teammate at Seattle who was given

$85 million to throw passes for seven more years. Everything is relative.

'Look, Sam, six months ago they carried me off the field in Cleveland. I woke up twenty-four hours later in a hospital. My third concussion. The doctor suggested I give up football. My mother begged me to quit. Last Sunday, I woke up in the dressing room. I stayed on my feet, walked off the field, I suppose I celebrated with everybody else. But I don't remember it, Sam, I was knocked out again. Number four. I don't know how many more I can survive.'

'I understand.'

'I took some shots this season. It's still football, and Maschi hit me as hard as anybody in the NFL.'

'Are you quitting?'

'I don't know. Give me some time to think, to clear my head. I'm going to a beach for a few weeks.'

'Where?'

'My travel consultant has decided on Apulia, way down south, the heel of the Italian boot. Been there?'

'No. This would be Livvy?'

'Yes.'

'And the visa thing?'

'She's not worried.'

'Are you kidnapping her?'

'It's a joint kidnapping.'

* * *

They boarded the train early and sat in the heat as other passengers hurried on. Livvy sat across from him, her shoes already kicked off, her feet in his lap. Orange polish. Short skirt. Miles of legs.

She was unfolding a schedule of train routes in southern Italy. She had asked for his input, his thoughts, wishes, and when he offered little, she was pleased. They would spend a week in Apulia, then ferry to Sicily for ten days, then catch a boat to the island of Sardinia. As August approached, they would head north, away from the vacationers and the heat, and explore the mountains of the Veneto and Friuli. She wanted to see the cities of Verona, Vicenza, and Padua. She wanted to see it all.

They would stay in hostels and cheap hotels, using his passport only until her little visa problem was fixed. Franco was hard at work on that challenge.

They would take trains and ferries, cabs only when necessary. She had plans, alternative plans, and more plans. Rick's only deal breaker had been his demand that two cathedrals per day was the limit. She negotiated but finally relented.

But there were no plans beyond August. Any thoughts about her family sent her into a funk, so she was trying to forget the mess back home. While she spoke less and less about her parents, she talked more about delaying her last year of college.

Fine with Rick. As he massaged her feet, he

told himself that he would follow those legs anywhere. The train was half-full. Other men couldn't help but gawk as they shuffled by. Livvy was off in southern Italy, wonderfully oblivious to the attention her bare feet and tanned legs were getting.

As the Eurostar moved away from the platform, Rick watched through his window, and waited. They soon passed Stadio Lanfranchi, less than two hundred feet from the north end zone, or whatever it was called in the rugby rule book.

He allowed himself a smile of deep satisfaction.

Author's Note

A few years ago, while researching another book, I stumbled across American football in Italy. There is a real NFL there, with real teams, players, even a Super Bowl. So the setting of this book is reasonably accurate, though, as usual, I did not hesitate to take liberties when faced with additional research.

The Parma Panthers are very real. I watched them play the Ancona Dolphins in the rain at Stadio Lanfranchi. Their coach is Andrew Papoccia (Illinois State), and his assistance was invaluable. Their quarterback Mike Souza (Illinois State), wide receiver Craig McIntyre (Eastern Washington), and defensive co-ordinator Dan Milsten (University of Washington) were extremely helpful. When it came to football, these Americans answered all my inquiries. When it came to food and wine, they were even more enthusiastic.

The Panthers are owned by Ivano Tira, a

warmhearted soul who made sure I enjoyed my brief time in Parma. David Montaresi walked me around that lovely city. Paolo Borchini and Ugo Bonvicini, former players, help run the organization. The Panthers are a bunch of tough Italians who play for the love of the game, and for the pizza afterward. They invited me to Polipo's after practice one night, and I laughed until I cried.

In these pages, though, all characters are fictional. I went to great lengths to stay away from real people. Any similarities are just coincidental.

Thanks also to Bea Zambelloni, Luca Patouelli, Ed Pricolo, Llana Young Smith, and Bryce Miller. Special thanks to Parma Mayor Elvio Ubaldi for tickets to the opera. I was an honored guest in his box and I did indeed enjoy *Otello* at the Teatro Regio.

John Grisham
June 27, 2007

Bleachers

John Grisham

An unforgettable novel about fleeting youth, legends and heroes.

High school All-American Neely Crenshaw was probably the best quarterback ever to play for the legendary Messina Spartans. Fifteen years have gone by since those glory days, and Neely has come home to Messina to bury Coach Eddie Rake, the man who molded the Spartans into an unbeatable football dynasty.

As Coach Rake's 'boys' sit in the bleachers waiting for the dimming field lights to signal his passing, they replay the old glories, and try to decide once and for all whether they love Eddie Rake - or hate him. For Neely Crenshaw, still struggling to come to terms with his explosive relationship with the Coach, his dreams of a great career in the NFL, and the choices he made as a young man, the stakes could not be higher.

'Grisham touches the soul and scores a winning touchdown with his sixteenth novel' *Evening Standard*

'I defy even the hardest jock not to shed a tear' *The Mirror*

'John Grisham is a copper-bottomed promise of reliable storytelling' *Independent*

arrow books

ALSO AVAILABLE IN ARROW

The Brethren

John Grisham

Trumble is a minimum security federal prison, home to drug dealers, bank robbers, swindlers, embezzlers, tax evaders, and three former judges who call themselves The Brethren. They meet each day in the law library where they spend hours writing letters. They are fine-tuning a mail scam, and it's starting to pay big. The money is pouring in.

But then their little scam goes awry. It ensnares the wrong victim, a powerful man on the outside, a man with dangerous friends, and The Brethren's days of quietly marking time are over.

'Grisham spins out a compelling, beautifully written thriller . . . it's all absolutely brilliant' *Independent on Sunday*

'An engaging and fast-paced story of powerful men in high places and blackmail gone awry, it will hook you from the first page and won't let you go' *New York Post*

'Completely gripping' *Mirror*

'A lively and fast-paced story' *Times Literary Supplement*

arrow books

The Summons

John Grisham

Ray Atlee, a Professor of Law at the University of Virginia, is forty-three and newly single. His father, a very sick old man who lives the life of a recluse in the ancestral home in Clanton, Mississippi, was once a beloved and powerful official who towered over local law and politics for many years.

With the end in sight, Judge Atlee issues a summons to Ray to return home to Clanton, to discuss the details of the family estate.

Ray reluctantly heads south, but the family meeting does not take place. The Judge dies too soon, and in doing so leaves behind a shocking secret which Ray believes only he knows. Until it becomes clear that someone else knows too . . .

'John Grisham is a copper-bottomed promise of reliable storytelling . . . the legal trappings are as persuasive as ever'
Independent

'Smooth, tough and addictive' *Mirror*

'Almost no one tells a story better than Grisham: there's an Ancient Mariner implacability about the way the story grips one . . . and doesn't let up' *Evening Standard*

'Compelling' *Times Literary Supplement*

arrow books